# Dreaming
## of You

## FRANCIS RAY

St. Martin's Paperbacks

This is a work of fiction. All of the characters, organizations and events portrayed in this novel are either products of the author's imagination or are used fictitiously.

DREAMING OF YOU

Copyright © 2006 by Francis Ray.

All rights reserved. No part of this book may be used or reproduced in any manner whatsoever without written permission except in the case of brief quotations embodied in critical articles or reviews. For information address St. Martin's Press, 175 Fifth Avenue, New York, NY 10010.

ISBN: 0-312-93973-6
EAN: 9780312-93973-1

Printed in the United States of America

St. Martin's Paperbacks edition / September 2006

St. Martin's Paperbacks are published by St. Martin's Press, 175 Fifth Avenue, New York, NY 10010.

10 9 8 7 6 5 4 3 2

## ALSO BY FRANCIS RAY

*Only You*
*Irresistible You*
*Any Rich Man Will Do*
*Like the First Time*
*Someone to Love Me*
*Somebody's Knocking at My Door*
*I Know Who Holds Tomorrow*
*Trouble Don't Last Always*
*You and No Other*

## ANTHOLOGIES

*Rosie's Curl and Weave*
*Della's House of Style*
*Going to the Chapel*
*Welcome to Leo's*
*Gettin' Merry*

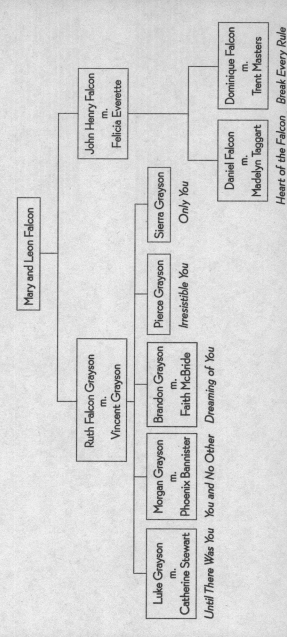

# THE GRAYSONS OF NEW MEXICO—THE FALCONS OF TEXAS

Cousins by marriage—friends by choice
Bold men and women who risk it all for love

Mary and Leon Falcon

Ruth Falcon Grayson
m.
Vincent Grayson

John Henry Falcon
m.
Felicia Everette

Luke Grayson
m.
Catherine Stewart

*Until There Was You*

Morgan Grayson
m.
Phoenix Bannister

*You and No Other*

Brandon Grayson
m.
Faith McBride

*Dreaming of You*

Pierce Grayson

*Irresistible You*

Sierra Grayson

*Only You*

Daniel Falcon
m.
Madelyn Taggart

*Heart of the Falcon*

Dominique Falcon
m.
Trent Masters

*Break Every Rule*

# Prologue

Brandon Grayson had cheerfully defied speculations and beaten the odds. He'd accomplished what his two older brothers had failed to do . . . remain single and unenamored despite being next on his mother's infamous marriage hit list.

Five months had passed since his second-oldest brother, Morgan, had married, yet to the amazement of Brandon's four siblings and many of the towns-people of Santa Fe, New Mexico, he remained, in his opinion, blessedly single. To top things off, the Red Cactus restaurant, his pride and joy, was thriving, he had a host of friends and a loving family, and tonight he was surrounded by some of the most beautiful women in the country.

Life was good.

That his mother and many of the other women in the ballroom in Casa de Serenidad Hotel in down-town Santa Fe who had come to help him celebrate his thirty-first birthday wanted to change his marital status was of no consequence to Brandon. He was more than willing to enjoy the women's company while they tried. It wasn't often that one of Ruth Grayson's five children got the best of her. Her middle child planned on enjoying every glorious second.

A wide grin split Brandon's handsome face as he sent his current dance partner, Andrea Cummings, in a double reverse spin on the hardwood floor, then pulled the willowy redhead back into his waiting arms. Pressing closer, she smiled seductively up at him, telling him without words that she was his for the asking. Brandon didn't even consider taking her up on her offer. He'd never gone in for casual sex, and for the time being he wasn't getting involved in anything serious.

He only had to glance around the room decorated in a southwestern theme of cowboy hats and boots and of course his favorites, cacti and chili peppers, and see his two married brothers to know that a woman in a steady relationship meant trouble. His smug smile faded.

His older brothers, Luke and Morgan, as they'd done most of the night, had their arms wrapped around their wives, blatantly ignoring the fast tempo of the music as they barely moved on the dance floor.

Before he married, Luke never danced in public, claiming he had two left feet. After his marriage to Catherine almost nine months ago, all she had to do was smile at him and he was on the dance floor. He'd walk through hell with a smile on his face to please her.

Morgan was the same love-smitten way about his wife, Phoenix. As next to the oldest, Morgan had cut a wide path among the ladies and was no slouch on the dance floor. He had vehemently declared that he had no intention of becoming serious about any woman, let alone getting married. Yet he'd caved faster than a marshmallow in a hot oven when Phoenix walked into his life. They'd hit a rocky patch in their courtship, but a tenacious Morgan hadn't given up until Phoenix accepted his proposal. A month later they were married.

Brandon admired his brothers and adored their wives; he just didn't want to be like them. He enjoyed his single lifestyle just the way it was. But if his matchmaking mother followed true to form, and there was no reason to suspect she'd divert from her plan, especially since she'd been so successful thus far, as the middle and next offspring he was next on her hit list.

Brandon shuddered. Not if he had anything to say about it.

*A wise man learns from the mistakes of others.* Brandon considered himself a wise man. His brothers had slipped up by exclusively dating one woman. If they had played the field they wouldn't have fallen into the marriage trap their mother had set for them. Well, they still weren't sure she had set Morgan up, but he'd ended up married just the same.

The trouble with Brandon's plan was that he'd been celibate since Morgan's marriage. He wasn't sure how much longer he could resist the soft lure of the women and the increasing needs of his body. He respected women, loved their softness, their smiles, their intelligence, even the odd way they thought, but he had healthy desires and it was becoming harder to control those desires.

"Brandon, you're not paying attention to me," Andrea said, her red lips pouting becomingly.

Brandon's attention snapped back to his dance partner. The music had stopped. Her slim, bare arms remained looped around his neck, her lush body pressed enticingly against him. He could feel the warm, seductive imprint of her body from her thighs to the tempting thrust of her rounded breasts against his chest. Her lips were pouty and mere inches from his. She was beautiful and willing. He could take her home for a wild night of sex with no recrimination in the morning.

He stepped back. He didn't use women. "No man could ignore you," he finally said.

The practiced pout turned into a smile. "Brandon," she purred his name in one final attempt, and slid her arms slowly from around his neck and down his wide chest.

Brandon took her arm and started from the dance floor. As was true of many of the women in the room, he'd known Andrea since grade school. They'd thought they were madly in love when they were in the tenth grade. Two months later each had happily moved on to someone else.

They'd only gone a short distance when a cousin of Catherine's asked Andrea to dance. From the flare of interest in Andrea's eyes Brandon knew that, like in high school, her interest had moved on. Brandon relinquished her without a moment's hesitation or regret. He had yet to meet a woman he couldn't walk away from.

Out of habit his gaze roamed the jovial crowd of two hundred plus in the Conquistador Ballroom to ensure that things were going well. Naturally his restaurant wasn't catering, but as the honoree he saw it as his responsibility to see that his guests enjoyed themselves.

His mother insisted that all her children have a party for their special day, and as usual she had picked the perfect location. The House of Serenity was a picturesque hotel surrounded by beautiful flower gardens and managed by a woman who wouldn't settle for anything less than perfection, Faith McBride.

He saw the woman he had been thinking about and waved. A strained smile flickered across Faith's pretty face before she was lost in the crowd. Concerned, he tried to locate her again. Faith could handle an event this size with her eyes closed. So why did she look so worried?

Brandon located her moments later speaking to the chef at the carving station. She quickly moved to the open bar and then to the buffet table to view the ravages caused by the hungry partygoers. Arriving on her heels were three waiters with fresh trays of fruit, raw vegetables, and a delicious array of tidbits. With a brief nod of approval, she was off again.

Thanks to Faith's guidance the waitstaff was doing an excellent job of keeping the food and drinks flowing. As part-owner and executive manager of Casa de Serenidad, she had taken the hotel from three stars to five in six years. He hadn't been surprised.

The pretty face and quick smile of the woman who barely came to his shoulder belied the tenacious spirit underneath. Faith wouldn't settle for anything less than the best. Meticulous and savvy, outgoing and vivacious, there wasn't a thing she put her mind to that she couldn't accomplish.

She was the main reason for the hotel's success. She genuinely cared about people, and it showed. She didn't need harsh words to reprimand; a raised brow worked just as well. Her staff was extremely loyal and devoted to her. He should know. He'd unsuccessfully tried several times to woo away the executive chef of their famed restaurant, the Pueblo. As at the Red Cactus, the employees here were like a big family. So what was bothering her?

Whatever the reason, he didn't like seeing her unhappy. He started to make his way through the crowd toward her. A familiar voice pulled him up short.

"How does it feel to be so old?" joked Cameron

McBride. He was dressed comfortably in a sports jacket and jeans.

Brandon grinned at the man who'd been his best friend since kindergarten. They matched each other in height at six-foot-two, but while Brandon had broad shoulders and hard muscles, Cameron had a long, wiry build that suited him for his life's passion, racing for NASCAR. "Since you're older by a week, you tell me."

"In a room full of beautiful women how do you think I feel?" Cameron replied, a roguish smile on his handsome face.

"With the McBride curse, it won't do you any good," came another voice.

Brandon glanced around to see Duncan McBride, Faith and Cameron's older brother, approach. Tall and rugged, Duncan had the loose-limbed gait of a man who spent long hours in the saddle and the conditioned muscles and calloused hands of a man who worked his sprawling Montana ranch.

Although Duncan and Cameron had personal reasons to disagree with him, Brandon didn't believe in the curse that no McBride would ever be happy in love, but the thought brought his earlier concern hurtling back. "Faith doesn't look happy."

Both brothers searched the room until they found their baby sister in a group of mutual friends. "She looks fine to me," said Duncan.

"Same here," Cameron agreed.

Brandon threw the brothers a disgruntled look. "How can you say that? There's obviously something wrong."

"I don't see a problem," Duncan told him. "There's someone I need to speak with. Bye."

"Your instincts are usually dead-on about women, but this time you're wrong." Cameron slapped Brandon playfully on the back. "Maybe it's old age." Brandon glared at him. His best friend laughed harder. "Despite Duncan's gloomy prediction, I might as well try to break the curse and find myself someone who won't mind taking a chance on me."

Brandon caught the sadness beneath the blithe words. "There are other women."

A shadow briefly crossed Cameron's pensive face. "Yeah. I keep trying to tell that to my stupid heart. I'll catch you later." He walked away.

Brandon wished he could do something to help, but only time or Caitlin's return would accomplish that. On the heels of that thought came one even more disturbing. Had a man put that look of utter misery on Faith's face?

"What has upset you?"

Brandon whipped his head around at the sound of his mother's worried voice. She was a tall, beautiful woman with sharp cheekbones and unblemished golden skin. She had the trim figure of a woman who took care of herself, and onyx eyes that saw too much.

Admitting his concerns about Faith would send the wrong message. "What's there to be upset about?

I'm happy and single and I plan to remain that way for a long, long time."

"We shall see," Ruth said, her voice calm and self-assured.

Brandon fought back a frown as he recalled all the other occasions in his life he'd heard his mother utter those words. In each case she'd emerged victorious. He was determined that this time it would be different. If he showed even the slightest hint of weakness or doubt, she would use it to her advantage. She was relentless when it came to doing what she felt was best for her children—even if they disagreed with her. "I'm winning this time, Mama. Admit it."

"I admit that I love you and only want what's best for you."

She hadn't given up. She stared up at him with utter devotion and steadfast determination. She wouldn't be satisfied until he was shackled to some woman. It was useless to argue or ask her to stop. Love drove her.

"I make my own decisions," he told her.

She briefly palmed the smooth line of his jaw with her soft hand. "I wouldn't have it any other way. Now, go circulate with your guests."

Brandon's black eyes narrowed for a moment. To anyone else his mother's words might have given the impression she was quitting. He knew better. She had the uncanny ability to use your assets against you. "I'm on to you. This time it'll be different." Bending, he kissed her on her unlined cheek, and then he walked away.

Almost immediately Felicia Falcon, Ruth's sister-in-law, came up beside Ruth. "Is everything in place?"

"Finally. I surmised getting them together would be difficult, but I hadn't anticipated to what extent." The irritation in Ruth's voice turned to undisguised satisfaction. "It begins tonight."

A pleased smile on her beautiful face, Felicia handed Ruth one of the flutes filled with sparkling cider. Dangling from the stem was an *N* for nonalcoholic and, in honor of Brandon's birthday, a second charm of cowboy boots. "I wish I could be here to see them start falling in love."

Ruth smiled over the rim of her glass. "You are. It's already started."


Faith McBride saw the troubled expression on Brandon's face and immediately excused herself from the group she'd been chatting with. "Brandon, is there a problem?"

Blowing out a breath, he shoved his hands into the pockets of his slacks. "Mama is at it again."

Faith's gaze jerked to Ruth Grayson standing across the room with her sister-in-law, Boston socialite and art patron, Felicia Falcon. The pleased expressions on their faces were a marked contrast to Brandon's unhappy one. Faith felt her stomach clench. "You mean—"

"She won't be happy until there's a ball and chain around my neck," Brandon said, gritting his teeth.

"She loves you," Faith offered. It was the truth and the best Faith could come up with at the moment. She had thought she had more time.

"I know and that makes it worse." One hand came out of his pocket to swipe across his handsome face. "She'll never give up because she wants each of her children to be happy. But her idea of happiness isn't mine."

"Your brothers are happy," Faith said, pointing out the unmistakable truth.

"More ammunition."

*True and all the worse for me,* she thought, but she'd always known the odds weren't in her favor. "Smile or people will think you're unhappy with the services of Casa de Serenidad." she told him, trying to tease him out of his unhappy mood.

The corners of his mobile mouth tilted. "Next to the Red Cactus, this is the best place to throw a party."

Her naturally arched brow lifted. "Is that why you keep trying to steal my executive chef?"

Brandon somehow managed to look offended. "Would I do that to an old friend?"

"In a heartbeat," Faith answered without a moment's hesitation.

He laughed, a deep, rich sound that sent goose bumps skipping over her body. "You know me too well."

"Brandon, dance with me." Elizabeth Jackson, sleek, thin, and wearing a black mini cocktail dress that hugged her ample bust and long legs to eye-popping perfection, ran her fingers down Brandon's wide chest.

Faith briefly wondered what Elizabeth would look like with every strand of her thick auburn hair on the floor, then shook the uncharitable thought away. It wasn't Elizabeth's fault that she was bold enough to speak up and go after what she wanted, whereas Faith hadn't the courage to do so.

Brandon gave Elizabeth a dimpled smile that caused the slim, beautiful woman to sigh with pleasure. "Let me take a rain check. Right now Faith and I are going to show the people on the dance floor how it's done." Catching Faith's hand, he started toward the dancers.

Elizabeth blinked as if she couldn't believe she had been rebuffed or who Brandon had chosen in her place. Faith was having a difficult time believing it as well and wishing she weren't twenty pounds overweight—all right, it was more than that, but if she thought about the exact number it would spoil the moment.

A teasing glint entered Brandon's midnight black eyes when he stopped in the midst of the dancers. "You do remember how to dance, don't you?"

Faith caught his playful mood and forgot about Elizabeth and the extra pounds she'd carried since she was a child. "I might."

"Let's see." With no more warning than that, Brandon pulled Faith into his arms, only to send her spinning in a succession of fast circles before he caught her around the waist to sway and dip to the pulsating beat of the music. "You didn't forget," he whispered against her ear.

Shivers raced down her spine at his warm breath. She'd never forgotten one precious second with Brandon. "I had a good teacher."

Twirling her away, then back in quick repetitions, he stepped away, and they danced around each other in a synchronized beat that had couple after couple stopping to watch and clap their hands. Brandon caught Faith again, pulling her back against him as they went halfway to the floor, then back up, wiggling all the way.

Hand in hand he swung her out on the floor as if it were yesterday instead of eleven years since they'd danced together. Grinning at each other and out of breath, they finished with his arm clamped tightly around her waist. Applause erupted. Stepping to one side, they gave exaggerated, laughing bows and left the dance floor.

"Let's get something to drink." Brandon's arm remained curved with easy familiarity around her.

Fanning her flushed face, Faith tried to keep her voice normal. "You need to be with your guests."

He shook his dark head, sending his thick black hair confined at the base of his neck with a thick silver band skimming sensuously down his back, and kept walking. "I'm sticking with you while Mama is watching."

Faith stopped abruptly and looked up at Brandon's handsome, strong, and, so she thought, intelligent face. "So I'm safe," she said, trying to keep the hurt and anger out of her voice.

Eyes that she dreamed about stared down into hers. "You're the only woman I can be sure of. I can relax with you. You aren't after me."

*I want you more than all of the others put together,* she thought. She knew she could never voice the words.

Apparently taking her silence for agreeing with his assessment, Brandon straightened, slinging his arm around her shoulders in a brotherly fashion as he'd done so many times in the past. "We're just friends."

Faith swallowed the knot in her throat. *Just friends.* He didn't see her as a desirable woman. He probably never would. At least she had his friendship. As they walked to the bar she tried to tell herself that was enough.

I

"Thank goodness this is the last trip." Pierce Grayson, Brandon's younger brother, set the coffee bean grinder on the gleaming black granite counter in Brandon's spotless and ultramodern kitchen with a relieved sigh. The counter was filled with birthday gifts of various kitchen utensils and cooking appliances.

"What's her name?" Brandon didn't even try to keep the sarcasm out of his voice as he placed a twelve-speed stainless-steel blender and a rice cooker and steamer next to the coffee bean grinder.

A grin flashed across the sculpted face that women couldn't seem to get enough of. "Carmella."

Brandon folded his arms and leaned back against the counter. "You could at least pretend not to be having so much fun while I'm having none."

Pierce's manicured hand slapped Brandon on the back. "I appreciate your sacrifice, big brother."

"Only a nitwit would believe that," Sierra Grayson, their baby sister, mocked as she nudged over a sleek stainless-steel can opener to place an assortment of gourmet cooking oils on the breakfast table.

Pierce tried and failed to look contrite. "I'm just storing up memories."

Sierra made a face. "You've been using that lame excuse since Luke bit the dust."

"Just proves me right, since Morgan fell so quickly." Pierce turned to his older brother. "Brandon here is made of sturdier stuff."

"I might not be able to hold out much longer." His glance slid away from Sierra, who promptly rolled her eyes. He didn't like talking about sex in front of her.

"Pierce certainly couldn't have held out this long," Sierra said, running her fingers through shiny black hair that tumbled to her tiny waist.

Pierce shuddered and once again clasped Brandon's shoulder. "She's right. I couldn't. Are you sure this is the only way?"

Morose, Brandon nodded and unfolded his arms. "I've thought about this a lot. Playing the field is the only way."

"Then why aren't you playing?" Pierce demanded with his usual straightforwardness to get to the bottom of a problem.

"And don't act as if I haven't ever heard the word 'sex' before," Sierra said. "Pierce has a point. You dated before. Why stop now?"

"Because before Mama wasn't in the mix," he said a bit impatiently. "She has the uncanny ability to pick out the right woman. I can't take a chance that the woman I date is the one."

"I see your point," Pierce said slowly, then hung his head, only to lift it moments later. "Sierra, if Brandon falls, you might as well start picking out your china pattern."

Sierra swatted her brother on the chest. "Because we all know you can't go two days without a woman," she said with disgust.

"Women like me," Pierce said, his broad smile returning as he straightened the silk tie that exactly matched the pocket square in his fifteen-hundred-dollar wheat-colored sports jacket.

"They used to like me, too," Brandon said, his shoulders slumped.

Pierce and Sierra traded worried glances. Both knew one of the perks of Brandon's popular restaurant was all the women who came there. He adored women. Sierra lightly touched Brandon's arm in sympathy. "If it's any consolation, I'm not dating, either."

"You're too picky," Pierce said.

"Just like my brothers taught me to be," she said. "Whereas you, my dear brother, could use some of the same discretion. Carmella De La Vegas is a temperamental flamenco dancer who has a reputation for shredding her lovers once she's finished with them."

"Until now," Pierce said with confidence. "If there is nothing else, Carmella is waiting."

Sierra wrinkled her nose. "Since her group's last

performance was tonight, I guess we won't hear from you until after she leaves Tuesday morning."

Pierce's dark eyes narrowed. "She's staying in a hotel, not in one of your lease properties. How do you know her itinerary?"

"Trade secret," she said sweetly.

"Get out of here," Brandon urged. "I would tell you to think of me, but it would be ungentlemanly."

With one last puzzled look at Sierra, Pierce left. As soon as the door closed, Brandon asked, "How did you know?"

She laughed. "I read it in the newspaper."

Brandon chuckled. "He'll worry about it all night. He likes everything neat and tidy."

"Exactly." Opening a drawer, Sierra pulled out a box cutter.

Brandon promptly took it away from her. "I can do this in the morning." He put the box she had been about to open under his arm and ushered her to the door. "Good night, and thanks."

With her hand on the doorknob, she paused. "If you need any help taking the old appliances to the Women's League, let me know."

Brandon shook his head. The Women's League was a nonprofit organization to help the disadvantaged of Santa Fe. His mother was an active member and past president. "Mother and Mrs. Poole are coming to pick up everything Monday. I understand they already have a waiting list."

"And you'll go over Tuesday night to give cooking

instructions and food demonstrations and then feed the fifty or so extra men and women who show up at no charge," Sierra said.

He shrugged carelessly. "I enjoy doing it."

"And they enjoy having you." Sierra opened the door. "See you then, if not before. We know we won't see Pierce much before then."

Brandon grimaced. "Don't remind me."

She bit her lip in an uncharacteristic indecisive motion. "Perhaps dating just a bit wouldn't hurt."

Brandon threw his free arm around her slight shoulders. "That means a lot coming from you, and I *might* have to dip my toe in the dating waters again, but I'm going to try to hold out a little longer. Mama seemed too pleased with herself tonight."

Sierra's ebony eyes widened. "You think she's picked out your wife?"

Brandon sighed. "Yes."

"I don't suppose you have any idea who she is?" Sierra asked.

"Not a clue," he said with disgust. "Catherine and Phoenix were both from out of town. And we're still unsure if Mama had a hand in bringing Phoenix and Morgan together."

"I'm not," Sierra said. "Mama doesn't leave anything to chance. Remember, one of the cities Phoenix visited before she came here was Boston. Aunt Felicia might live with Uncle John Henry on his ranch in Oklahoma, but she grew up in Boston, her parents are there, *and* she has strong ties to the art community there. My guess is that Aunt Felicia had a hand in it somehow."

"Aunt Felicia and Mama spent a lot of time together tonight," Brandon said thoughtfully. "But they've always been close, even when Uncle John Henry and Aunt Felicia were separated."

"Besides being from out of town, the women she chose were talented and gifted. Catherine is a noted children's author; Phoenix, a renowned sculptress."

"So you think the woman Mama's picked is an artist or a woman with a special talent or gift of some type?"

"I'd like to say yes, but we both know how unpredictable Mama is."

"So, basically, I'm screwed."

"Not for a while," Sierra said, deadpan.

Brandon burst out laughing and hugged her again. "Get out of here. Drive safely, and call me when you get home."

It was a ritual Sierra was familiar with. "Happy birthday, and may you have many, many more."

"Hopefully as a single man."

Giving him one last smile, she went through the open door and closed it softly behind her.

Brandon turned with the boxed can opener and yawned. Opening the gifts and putting them away could wait. Setting the box on the kitchen table, he headed to the bedroom. By the time he reached the middle of the room his shirt was off.

Plopping on the side of the king-size bed, he pulled

off his favorite Red Cactus boots, then shucked his slacks. He preferred jeans but had worn the pants to please his mother. Thank goodness he hadn't had to wear a tie. He'd leave that to Morgan and Pierce.

Opening the door to his bathroom, Brandon was three feet inside when he stepped in water. He glanced down and muttered an oath. Water trailed from the baseboard a few feet away.

Crouching, he discovered the wall behind the commode was wet. Straightening, he went to the phone in the bedroom and speed-dialed. With a restaurant, he never knew when he might need a plumber or electrician or any number of services.

"Reliable Plumbing answering service."

Brandon recognized Kay Smith's dry smoker's voice immediately. She was the owner's mother-in-law. "Good evening, Mrs. Smith. This is Brandon Grayson. I need Mr. Montgomery right away. I think a pipe in my wall burst."

"In your restaurant?" asked the efficient voice.

"My apart—" The bathroom was directly over the restaurant's storeroom. "Please tell Mr. Montgomery I'll be downstairs." Hanging up the phone, Brandon snagged his pants and rushed downstairs.

"Please reconsider and wait until tomorrow to leave." Faith stood on the bricked sidewalk in front of Casa de Serenidad with her two brothers. Their luggage was already inside the trunk of the luxury rented sedan.

"I wish I could, but I need to get back to the ranch," Duncan told her. "It's haying time."

"I have to meet one of my race car sponsors in Chicago on Monday," Cameron explained.

*And if you stay, you might be reminded of too many memories.* "I love you."

They hugged her, then started to the car, only to stop and come back. "You changed your mind?" she asked, meeting them halfway.

Duncan stared down at her. "Brandon seemed to think you weren't happy tonight. You'd tell us if there was a problem, wouldn't you?"

Faith's heart thumped. The last thing she needed was her brothers knowing how she felt about Brandon. "Brandon's mistaken."

Cameron frowned. "Obviously what we know about women you could put on the head of a pin."

Faith had never felt so helpless. She could cheerfully have wrung Caitlin's neck for what she'd done to Cameron. "Some women can't see what's in front of them."

"I'd hate like hell for you to fall prey to the McBride curse," Duncan said.

Pain and shadows crossed her brother's dark face. When Faith finished with Caitlin, Duncan's ex-wife, Sheryl, was next. "I have to believe one day things will change in our favor."

"We pray that's true for you," Duncan said. What he hadn't said was that for him and Cameron there was no hope. Hugging her, he passed her to Cameron's waiting arms.

"Take care." Cameron tweaked her nose. "Stay safe."

"You both do the same. Good-bye." She watched Cameron climb into the driver's seat while Duncan got in on the passenger side. Cameron was happiest when he was behind the wheel.

It wasn't often that they could get together. Duncan was busy with his ranch in Montana, and Cameron was on the NASCAR circuit. Both had fled Santa Fe after their disastrous relationships. In that, they'd done as their father had done when their mother had left him the day Faith graduated from college six years ago.

The McBrides could turn a dime into a dollar, as her grandfather had often said, but they weren't worth warm spit when it came making their women stick around. With Faith's birth, the first female in six generations, they'd all thought their luck had changed. So far, it hadn't.

Turning, Faith followed the well-lit path through the bricked archway into the courtyard flush with blooming flowers in bright hues of red and purple, then continued into the open lobby of Casa de Serenidad, her pride and joy. After her mother left, Faith's father had lost interest in the hotel that had been in the family for two generations.

With Duncan and Cameron gone, the job of running the establishment had fallen to her. It had been scary for a woman fresh out of college, armed only with a business degree and zeal, to succeed. She'd put her plans of traveling the world on hold and settled down to running the family business.

Her heels clicked softly on the terrazzo floor. Her practiced eyes surveyed the area, pleased with the comfortable jade green leather sitting area, fresh floral arrangements, and muted colors of red, green, and yellow in the throw pillows and the area rug. As usual, she stopped by the front desk before retiring for the night.

"Hello, Pamela. Everything is going well, I see." One thing she'd learned was to always phrase a question as a positive statement.

"Yes, Ms. McBride." Pamela Houston was a new hire and overflowing with good cheer. Cute and petite, with big brown eyes, she had a knack for soothing the ruffled feathers of disgruntled travelers who'd had delayed flights, car trouble, or other problems before arriving. "A number of the guests at the Grayson party stopped by and asked for information on the guest and banquet facilities. We gave them the gift bags you had prepared. They were all thankful and were only too anxious to provide their mailing information."

"Excellent." The note from her offering 15 percent off their first stay for completing the form probably helped. Everyone liked a bargain.

"They were disappointed that we're booked solid through summer," Pamela added.

"Thanks to the efficient employees like you, we will stay that way." The only reason Faith's brothers had a room was that she had known when Brandon's party was scheduled and had reserved the suite far in advance. Another guest had late check-in Sunday afternoon. "Good night."

"Good night, Ms. McBride. Sleep well."

"Thank you," Faith said, knowing that sleep depended on whether she had the nightmare of Brandon at the altar waiting for his bride or the erotic one with Brandon doing things to her body that left her breathless with desire. She dreaded both. They were a painful reminder of what she could never have. And if he learned her secret she'd never be able to face him again.

Was there any misery worse than loving a man who didn't love you back? If there was, Faith didn't want any part of it.

In a long silk lilac-colored nightgown Faith stood in front of the vanity in the oversize bathroom decorated in muted tones of blue and beige and tried to objectively assess herself. She started with her face—mocha-colored, unblemished, with naturally arched eyebrows and an average nose and mouth. She would never drive a man wild with lust, but she wouldn't make him run screaming from the room, either.

Inhaling deeply, she let her gaze drift downward,

quickly running over the ample breasts that she had
tried to hide in high school with oversize shirts in the
summer and sweaters in the winter. Then she viewed
her entire body. *They're still there* . . . the thirty, all
right, fifty-three and a half pounds that, no matter
how she starved herself or how many miles she ran,
clung to her like a burr.

Her mother fondly called her daughter and youngest child "curvy." Those less charitable called her
fat. She lifted her arms and vigorously shook them,
pleased that no loose skin jiggled. She might be ample, but she was toned. As if that would help her get
Brandon to notice her.

Faith left the bathroom, cutting off the light as she
went into the adjoining bedroom, and climbed into
the ornately carved queen-size bed with a six-foot
scalloped headboard upholstered with blue check
silk. The pale blue damask coverlet edged with silk
trim matched the drawn striped silk draperies. Vintage beams crossed overhead to meet in the middle,
where a handblown glass chandelier with crystal drops
hung. On the opposite wall over her fireplace was an
1850 French tapestry.

Drawing up her knees, she stared out the French
casement double doors leading to the lit terrace.
Outside, Wave petunias, Dragon Wing begonias, im-
patiens, and moss roses in full bloom spilled over
urns and terra-cotta pots. Pink peace roses trailed
over the brick wall at the back of the enclosure.

Since she couldn't travel to Paris, she had decided

to incorporate a French flair when redecorating her home. Countless times she'd imagined Brandon here with her.

He thought of her as the little sister of his best friend. She thought of him as her knight in shining armor, her prince charming, the man she had secretly loved since he had saved her from going to her sophomore dance without a date. She'd assumed Cameron had put Brandon up to asking her, but when she'd asked him he'd grinned and said it was his idea.

Faith hadn't been able to contain her happiness until she remembered she couldn't dance and sadly admitted as much to Brandon. Ignoring the good-natured jibes and instructions from Cameron, Brandon had proceeded to teach her.

The night of the dance was magical. He'd given her a gardenia corsage and acted as if it were a real date. She'd even been able to talk him into briefly playing the saxophone of one of the band members. She knew he played a musical instrument, as all the Grayson siblings did, but had never heard him play. Each note had resonated in her heart. Loving Brandon was the easiest things in her life to do. The hug at her front door was almost as good as a kiss. He cared.

Whenever she had a problem, Brandon had always been there to help her solve or get through it. And he might be lost to her forever.

Everyone in Santa Fe knew that Brandon was next in line to get married. It was only a matter of time before his mother threw a woman in his path whom he couldn't resist . . . just as she had done with his older brothers. When that happened, Faith would lose any chance of making Brandon notice her. He was the kind of man who would love one woman deeply, completely. Once he found his soul mate, it was all over for Faith, and there was nothing she could do about it.

"Pipe busted all right." Jerry Montgomery, in overalls and a starched chambray shirt, hunkered down in front of the wet wall behind the commode.

"You're sure? I mopped the water off the floor and it's still dry." Brandon squatted beside the thin man. "Maybe I was mistaken."

Jerry turned, his bushy salt-and-pepper eyebrows arched at a haughty angle. "You questioning me?"

Mr. Montgomery was more than twice Brandon's age and a master plumber. He'd been Brandon's mother's plumber for as long as he could remember, charging her a fraction of what it cost for repairs while she raised five children on her teacher's salary. "I—"

"I turned off the water outside before I came in."

"Oh!" Brandon mumbled, and barely kept from ducking his head.

"What would you tell someone who tried to tell you how to cook one of those fancy dishes of yours?" Mr. Montgomery asked.

" 'Take a flying leap,' " Brandon answered almost immediately.

"Thought so," the plumber said, slowly coming to his feet with a wrench in his hand.

Brandon thought he heard bones crack. He knew the discussion was over. "How soon can it be fixed?"

"Depends on what I find when I get in the wall. In the meantime, you won't have water."

Panic rushed through Brandon. "The restaurant can't run without water."

"Won't have to." Jerry started from the room. "Different water lines."

Brandon's relief was short-lived. "I can't stay here without water."

"You could for a while, but like I said, I'm not sure how long the job will take until I get in that wall." He stopped at the door. "I don't like working on the Lord's Day, but I guess this is an emergency."

"I'd consider it one," Brandon said.

"Thought you might. I suppose you'll be here to let me in tomorrow afternoon after church."

"I'll be here." Brandon blew out a disgusted breath. "This couldn't have happened at a worse time."

"Plumbing problems seldom happen at a good time."

"I suppose you're right. I'll see you out." Opening the door, he led the elderly man down the stairs to the first floor, then unlocked the front half-glass door. "Thanks for coming."

"Keep that thought when you see my bill."

"I'll try. I'll see you tomorrow. Good night."

"Night."

Brandon watched until Mr. Montgomery climbed into his white van. When the headlights came on, Brandon waved, then closed and locked the door. Slowly he trudged back up the stairs.

In the bathroom, he knelt down and felt the wall, almost tempted to get a hammer and see the damage for himself. The only thing stopping him was the possibility of doing even more damage. He came to his feet, hoping the problem could be fixed easily. In the meantime, he needed a shower and a place to stay.

He discarded his mother immediately. She had three empty bedrooms, but she'd have women lined up at the door when he woke up in the morning. At this point he wasn't sure he wouldn't succumb.

Obviously Luke and Morgan were still honeymooning. Pierce wasn't home. Sierra, who had called when he came back upstairs with Mr. Montgomery, had had her extra bedroom lined with cedar and turned into a closet. She had more clothes than a store.

He had friends, but it was close to one in the morning. Just because he was sleeping single didn't mean his friends were . . . except Cameron.

Brandon reached for the phone, then let his hand fall. Cameron might have gotten lucky with the dark-haired beauty he left the party with.

Pulling a duffel bag from his closet, Brandon began to pack. During the summer the area hotels were booked solid. Perhaps by the time he finished he'd have figured out where he was spending the night.

# 2

"Casa de Serenidad, House of Serenity, how may I assist you?"

"Cameron or Duncan McBride, please." With his duffel bag all packed, Brandon had come to a decision. It wasn't likely Cameron or Duncan had brought a woman back to a hotel room they were sharing. No man worth a nickel would do that; neither would they disrespect Faith that way. Brandon had crashed at their place on the floor when they were growing up just as they had at his. It wouldn't hurt for a night to do so again.

"They checked out."

Brandon's initial surprise quickly faded. Santa Fe and Casa de Serenidad held too many bad memories for both men. But if they'd checked out that meant their room was empty until the next guest checked in "Ms. McBride."

"I'm sorry, sir. Ms. McBride is off duty. Can the night manager assist you?"

Brandon rubbed the back of his neck. "This is Brandon Grayson, a family friend. Please connect me. It's important."

"Certainly, Mr. Grayson."

Faith came on the line almost immediately. "Brandon, is everything all right?"

"No, but you can certainly help with a major problem." He sat on the bed. "A pipe burst in my bathroom and the water is off. Since Cameron and Duncan left, I thought I could throw myself on your mercy and have their room for the night."

"Of course, but another guest is scheduled to arrive this afternoon."

"That's all right. I just need a place to crash and take a shower."

"Oh," she said, sounding strange. "I'll call the front desk. It's the Conquistador Suite. One of our best."

"Just so it has a bed and a shower."

"That and a lot more. See you in a bit."

Standing, he picked up his bag. "You don't have to get out of bed."

"Brandon, have I ever tried to tell you how to run the Red Cactus?"

He smiled. "That makes twice I've been told off tonight. First Mr. Montgomery and now you."

"He's such a sweet man."

"I hope you understand if I don't comment."

Laughter drifted through the receiver. "I'll tell the front desk to expect you. It's the room to the immediate left of mine."

He knew her room because he had been in and out of it hundreds of times when her father was the executive manager. Since he'd retired, Brandon didn't recall ever going there again. "Thanks, Faith. I really appreciate this."

"You've come to my rescue a number of times."

Although Faith was popular in high school, she had few prospects for school dances. Hanging around her house, he'd seen how bad she felt and stepped in. On the other hand, Sierra always had too many boys wanting to take her out in his and his brothers' opinions. Brandon had never figured out why boys preferred a girl who kept them waiting, was picky about where they went and bossy to boot, to one who was always sweet and agreeable. "I was happy to do it."

"I know. I'll be waiting."

"Bye." Brandon hung up, unaware of the smile on his face.

As she was used to dealing with unexpected crises at the spur of the moment, it didn't take Faith long to slip out of her nightgown into undergarments, then pull on a loose-fitting white blouse and black slacks. Bemoaning the fact that she didn't have time to reapply her makeup, she raked a comb through her curly black hair and swiped on lip gloss, grabbed her master key, and hurried out the door. Brandon's place was only a short five-minute walk away. She wanted his room ready when he arrived.

Opening the heavy wooden gate that separated her private quarters from the hotel grounds, she hurried to the linen closet located just inside the hotel. The cart was already stocked and ready for the morning shift to begin cleaning. Rather than take time gathering the necessary items, she grabbed the metal handles and was out the door in seconds.

The two housekeepers on duty were probably in the lounge watching television or asleep in two of the recliners. Faith didn't even think of disturbing them. The hotel billed itself as having twenty-four-hour room and maid service. She could make up a bed and replace the toiletries as well as they could. Duncan and Cameron, unlike Brandon, were relatively neat, so she didn't expect the room to be a disaster. As for sanitizing the bath, all three had roomed together many times, so that wasn't an issue.

Opening the door to the suite, she was pleased to see that she was right. Except for the newspaper in the trash can, the room looked as if the maids had just left. Going into the spacious bathroom, she replaced the toiletries and cleaned the mirror, smiling as she did so. Duncan still liked to brush his teeth within inches of his reflection.

In the living area, she dumped the trash and put a fresh liner in the ice bucket; then she moved to the bedroom. She had just folded the abstract coverlet onto the covered bench at the foot of the king-size bed when she heard the door open. She froze, then

drew a calming breath and went to the bedroom door.
Her mouth watered; her heart yearned.

Brandon in a black T-shirt and jeans was a sight
that would make any woman's pulse race. The T-shirt
stretched across a muscled chest before tapering down
to a hard, flat stomach. The faded denim hugged muscled thighs with wanton pleasure.

Brandon's gaze flickered to the cart, then back to
her. "Tell me there's someone here with you."

"You forget, Brandon, that I've worked in almost
every capacity of this hotel since I was nine."

"You weren't the executive manager then," he told
her, crossing the room in a lazy gait.

No matter how impossible it was, she wished he
was coming to her as a man who desired a woman,
wished he was taking her to bed, where they'd rum-
ple the sheets and drive each other crazy. She turned
away before he could see the desire she kept care-
fully hidden from him and went back to the bed.

As she reached for the sheet, his strong fingers
closed gently but firmly around her upper forearm.
"Leave it and go to bed. It's almost two."

Her pulse skidded. He was so close. Too close.
Wide-eyed, she stared at him.

His midnight black eyes narrowed for a moment.
His fingers loosened. "Faith?"

"Stop being bossy and go around to the other side
and help," she said, refusing to look at him.

For a long moment he didn't move; then mercifully

he did as she'd asked. But as she tried to pull the sheet back he simply held his end. She was forced to meet his gaze.

"You'd tell me if there was something on your mind, wouldn't you?"

"Brandon, as you pointed out earlier, I'm executive manager. There's always a lot on my mind," she said with a smile. "Now, let's get this done. Unlike you, I like to start the day with a good breakfast."

That got him rolling. "The best sleep is in the morning."

*The best sleep would be in your arms.* The thought popped so suddenly into Faith's head that for a scary moment she thought she might have voiced the words. Thankfully, Brandon had gathered the old sheets in his arms and was placing them on the easy chair.

Her face warm, Faith grabbed the fresh bottom sheet and flipped it to the other side. "The restaurant didn't have any plumbing problems, did it?"

"No, thank goodness," he told her, following her lead in making the bed. "We're on two different water lines. We'll be able to open as usual tomorrow for lunch."

Expertly she encased three pillows while Brandon was trying to do one. She simply held out her hand after she finished the fifth one. He handed his over without an argument.

"Guess I wasn't much help."

"Your expertise lies in the kitchen, not the bedroom." Her eyes widened at the slip. She could have bitten off her tongue.

"Not anymore," he mumbled, then seemed to realize what he'd blurted. A dull flush climbed up his neck.

Hugging the pillow, Faith couldn't have been happier with the news. "I'd heard you weren't dating very much."

"Try 'at all.'" His hands rested akimbo on his narrow waist. "And it's Mama's fault. Her and her wild scheme to get all of us married."

"So you're not dating to escape the odds of falling into your mother's plans for you to be next?" she reasoned.

A pleased smile crossed his face. "It's great that I don't always have to explain everything to you. I might worry about it if you weren't my friend."

"That's me, friendly and safe." Stepping around him, Faith gathered the linens.

Brandon caught the sarcasm in her voice and trailed after her. "I think I know what the problem is."

Clutching the bedsheets, she stared up at him, her eyes wide with foreboding. "I told you there is no problem."

His long-fingered hands clamped on her shoulders when she started to turn away. "Is some man giving you a tough time?"

Her jaw slackened.

He emphatically nodded his dark head once. "Thought so. You're too sweet and trusting."

*Sweet.* She gritted her teeth so hard they ached. She bet he'd never called any of the women after him tonight sweet.

"Forget him and move on," he advised, and straightened, letting his hands fall to his sides. "Don't let the McBride curse stop you."

"That's the least of my worries." Finally dumping the linen in the hamper attached to the cart, she grabbed the handles. "Good night, Brandon. Sleep well."

"I don't suppose you'd let me walk you back to put that up."

"As you said, we know each other too well."

"Stubborn," he said, but affection laced the word.

"Practical."

Opening the door, he yawned, then lifted muscled arms over his head, causing the thin black material to stretch and strain across his impressive chest. "Thanks again."

Her mouth as dry as cotton, Faith hurried through the door Brandon held open. It closed behind her with a soft click. Biting her lip, she glanced over her shoulder. Elizabeth wouldn't be out here; she'd be in bed with Brandon. But the hard truth was that where Brandon might want the other woman in his bed, he'd relegated Faith to the role of a friend.

Swallowing the sudden lump in her throat, she resumed pushing the cart.

• • •

Brandon woke tangled in the sheets and sprawled facedown. The uncomfortable sensation in his lower body was a blatant reminder that he'd been without a woman for too long. He'd dreamed of a woman last night, but he hadn't been able to get her, either.

One eyelid lifted, then quickly shut as bright sunlight streaming through the French doors assaulted him. Groping around, he found one of the pillows and pulled it over his head. There had been something oddly familiar about the dream woman who'd remained just beyond reach no matter how desperately he'd tried to touch her.

Turning over on his back, he dragged the pillow away and stared at the recessed ceiling, his thoughts returning to the mystery woman, since it wasn't likely he'd have a real woman in his bed anytime soon. He couldn't remember if she'd been short or tall, slender or voluptuous, dark or fair; all he was certain of was that she could assuage the aching need of his body.

Since he was so sure of it, she was probably a woman from his past. There had been times when he'd run into an old girlfriend and they'd ended up in bed. They'd go out a couple of times before realizing it wasn't going to work that time, either.

Strange he didn't have any sensory memory of the woman. After making love to a woman over a period of time you learned her body . . . the taste of her heated skin, the softness of her body, the unique scent of her, the sounds she made when she was aroused or reached orgasm.

Last night he'd drawn a blank . . . just like in real life.

Aware that sleep was impossible, he glanced at the small clock on the bedside. 9:37. Muttering an expletive, he sprang out of bed and headed for the shower. Time had gotten away from him.

Instead of daydreaming about some woman, he should have had his mind on his restaurant. The cleaning crew was due to arrive at 10:00 along with the first shift. The restaurant opened at 11:00. Since today was Sunday, they'd be busy from the time the door opened.

The black marble-tiled shower with its glass enclosure was large enough for three people or two people intent on pleasuring each other. Brandon gritted his teeth and switched the water temperature to cold. Enough was enough. He wouldn't make the week if he didn't get his mind off women . . . or one woman in particular.

Less than ten minutes later he was dressed in his usual blue jeans, white shirt, boots, and out the door. His strides long and purposeful on the flagstone walkway, he headed for the hotel. The bungalows were situated on a meandering maze. Thankfully his was only a short distance away from the lobby.

"Mr. Grayson."

Brandon pulled up short in the lobby to see a man in his midfifties wearing a light gray suit hurrying toward him. "Yes?"

"Compliments of Ms. McBride. She left this for you." The man, whose gold name tag read JENSON, offered Brandon a handled bag with MESA, the name of the hotel's restaurant for casual dining, printed in blue letters. "Enjoy."

Brandon hooked three fingers through the handle and briefly lifted the bag upward. The distinct aroma of fresh-baked breakfast pastries wafted up to him from the white bakery box inside. His mouth watered. "Henrí?" Brandon named the executive chef, an artistic genius who liked to "relax" by baking irresistible breads and pastries, and who Brandon had been trying to sway to leave Casa de Serenidad for months.

The other man nodded with a pleased smile and patted his slightly extended stomach, which tested the fit of his buttoned jacket. "He's the best, and a thermos of Blue Mountain."

Blue Mountain coffee was often called liquid gold because of the expense, but the taste was worth it. "Where is she?"

Jenson shrugged and pulled his cell phone from the pocket of his jacket. "She could be anywhere on the premises. She works harder than any two people. No task is too menial, and she always does it with a smile." He pressed his hand to his earpiece. "Shall I call her?"

Brandon shook his head. "Please tell Ms. McBride I said thanks and I'll call her later."

"Yes, sir. Have a great day."

"Thanks." On the sidewalk, Brandon glanced at

his stainless-steel watch, then set off at a brisk pace. 9:53. Maneuvering through the sidewalks, already crowded with summer tourists, with his hands full was more difficult than it had been early that morning.

Since the hotel was so close, instead of driving he had left his car in the garage behind the restaurant. Now he wished he had driven. He increased his pace.

Just shy of five minutes later Brandon rounded the corner and saw the Red Cactus across the street. He immediately recognized his brothers' and sister's vehicles, but what made his blood run cold was the police car.

# 3

Unsure of what he'd find, his skin clammy, Brandon burst through the open doors of the restaurant. Seeing his sister, worry on her face, her arms folded around herself, his brothers with their arms protectively around their wives, Pierce's head bowed, almost sent Brandon to his knees. "Mama?"

They all rushed forward. Sierra, always the volatile one, spoke first. "Where have you been?"

Brandon's worried gaze went to his oldest brother, Luke, always the leader and always calm. "Is . . . is Mama all right?"

"She's fine," Luke said, clasping a large hand on Brandon's shoulder. "It's you that had us worried."

"And pulled me from some very nice company," Pierce complained.

"Looks like I'm not needed here," the policeman said. "Sierra, looks like I can close the case on this."

"Sorry, Dakota," she said, then glared at Brandon.

"If someone would have had his cell phone this wouldn't have happened."

Dakota chuckled. "You're in for it now, Brandon. Hate I can't stay for the fireworks. Bye."

"Bye. And thanks, Dakota," Luke said. "Dinner is on me tonight."

"Anytime." Tipping his hat, the policeman left.

"Explain."

The one short command came from Brandon's sister, the Little General, fiercely loyal to her family, and who loved her brothers unconditionally.

"Mr. Montgomery had to cut off the water, so I stayed at Casa de Serenidad. Cameron and Duncan had checked out, so I took their room."

Pierce turned to Sierra. "I will never let you forget this."

Sierra waved his words aside. "It will show Carmella that she has to work harder to get you to be solely in her power."

A slow smile spread over Pierce's face. "You're forgiven."

"I'm glad you're all right, Brandon," Catherine, Luke's wife, said from beside him. "We were all worried."

"It's a wonder Dakota didn't give Morgan a ticket," Phoenix, Morgan's wife, added. "He bumped stop signs and went through three signal lights on yellow."

Brandon wasn't surprised by their concern. They had always been close. "I hope you didn't call Mama."

"Luke said not to," Sierra told him. "He said if you were breathing you'd be here at ten to let in the first shift."

Brandon glanced around and saw two of his staff behind the bar, another replacing the condiment containers. The cleaning crew was stacking chairs. "I tried to get here as fast as I could."

"Seeing your car here and knowing how you'd rather drive than walk across a street made us worry," Morgan said. "Next time, call."

"Yes, Mother," Brandon said, then laughed. The others joined in.

"What's in the bag?" Sierra said, pulling open one side.

Brandon pulled it out of reach. Sierra might be small, but she ate like a lumberjack and was always hungry. "These are mine. You've already had breakfast."

The brief flash across her face spoke more clearly than words. "What time did you start calling?"

Sierra shrugged and shoved her hands into the pockets of her short stylish black jacket. "Not until nine, since you're such a sleepyhead."

"I got the call at nine nineteen." Luke put his arm around Catherine's shoulder.

"Nine thirty," Morgan answered before he was asked.

"Nine thirty-seven. At a very inopportune moment," Pierce added, then folded his arms. "What were you doing at that time?"

Brandon thought of the dream and tucked his head. It came up when Pierce gave his shoulder a good-natured shove. "You were with a woman after all that talk of not dating?" his baby brother accused.

"You had me worried sick and you were with some woman." Sierra put her hand on her hips, then with the other yanked the sack from his loose grip. "This is definitely mine."

"I wasn't with a woman," Brandon admitted slowly, then continued at the skeptical looks from Pierce and Sierra, the sympathetic ones from his sisters-in-law, the understanding ones from his older brothers, "Come on sit down, and I'll tell you."

"This had better be good." Sierra led the way to the family table near the back of the restaurant.

While they slid onto the wooden benches, Brandon grabbed flatware, saucers, and cups and put them on the table. By the time he returned, Sierra had the container open and was munching on a flaky croissant. A quick look into the box confirmed his fear. There was only one.

"You could have waited."

She smiled and licked a golden flake from the corner of her winsome mouth. "You would have given it to me anyway. I just saved you the trouble."

*True.* All of them were putty in her hands. "But I want at least a sip of Blue Mountain."

"Blue Mountain," Pierce and Morgan cried in unison, and straightened.

Brandon might have known. If it cost money, Pierce

and Morgan knew about it. He said good-bye to his coffee and signaled Ruben at the bar to bring glasses and a carafe of orange juice. Catherine and Phoenix helped him serve, graciously declining pastries of their own in favor of sharing with their husbands.

"Talk, Brandon," Sierra said, taking another healthy bite.

"I wasn't with a woman. I was thinking about one I'd dreamed about," he said.

Forks clattered on the plates. Sierra and Pierce stared with wide accusing eyes at him.

"Last night you said you weren't interested in a woman." Pierce swiped a shaky hand across his face. "My days are numbered."

"There *isn't* a woman." Brandon wrapped his hands around his glass of juice. "She was in my dreams. I couldn't see her, but there was something familiar about her." He shrugged. "I lost track of time trying to figure out why I thought she was familiar."

Sierra relaxed in her seat. "You scared me . . . again."

"Same here." Pierce looked thoughtful. "I don't think I've ever dreamed about a woman."

"Capital assets and gains would be more your style," Morgan said drolly.

Unoffended, Pierce nodded. "Much more challenging and mysterious."

"On behalf of women everywhere, I have to disagree." Catherine placed her arms on the wooden table.

Morgan lifted Phoenix's hand and kissed it. "Phoenix was both, and a lot more."

"I didn't mean to be," Phoenix said. "It still scares me sometimes to think of what my life would have been like if we hadn't fallen in love."

"I don't want to think of a time without you," Morgan said.

Catherine put her head on Luke's shoulder and stared across the table at Pierce. "She's out there waiting for you."

"She'll have to catch me first." Sliding out of the booth, Pierce stood. "In the meantime, good-bye."

Brandon watched Pierce stroll from the restaurant. "The woman hasn't been born that can make Pierce a one-woman man."

"Then I'm safe." Sierra polished off her croissant and stood. "I'm picking up Mama for church." A pained expression crossed her face. "Afterwards we're going to Mrs. Poole's for lunch."

Amanda Poole was their mother's best friend and they dearly loved her, but she couldn't cook. Her food was always over- or undercooked. Brandon had tactfully tried to help her, but she just didn't have the knack. Her husband said he and their children had grown accustomed to it. No one had the heart to tell her. "I'll see you later for dinner."

"Did I say you were forgiven?" Sierra smiled. "See you this afternoon."

"Brandon," Catherine said. "I know you asked me

to never try to analyze you, but dreams or the lack thereof have meaning."

His sister-in-law was a noted child psychologist, children's author, and lecturer at St. John's College. He'd been joking at the time, but now looking at her serious expression he became a bit uneasy. "No offense, but I'll still pass."

Her hand gently covered his. "I understand. Life is much more interesting if there are a few surprises around the corner."

He wondered, just as he wondered about the mysterious woman of his dreams.


As soon as his last family member left the restaurant, Brandon went through his daily routine of speaking to each employee and checking to see that everything was in place for the day's operation. If there was a problem, either personally or with supplies, he wanted to know up front. He prided himself on customer satisfaction, which was tied to happy employees. Assured that all was in order, he headed for his apartment.

Inside, he tossed his duffel bag on the bed and went into the bathroom. Kneeling, his fingers brushed across the damp wall, the baseboard. Hoping the problem was minor, he pushed to his feet and returned to his room to charge his cell phone. He found it on top of the dress slacks he'd tossed on the bed. Perhaps if he wasn't such a lousy housekeeper he would have noticed it last night.

Plugging the charger in, he glanced around the room. The functional area was comfortable rather than stylish, with a mismatched overstuffed gray plaid sofa and blue easy chair. They were a far cry from the luxurious yet somehow homey feel of the room last night. When he'd moved in five years ago, where he slept hadn't mattered as much as finding the right location for his restaurant.

Being able to convert the upstairs into an apartment was an added plus. He'd put his money into purchasing the best equipment for his restaurant and the kitchen in his living quarters. He enjoyed developing new recipes and trying new ways of preparing old ones. For as long as he could remember, he'd been cooking.

As she had with all her children, his mother had encouraged him to follow his passion. While his friends were buying records or Atari games, he was spending his money on cookbooks and supplies. It never occurred to him to worry about how people perceived his plans to be a chef. Their mother taught her children to be self-sufficient, independent thinkers. If people were too narrow-minded to accept who or what you were, that was their problem, not yours.

He had a great mother and family. Luke and Morgan insisted on loaning him the money to get started. He'd paid them back with interest the first year. They were good men and had chosen good women. Phoenix was more introspective than Catherine, who had a way of seeing through the crap to the heart of the matter. But this time Brandon was ahead of her.

It was a good chance that he had at least met the woman from his dreams. Maybe she had turned him down and he was fantasizing about her. Maybe he had fixated on her because she was safe. It didn't matter. He wasn't going to waste any more time thinking about it.

Going to the table, Brandon slowly opened the lid of the bakery box. A Danish oozing with fresh strawberries and swirls of freshly made cream cheese icing lay inside. Phoenix had closed the box just before she left with Morgan and shoved it across the table to him.

Brandon inhaled. Anticipation was a big part of savoring food or a woman. Chastising himself for that lapse, he grabbed a fork from the drawer and took a bite of the pastry, chewed, savored, then swallowed. Delicious.

He was the pastry chef since the previous one had married and relocated. Neither he nor the one he'd lost was the culinary genius Henrí Fountain was. The wiry little Frenchman with the drooping mustache and snapping black eyes could make an angel weep with his cooking. Picking up the box, Brandon went to the phone and dialed.

"Good morning, Casa de Serenidad, House of Serenity Hotel, may I help you?"

Hastily he swallowed. "Ms. McBride, please."

"Certainly, sir. Have a good day."

Brandon leaned against the counter and took another bite. The day was certainly looking up, thanks to Faith.

"Good morning. Faith McBride. How may I help you?"

Her voice had always reminded him of sunshine on a beautiful spring day, bright and beckoning. "Good morning, Faith, and you already have," Brandon said. "Thanks for the pastries and coffee. Delicious. Although I had to share them with the family."

"Thanks. That's high praise coming from you. You dropped by your mother's house?"

Brandon ate another small bite, then told her what had happened. "Sierra grabbed the only croissant."

Soft laughter made him smile. "I'll ask Henrí to make enough for both of you tomorrow morning. They'll be waiting at the concierge desk after eight."

Her generosity didn't surprise him. "You make me almost think about stop trying to sway Henrí to work for me."

Faith harrumphed. "Try all you want, but Henrí will never leave me."

Brandon's lips curved. Faith never lacked assurance. She also inspired loyalty. Just as she had last night, she always went beyond what was expected of her. It was easy to return the favor and give back. "How about lunch or dinner? Whichever works for you."

A soft sigh drifted to him over the phone line. "I

wish I could, but Sundays can be hectic with so many people checking out and checking in."

He was surprised at the disappointment he felt. "Maybe some other time?"

"I'd love to."

Taking a pen from the coffee mug on the counter, a Red Cactus logo emblazoned on the white background, he wrote a note to remind himself on a recipe pad. "I suppose a guest has already checked into my room?"

"He's scheduled to arrive late this afternoon."

"He's a lucky man." Brandon glanced around his place with its out-of-style furniture and dark curtains. He'd adamantly refused to let his mother or Serena decorate his place. "I can see why you've gotten all the accolades. Casa de Serenidad is aptly named."

"Thanks. I'm glad you think so." He could tell from the inflection of her voice that she was moving. "I hope the plumbing problem is easily fixed."

"You and me both. I'll let you go. Bye."

"Bye, Brandon."

"Bye, Faith." He hung up the phone, looked around, and wondered why he felt a bit off. His gaze drifted to the bathroom and his question was answered. He was just annoyed with the inconvenience of no running water.


Faith took a seat in her executive chair and tapped her pen on her day planner. Brandon had been raised right. He'd called to thank her, then politely tried to repay her by inviting her to his restaurant. She'd declined because she didn't want him speculating anymore about the reason for her being unhappy last night.

He'd always been able to read her. Once that had pleased her; now it made her uneasy. Perhaps it was best this way. No matter how much she wished it were different, Brandon would never look at her with desire.

Faith accepted another hard truth. Brandon meant well, but his life was as busy as hers. Before his party last night she had seen him exactly twice in the last month. Once at the gallery opening of Phoenix's sculptures and another time when Faith had eaten at his restaurant.

At the opening, he'd been catering and as busy as she had been last night. The only time they'd spoken was when he'd served her a drink. At the Red Cactus, he'd been circulating and chatting with the dinner guests as he did nightly. There had been nothing special about his dropping by her table as she dined with a girlfriend, Martina Royal. Martina was ten years older than Faith, happily married, with a beautiful daughter, yet she'd still stared after Brandon with a hint of longing in her dark eyes, the same way Faith and many of the other women had done that night.

Brandon was popular not only because he was so handsome it made a woman's heart race just looking at him but also because he was a wonderful, caring guy. Even before his mother started her campaign to marry off her children, starting with the oldest, Brandon had topped the lists of many women as a prospective husband. Wealthy, successful, gorgeous. He could have his pick of women.

Faith had no experience enticing men. For as long as she could remember, boys and then men confided in her; they didn't lust after her. And because so many boys were her friends, the girls gravitated to her to get to the boys. She'd like to think they stayed her friends because they saw something in her they liked.

After her parents' divorce she'd been thrust into the role of managing the hotel, which meant long days and lonely nights. There had been no time to date even if she hadn't had a crush on Brandon. Only recently had she been able to take days off, and that was to visit Duncan or Cameron to check on them.

Their father was off with his new passion, competition trout fishing. He'd seemed happy three months ago when he'd visited. At least he'd lost that haggard look he'd worn for so long after her mother left. Her mother's marriage last year had sent him into a tailspin. He still loved her.

She loved another man.

Faith's fingers ran over the family picture of happier times in the McBride family. She of all people knew the odds of a McBride finding happiness in a relationship. Her brothers and father certainly hadn't.

She'd missed her chance with Brandon, although she couldn't see what she could have done differently to change things. Going over it again and again wasn't like her. *Stop feeling sorry for yourself, Faith.* She wasn't a woman who bemoaned what couldn't be changed.

She'd do better by working on the new initiative for Casa de Serenidad to remain unique and innovative. She'd come up with the idea after viewing Phoenix's breathtaking work at the gallery.

Flipping through the Rolodex, Faith picked up the phone and dialed, then sat back as the phone rang for a fifth, then a sixth time. She was about to hang up when the phone was picked up in the middle of the seventh ring. A deep male voice said, "Make it quick and make it good."

She didn't have to think long as to the reason she heard the impatience in Morgan's raspy voice. She flushed. "This is Faith McBride. I can call back if this isn't convenient."

"Faith? Did Brandon check back into your hotel?"

"No." She twisted uncomfortably in her seat. "I wanted to speak with Phoenix about a business idea I had."

"Hold on."

"Hello, Faith."

Phoenix's voice sounded breathless. Faith decided a quick out was needed. "A problem at the hotel just came up. Can I call you back tomorrow afternoon?"

There was a brief pause, as if Phoenix was trying

to gather her thoughts. "I lose track of time in the studio. If it's all right, I'll call you in the morning."

"Perfect." Faith gave her the number. "Thank you. Good-bye."

"Bye."

"Come here," she heard Morgan say just before the phone was disconnected.

Faith's face heated. She quickly hung up her phone. Morgan hadn't meant for her to hear those words filled with desire and so much love.

Too keyed up to sit, Faith rose and went to stare out the window at the small garden. Would she ever know the rapture of loving Brandon, the feel of his skin against hers, his deep voice hoarse with passion and need just for her?

Her arms wrapped around herself. She knew the answer before the question completely formed, and it brought a lump to her throat and tears to her eyes.

# 4

"I'll have to tear out the entire wall to get to all the pipes to check them."

"What!" Brandon shot up from his seat, disbelief etched on his face. He didn't notice the diners turning; his attention was focused on Mr. Montgomery. Brandon had joined Sierra and his mother at the family table while Mr. Montgomery was upstairs.

Apparently used to the shocked response of customers, the plumber remained unfazed. "Wasn't what I expected, either. The ones I saw were in pretty bad shape. The good thing is, the leak warned you before it burst. You might have had to shut down the restaurant. I can fix just what I see and hope for the best, but I wouldn't take that chance if I were you."

Brandon shuddered. Put that way, it brought everything back into perspective. "How long?"

"Three days. Maybe a week." He shrugged thin shoulders underneath his coveralls and blue cotton shirt. "I won't know until I finish tearing out the wall and see if any more pipes need replacing, but like I said, I suspect they will."

Brandon was already shaking his head. "That's impossible. I can't be out of my place for that long."

"You won't have to if you can live without water," came the plumber's answer.

The man's calmness made Brandon want to shake him.

"You're welcome to stay with me," Brandon's mother said from her seat in the booth.

"You know you're welcome at my place," Sierra echoed.

The reason for him not staying at his mother's or Sierra's home was still valid. Sierra had on a different outfit from the nifty one she had on earlier. This one was lime green with a short jacket and slim pants. All that fussing with clothes would drive him crazy.

But the decisive point was her kitchen. The only appliances she had besides the built-in ones that came with her condo were an espresso machine Morgan and Pierce had given her and a juicer, a gift from a friend who was a vegetarian. The juicer was still in the box.

"Thanks, but I need to be able to cook, and I couldn't do it in your kitchen." He rubbed the back of his neck. "I'll work something else out."

"You're turning your mother down?" Ruth asked, obviously annoyed with her middle child and ready to let him know it.

"It would be too good of an opportunity for you to pass up," he frankly told her.

She had the grace to flush. "A missed opportunity can never be recouped."

Brandon shook his head, then turned to the plumber and indicated the older man should take a seat in the booth. "Can I order you anything?"

Mr. Montgomery slid into the booth beside Ruth. "The missus did say she'd like some of your special fried catfish."

Brandon signaled Elaine, a bubbly college student, over and put in the order. "When can you start?"

"I can start on the tear-out tomorrow. I should know by the end of the day what we're looking at and the cost."

"You'd better sit down, Brandon, when he tells you," Sierra said. "One of my clients had to deal with the same problem in her rental property recently. She said for what it cost she could have renovated the bathroom twice over."

Brandon pinned Montgomery with a look. "How much are we talking about?"

Montgomery's gaze didn't waver. "Ballpark, from one thousand to three thousand."

Brandon's jaw became unhinged. He eased down onto the bench beside his sister.

Sierra whistled. "In that case, you might as well go for the remodeling and just bring your bathroom out of the nineteen-fifties. You could retile the floors and walls with marble, replace the fixtures with the nickel ones, get a decent three-light wall mount for over the sink, and have him install multiple jets in the shower or perhaps a Jacuzzi tub," Sierra ticked off.

Ruth perked up. "I know just the designer."

"I don't need all that," Brandon said. "I just want things repaired."

"You'll kick yourself later." Sierra sipped her diet cola.

"Here is the order you wanted, Brandon." The waitress placed the order on the table.

"Thank you, Elaine." Brandon stood and handed the food to Mr. Montgomery. "Can you be here at eight in the morning to get started?"

Taking the bag, Mr. Montgomery stood. "Can you?"

Brandon didn't hesitate. "I'll be here."

"See you then." Tipping his hat, he moved away.

Brandon slid back into the booth beside Sierra. "Yesterday started out with such promise, then turned bad when I came back to my place, and it just keeps getting worse."

"Not necessarily," Ruth said. "If you would just consider the decorator I mentioned, she could do wonders for your place."

"I bet she's single, gifted, and talented," Brandon said mildly, too mildly.

Sierra sat up straighter.

"She happens to be single and has won several awards, but I'd think you'd want the best." Ruth placed her hands on the table. "You are certainly proud of your culinary achievements."

"Yes, but I'm not looking to get married." He got to his feet. "I'm going to the kitchen and try not to stick my head underneath a running faucet."

"Brandon, where are you going to stay?" his mother called after him.

"A friend's place," he tossed over his shoulder, although he had absolutely no idea who that friend might be.


"Faith, you won't believe this," Pamela said, hanging up the phone behind the four-foot-high oak reception desk.

"Try me." Faith walked around the desk to stand beside the petite clerk. It was half past nine at night and things were finally settling down. The Mesa restaurant and bar were closed. The Pueblo restaurant for fine dining would soon follow. A few guests were clustered in the lobby or on the lit patio near the pool.

"That was Mr. Nolly's secretary. He was the guest scheduled to check into the Conquistador Suite today for two weeks. She said he had an emergency and canceled his reservations." The clerk picked up several slips of paper. "We shouldn't have any problems finding another guest from the list of names given to us last night. Who should it be?"

Faith took the papers from Pamela. She knew who she'd like to give the room to. "I'll take these to my

office and go over the requests. It's too late for anyone to check into the room tonight in any case."

"You're going to make someone very happy."

Trying to match the clerk's enthusiasm, Faith
stuffed the papers into the pocket of her jacket and
went to her office. Taking them out, she went through
the names, once, twice. Last-minute cancellations
were rare, since the hotel required forty-eight hours'
notice or one night of room rental was automatically
charged. Rooms started at $290 a night and rose
sharply. The Conquistador went for $675 a night. Casa
de Serenidad prided itself on being worth every penny.

She laid the requests aside. There was no rush to
call, she told herself, very much aware of why she
was procrastinating. Brandon.

She hadn't been able to get him off her mind.
Usually she was a woman who took advantage of
opportunities when they presented themselves. She
didn't usually stand around and wring her hands.
Feeling sorry for herself wouldn't get Brandon in
her arms. She'd done enough of that.

If she wanted him, she'd have to do something
about it.

Before she lost her nerve, she went into her bathroom to freshen up. It was too late for dinner, but
perhaps she and Brandon could share a dessert.


Brandon had a place to stay. In fact, he had several.

Marlive, his head waitress, had overheard a bit of

the conversation and mentioned it to another waitress. And, like wildfire, the news had spread to his staff and then to friends. While he was thankful for the offers, he hadn't stayed with anyone past one night since he was a freshman in college. He might have grown up with three brothers and a sister, but he liked his space. Plus, he wasn't the most pleasant person to be around in the morning. Sierra called him a grouch.

He was grateful that only a few customers remained, so he didn't have to continue to turn down invitations from women as well as men. He was returning from the front when Glenda Garriety waved him over. His steps didn't falter, but he wanted to.

Glenda was pushing fifty and trying desperately to be thirty, with a nip here and a tuck there. Sitting at the table with her was her younger sister, Sonja. The exact age difference depended on who you asked. Both women wore summer dresses that bared their shoulders in the bright colors the sisters were partial to. Their dyed hair was a shocking red.

"Brandon, I heard you're in need of a place to lay that gorgeous head of yours. You know you'd be more than welcome at my place," Glenda said slowly, with just a hint of the South Carolina accent from her home state.

"Or mine," Sonja added.

Brandon could almost hear the women thinking, *And in my bed.* The widowed sisters lived next door to each other, owned a florist shop, and liked chasing men in their spare time. There wasn't a shred of doubt in his mind that if he took them up on their offer, before the night was out one or both would try to find a way into his bed.

"Thanks, ladies. If things don't work out, I'll give you a call."

Both giggled like schoolgirls and batted their long eyelashes. Brandon started back to the kitchen but looked around when he heard the hostess greet someone. Seeing Faith, he smiled and went to meet her.

"I'll take it, Carol," he said to the hostess as he took Faith's arm. "Glad you could make it. What will you have?"

"Aren't you closing shortly?"

He didn't have to glance at his watch to know they were closing in less than fifteen minutes. "For you, the kitchen is always open." He pulled out a chair from a table for two. "What are you hungry for?"

Faith ducked her head for a moment. "I thought we could have dessert."

"Sure. I was just finishing making the rounds. Do you know what you want or do you need a menu?"

Faith placed her small purse on the far side of the table. "Surprise me. Then I can see if your pastry chef is in the same league as Henrí."

Brandon flashed a killer grin. "No, but he's a close second."

Returning Brandon's smile, she placed her elbows on the table, laced her fingers together, and propped her chin on top. "You?"

He bowed his head. "Me."

She chuckled. "Take care of your customers. I'm fine."

Brandon straightened. "What will you have to drink?"

Unfolding her hands, Faith wrinkled her nose. "Diet cola, and don't you dare laugh like Cameron and Duncan always do when we're out."

Lines marched across Brandon's strong brow. His hand came back to rest on the top rung of her chair. "Why would I do that?"

Surprise widened her eyes. "It's counterproductive and nonsensical to mix a diet drink and a high-caloric dessert."

"You're a woman. You're allowed," he said. "Be back as soon as I can."

Faith watched Brandon walk away and sighed. He seemed to understand women so easily. It was no wonder that so many were after him.

"Hi, Faith."

Faith looked up and saw the Garriety sisters. "Hello, Glenda, Sonja."

"Don't usually see you in here," Glenda said, her eyes narrowing suspiciously.

Another woman who wanted Brandon. "You must be regulars," Faith countered. In management she'd learned not to volunteer information.

"Every Wednesday and Sunday night," Sonja said proudly.

"That would certainly qualify you as regulars," Faith said.

"Come to try your luck with Brandon?" Glenda asked, watching Faith closely.

Faith couldn't help the start of surprise. Had she been that obvious? "What are you talking about?" she asked, trying to keep her voice level.

Both women stared at her a long time before Glenda leaned over and whispered, "Owning that hotel, it would be a snap to offer him a room while his bathroom is being repaired."

Faith let out a relieved sigh. "The plumber was scheduled to repair the problem this morning. Brandon doesn't need a room."

Glenda sat in the chair across from Faith. Sonja appropriated one from the next table. Both women scooted closer to Faith, then braced their arms on the table. "You don't know?"

"Of course she doesn't, Glenda," Sonja answered. "You can see it on her face."

"Could one of you please tell me what is going on?" Faith asked, but her heart was already racing with excitement.

"Old Man Montgomery told Brandon that it might be anywhere from a few days to a week before the repairs are complete," Glenda offered. "A lot of us figure it's a good time to offer Brandon a place to stay. Of course, if someone walks in their sleep we're all consenting adults here."

Both women giggled.

"Did he take you up on your offer?" Faith asked, hoping her dread didn't show on her face.

"Turned us down flat, but he did it with a smile. You might have better luck." Glenda leaned closer. "About time one of our own got a crack at one of the Grayson men."

"We're just friends." Faith mouthed the words that almost stuck in her throat. "He doesn't see me that way."

"Yeah." Glenda sat back in her seat. "You're probably right. No offense, but he likes them a bit on the lean side."

"None taken." Faith had been called overweight in nicer and crueler ways.

"Well, we'd better get going." Glenda stood and Sonja followed. "Have to get an early start in the morning. A lot of orders to get out. Good-bye."

"Good-bye."

As soon as they left, the waitress appeared. "Here's your drink and Brandon's. He said to start on the carrot cake without him."

Faith ignored the huge slice of the cake heavily layered with buttercream icing and loaded with chopped pecans, finely grated carrots, and coconut. "Where is he?"

"Probably fending off more invitations." Marlive shook her dark head and blew out a breath. "If I don't get fired over this, it will be a miracle."

Marlive had been Faith's waitress the last time

she'd eaten there. She'd instantly liked the bubbly woman. "What do you have to do with that?"

"Plenty," the waitress said, then explained. "I broke the first rule of employment of not gossiping. And about Brandon, of all people." She swallowed. "He's never said a word when I've had to take off unexpectedly with my youngest that has asthma or when I have to take my mother to one of her many doctors' appointments. If he fires me, I don't know what I'll do."

Faith was on her feet, her arm around the distraught woman in an instant. "You know Brandon better than that. He wouldn't dream of firing you for such a minor infraction and, if he did, I'd hire you."

"Trying to steal one of my best waitresses in my own restaurant, Faith?"

Marlive whirled around to face Brandon. He wasn't smiling. Expertly he balanced a platter of quesadillas and chips on one arm and two plates on the other. The older woman gulped.

Backing down never entered Faith's mind. "It's no more than what *you've* tried to do."

Up went his dark brow. "Says who?"

"Six managers or owners of restaurants that I can think of," she told him. "Anyone who owns a restaurant starts to worry when you eat at their establishment more than once for fear you're stalking one of their chefs. They're usually right."

He placed the food and plates on the table. "They should be pleased that they had the sense to hire a talented chef."

"And not be bothered by the little task of finding his or her replacement, I suppose?" she asked with dripping sarcasm.

"Change is good."

"Except when the shoe is on the other foot?"

Brandon sobered. "Marlive wouldn't leave me, would you?"

The woman was already shaking her head. "No."

"See," Brandon told Faith triumphantly. "Now, let's eat."

Faith took the chair he pulled out. "You are too sure of yourself."

He said grace over the table, then divided the food between them. "Since when was that a bad thing?"

"Never that I can recall in the McBride or the Grayson household." Faith dunked a chip in the salsa swimming with red and green chilis. "But I'm warning you, keep trying to steal Henrí at your own risk."

Brandon paused with the quesadilla near his mouth, then took a bite. "You know I could never walk away from a challenge."

"You will this time because I'm in a position to make you a very interesting offer." She had the satisfaction of seeing puzzlement replaced by speculation chase across his gorgeous face. She bit into her quesadilla with gusto, suddenly famished.

"Your staff already recommends the Red Cactus as one of the best places besides your own restaurants for dining." He finished off his food and reached for his raspberry lemonade. "So do many of the hotels and the Chamber."

"I'm talking about on a more personal level." She watched him closely over the rim of her glass and was disheartened and disappointed to see unease cross his face. "You know Casa de Serenidad has a forty-eight-hour cancellation policy."

He straightened, his glass hitting the table with a thud.

"What if we had a cancellation within the last hour?" she asked.

"You'd have a room." Rising, he scooted his chair over and sat back down closer to Faith, their elbows brushing against each other. "Please tell me you're not just making conversation."

He smelled of lemons and another overlying sexy scent that made Faith want to lick her lips and investigate. Instead she moistened her lips and concentrated on breathing. "I might if I knew I didn't have to worry about my chef."

Brandon sat back. "You'd try to blackmail a desperate man?"

"Brandon, you've never been desperate for or about anything," she told him, finding herself enjoying bantering with him. "Besides, who said this is anything but dinner conversation?"

"And what if it wasn't, and I said I might consider laying off Henrí for a week or so."

Brandon was no pushover, but then neither was she. "Thank you for dinner, Brandon."

His hand clamped down on hers when she started to stand. He stared into her eyes a long time. "Your pulse is racing."

His strong, calloused hand made her skin tingle and her body want. "Caffeine in the cola."

"You aren't going to eat your dessert?"

She tested the strength of his hold before answering. He wasn't about to let her go until he was ready. "I couldn't eat another bite, thank you."

"I could call the hotel."

"If you'll release my hand I'll get my cell phone." Her lips quirked upward. "It's on speed dial."

He stared at her a few minutes longer, then released her arm and sat back. Although her insides were jumping, she waited for his final answer.

"My wanting Henrí is not a whim. I need a pastry chef who can also do the main dishes. My last chef married and relocated to New Orleans," he told her. "You must know how much time it takes away from my other duties to prepare the desserts and cook."

"If you weren't so territorial you could let someone else do the finishing touches on the desserts or you could purchase them," she suggested. Around her she heard the soft conversation of the staff, the scraping of the chairs, as they closed the restaurant down for the night.

Brandon looked offended. "We serve five specialty desserts and a number of entrées as well. If I start a dish, I finish it."

"Territorial, as I said." Picking up her purse, Faith rose to her feet. "Good night, Brandon, and thanks." Her fingernails bit into the soft leather as she walked away. She had overplayed her hand. Cameron and Duncan knew how to bluff; apparently she had a lot to learn.

# 5

Just as she was about to reach for the brass door handle, it opened. In strode the rest of the Grayson clan. Any hope Faith had of winning the war of wills with Brandon evaporated.

"Hello, Faith," they said in greeting.

"Hello," she returned, then sensed Brandon behind her.

"Does your being here mean I won't have to creep around in the morning when I get up?" Sierra asked.

"I certainly hope it means I won't get any more phone calls," Pierce said, but there was no heat in the words.

"Faith *might* have a room *if* I agree to lay off trying to hire her chef when I desperately need one," Brandon said, his voice tight.

"Then all you have to decide is which one you need the most, the room or the chef," Luke reasoned.

"Knowing how you like your space and your sunny disposition in the morning, I hope your stubbornness doesn't get in the way of common sense," Morgan reminded him.

"She's trying to blackmail me!" Brandon protested.

"Is that slander or character assassination, Morgan, and can I sue?" Inadvertently his outburst made Faith feel better. He always did the same thing when he was playing cards with Cameron and was losing. Brandon hated to lose.

Brandon stepped around to face her. "To sue you'd have to prove I was wrong, which I'm not."

"Actually, since you made the accusation in public, she doesn't," Morgan glanced around. "I believe she has several witnesses. Although I'd have to recuse myself from the case, since I'm both of your lawyers."

Faith thought she saw steam coming out of the top of Brandon's head.

"Stop being mule-headed. You're going to kick yourself if, while you're dithering, the room is taken," Sierra pointed out. "Besides, if you stay anyplace else you'll hurt Mama's feelings."

Incredulous, Brandon moved closer to Faith. "You mean while you were leading me on, someone could have taken my room?"

"Brandon," Faith said patiently, as if speaking to a small child or a senile adult. "That's what hotels do. Rent rooms."

A sound like a growl came through clenched teeth. She'd never seen that particular odd flushed shade on Brandon and didn't think she ever wanted to see it again. She eased toward the door. He followed.

"Well, I guess I should be going. Good-bye, every-one." She turned to flee. A vise grip closed around her upper forearm.

She swallowed and managed, "Brandon, was there something else you wanted to say?"

His other hand clamped around her other arm. Before she could draw another breath, her feet were dangling several inches off the floor. She was so awed by the notion that Brandon had picked her up that she smiled at him.

His scowl deepened. "You think you've gotten the best of me, don't you?"

Faith was pretty sure she had. She stuck her tongue in the roof of her mouth and remained silent. Her mother had always told her to be gracious in winning.

"Well, Faith Allison McBride, I accept your black-mail terms, and that's what they are no matter what my hotshot lawyer brother says, and I had better have a room or guess where I'm spending the night."

Faith gulped. She should have remembered that when pushed, Brandon pushed back.

"You know you owe Faith an apology. You're not go-ing to be able to sleep until you give it to her."

Brandon scowled and let himself into the Con-quistador Suite at Casa de Serenidad. His brothers and sister had said the same thing in varying ways since they left him at the restaurant. Their censure didn't bother him nearly as much as the flush of embarrassment on Faith's face. He'd wished he could recall the words the moment they were out.

She'd tucked her head. He'd set her on her feet. He hadn't even been aware of picking her up. He'd never manhandled a woman. He was still in shock when she finally lifted her head and said the keys to his room would be waiting at the front desk.

Luke had chastised him with a look, then followed Faith out the door. Morgan had been right behind him. Sierra and Pierce weren't shy about telling Brandon what they thought of his outlandish actions. He couldn't explain to them why he'd lost it, or to Luke and Morgan, who came back after seeing Faith to her car.

"The pressure is getting to you," Pierce finally said. Then, when Sierra wasn't close enough to hear, he told Brandon to find a woman, and quick.

Brandon didn't want a woman. He tossed the duffel bag on the bed and went out the door to follow the lit path. Unhooking the gate, he went through, frowning as he did so. Anyone could get inside. He'd have to speak to Cameron about better security for Faith. He certainly couldn't talk to her about it; he'd be lucky just to get her to open the door.

At least the small porch was well lit, with a clear view from the peephole. The grounds were bursting with flowers. Some easily reached his waist in height. A stone path led to a curved padded bench. He could easily picture Faith sitting there after a long day. She worked hard. She didn't need the added aggravation he'd caused her.

Feeling worse, Brandon rang the doorbell, then shoved his hands in his pockets. A light snapped on in the living room. He heard locks disengage.

The door opened. Faith stood there staring up at him.

"I'm sorry." His hand came out of his pocket to shove through his unbound hair. "I don't know what got into me."

She wrapped her arms around herself and glanced away. "Forget it."

"I can't." He stepped closer, causing her to step back. "I wouldn't hurt you."

Surprise widened, then narrowed her eyes. "Of course not."

"You backed away from me."

"I'm not dressed to be dangled," she whispered softly.

Brandon let his gaze drift downward. She wore a long rose-print silk robe belted at the waist. His body stirred, but he had his mind on something much more important. "Did I hurt your arm?"

"I don't damage easily, Brandon," she said. "Remember, I used to follow after you and Cameron. I still have a scar on my knee from playing Evel Knievel with you two."

"If a man did that to Sierra, he'd answer to me," he said fiercely.

"The man hasn't been born that Sierra can't handle, and you know it," Faith answered.

Brandon relaxed a bit. "She has a mean left hook."

Puzzlement arched Faith's brow. "She's right-handed."

"We taught her to use her left and throw the opponent off guard." His expression became serious again. "Duncan and Cameron didn't teach you to take care of yourself?"

A shadow crossed Faith's face. "No need. The McBride curse keeps men away."

"If they let that old wives' tale keep them away, you're better off without them," Brandon said, obviously meaning every word.

"Hopefully there's a man out there who won't care about the curse," Faith said, staring at him.

"Yeah, well." He didn't know exactly what he wanted to say. "You're sure you're all right?"

"Positive."

"I don't suppose you'd let me see for myself?" he asked, only half-joking.

Up went her eyebrow; then to his amazement she slid the robe off her shoulder. He didn't expect the catch in his breath or the sudden impulse to touch the smooth skin beneath the thin straps with his fingers, then his mouth.

"See. I'm fine."

He had to get a grip. She was his friend, for goodness' sake. Celibacy was making him act weird. "I see." His stuffed his hands in his pockets and hoped they stayed there. "Thanks for the room. Good night."

She stepped out on the porch. "Breakfast is served until ten thirty tomorrow."

Brandon turned, then fisted his hands. The light behind Faith outlined her lush body in revealing erotic detail. "I'm meeting Montgomery at eight."

"How about a wake-up call at seven fifteen and we meet on the Mesa patio at half past?" she asked, hopeful and eager.

After his behavior he'd do anything to please her, but he also wanted her to go back inside and stop tempting him. "Fine. Night." He hurried back to his room, thinking a cold shower was definitely in order.


Locking her door, Faith crawled into bed. Brandon thought he had scared or hurt her. On the contrary, he'd inflamed her senses. Even angry, he had held her with gentleness. A thin line separated passion from anger. How would it feel if he touched her with passion instead of anger, used those strong hands and that sexy mouth to tease and coax her body to fulfillment? Her body craved the answer.

Brandon's mother wasn't going to give up until he was married. That left Faith only one option: she had to act before it was too late. She just had to figure out a plan.

Unfolding her arms, she sat up and leaned back against the padded headboard. She'd tackled difficult problems before. She just had to look at this the same way.

When she wanted to select servicepeople or staff, she learned their strengths and weaknesses. Brandon was a nurturer. He enjoyed feeding people. Quickly she discarded that idea. She didn't need to gain another ounce. But he also liked helping people, liked seeing them happy. So, what could he help her with?

The answer came to her almost immediately. She laughed. She'd ask him to teach her how to get a man. He'd refuse, of course, but possibly it would make him really look at her as a woman.

Throwing back the covers, Faith strode back into the bathroom and turned on the lights. Her fingers ran through the curly black hair that brushed her shoulders. Lifting the heavy curls up, she turned her head to the sides, trying to determine if she'd look better with short hair. She let the mass fall.

She'd never been into fashion. Most Santa Feans dressed casually. She liked the layered look, with unconstructed pieces that she could mix and match. Often she worked fourteen-hour days. She needed comfortable clothes that wore well and that could be dressed up with a jacket, jewelry, or a scarf.

It only took seconds to recall the women whom Brandon had spent the most time with at his birthday party. They'd worn short, form-fitted dresses that showed long legs and lush breasts. Faith had the bosom but not the long legs. There was nothing she could do about that; she could buy a few new outfits, perhaps get a new hairstyle. She wasn't going to get his attention in gabardine and cotton.

Leaving the bathroom again, she went to the secretary in the far corner of the bedroom, sat down, and wrote: *Operation Get Brandon* on the top of a notebook. "Look out, Brandon; I'm coming after you."

There was a ringing in Brandon's ears that persisted no matter how he tried to evade the irritating noise. Finally, blessedly, it stopped. Slowly uncurling from his protective knot, Brandon began to drift back to sleep . . . until there was a pounding on his door. His first thought was to toss whoever it was off the tallest building he could find. The pounding grew louder.

His eyelids jerked upward with the intent of carrying out his thought until he noticed the abstract-print draperies instead of the dark brown ones in his apartment. Everything came tumbling back. *The pipe burst in the wall. Mr. Montgomery coming at eight. Wake-up call at seven fifteen.* Brandon's gaze jerked to the clock on the nightstand. 7:19.

The pounding on his door continued. Throwing the covers back, he jumped out of bed and went to answer the door. He yanked it open. His mouth opened to tell the person he was awake, but the words were never uttered.

Faith stood there, her hand raised, her eyes wide, gaping. The expletive leaped from his mouth before he could stop it. He closed the door in her shocked face. She probably didn't count it as lucky for them both that he had on Jockeys, but he did.

"Sorry. I didn't mean to say . . . I didn't expect . . ." He blew out a breath and continued to speak through the door. "I'll meet you on the patio of the restaurant in fifteen minutes."

"Al-all right."

Muttering to himself, Brandon went to the bathroom. She'd sounded as if she had a vise around her throat. He had a tightness considerably lower than his throat. Stripping off his Jockeys, he stepped into a cold shower.

Faith sat at the black iron mesh table on the outside patio and sipped her orange juice. Ice cubes clicked against the side of the glass and brushed her lips. Two glasses of iced water hadn't help cool her down; the orange juice wasn't any better. But at least Brandon wouldn't see her chugging water and guess how he'd affected her. Lord, the man had a body on him. One she hadn't seen that much of in years.

He had roped muscles, hard thighs, and long, narrow feet. His hair had been unbound and flowing around his massive shoulders. He'd looked like a warrior. His eyes had been as dark as midnight and as piercing as a lance. He'd been annoyed for being woken up. It was obvious he hadn't known she was at the door.

She looked up and saw him. Her hand clenched on the glass. He was dressed now, more's the pity, hiding that magnificent body that she'd go to her grave remembering and wanting. She made herself meet his stare and smile. His briefs had covered as much as swim trunks. If it had been any other man, she would have probably been a bit embarrassed, not hot and bothered and wishing he hadn't closed the door so fast.

At the table his long-fingered hand gripped the back of the chair before he sat down. A dull endearing flush climbed from his neck upward. "Sorry about that."

Faith waved his apology aside and set down her orange juice. "No harm done. I took the liberty of ordering, since I know you're on a time schedule."

"Thanks."

A waiter in white shirt and black pants set up a folding rack, then began to place dishes on the table. "I didn't know what you preferred, so I ordered a bit of everything."

Brandon counted seven dishes. There were scrambled eggs, burritos, apple-cured bacon, smoked ham, pan sausages, crisp shoestring potatoes, and a basket of rolls and Danishes. "We might need sideboards."

Her lips twitched; then she bowed her head and said grace. "What do you plan to do while Mr. Montgomery works?" she asked him afterward.

"Change out the birthday gifts for the old appliances, then get a head start on the desserts." His gaze met hers as he bit into a buttered croissant. "You always get up this early?"

"I'm usually up by six." She picked at her French toast.

His fork stopped inches from his mouth. "You're kidding."

"Not at all. I like to make sure the staff is off to a good start." She took a bite of eggs. "Unless there is an event, I'm usually in bed by ten, so I get plenty of sleep."

Brandon sipped his coffee. "You've been up two nights because of me."

*More than that.* "Thankfully, I don't need much sleep." She reached for her orange juice.

"Neither does Cameron." Brandon reached for his second croissant and a second helping of eggs. "We'd stay up half the night talking when we were in high school, and the next morning he'd be ready to go and I'd just want to turn over."

The corners of her mouth tilted. "Is that why you don't serve breakfast?"

He polished off his croissant before speaking. "Why set yourself up for failure? I'd dread each day if I opened for breakfast. Now, I look forward to it." He made a face and picked up his coffee cup. "Until now at least."

The waiter returned, cleared the table, then was gone.

"Mr. Montgomery will repair the problem and

your life will be as before," Faith said softly, hoping there was a chance for her to be in it.

"That's not saying too much, if Mama has her way." Brandon braced his arms on the table. "She even tried to use the problem to her advantage and get me to hire some fancy decorator to redo the bath and the apartment."

"If it's anything like Duncan and Cameron's place, that might not be a bad idea," Faith told him.

"I admit I might like a shower like I have here in my room, but I'm not willing to dodge being hit on to have one installed. My bathroom can stay the way it is," he said stubbornly.

Ruth certainly didn't miss any opportunities, but Faith was learning to take advantage of them as well. "I helped with the decoration of Casa de Serenidad. I'd be happy to help you," she said casually.

He twisted uneasily in his seat and picked up his orange juice. "I'm not sure I'm ready yet."

"Of course. Just let me know." She placed her hands in her lap. It was now or never. "Brandon, we're friends, right?"

"Sure," he said slowly. A hint of unease crossed his face. Apparently, this wasn't the first time he'd heard those words.

She'd just have to see it through. What choice did she have? "I need to ask a favor," she said mildly.

"You can ask me anything," he said magnani-mously.

She needed no further urging. "Teach me how to get a man."

Shock, outrage, and embarrassment replaced indulgence. His juice glass banged down on the table. Faith wished she had a camera. "What did you say?"

"Teach me how to get a man."

"Are you out of your mind?" he shouted, drawing the attention of the diners around them. Noticing their interest, he leaned closer. "That's the craziest request I've ever heard."

"Is it crazy to want love?" she asked, unable to keep the longing out of her voice. She thought she saw compassion in his face; then it was gone.

"You know it's not, but what you're asking is." He tossed his cloth napkin on the table. "Cameron would kill me, and I wouldn't blame him."

"This is none of Cameron's concern. I'm old enough to make my own decisions."

"And mistakes," Brandon riled. "What's gotten into you? Not even Sierra has ever said anything so outrageous."

"Sierra doesn't need help. I do."

He snorted. "There's nothing wrong with you."

"Then why don't men find me attractive?" She whispered the question, her voice quaking.

"Because some men are plain stupid," he said with such heat it made her feel better.

She sat back in her chair. "All right, Brandon."

A relieved breath tumbled over his lips. "Glad to

hear you're giving up this crazy scheme." He came to his feet. "I may not see you for a couple of days. We close at eleven tonight, and tomorrow I'm cooking for the Women's League."

"I'll be busy as well. Have a good day."

"You, too."

He walked away and Faith took full advantage to view his fabulous butt at her leisure, something she had never done before. *Brandon, you're mine. You just don't know it yet.*

# 6

Brandon had been warned; he just hadn't believed the dust from the Sheetrock would be this bad. He'd been proven wrong . . . in spades.

The tiny gray particles were everywhere. He could have written his name on his counter, the pictures, the furniture—although he wasn't sure that all the chalk was from the Sheetrock—except that in his kitchen. It was always spotless.

"Once I finish tearing out the wall, you won't have to worry about any more dust," Mr. Montgomery explained, a white rubber mask over his mouth and nose. "I'm replacing the Sheetrock with mortar-board to absorb the moisture. You won't have the dust problem if you have this done again."

Brandon barely kept from shuddering as he glanced at his poor counter. "Don't even think that."

The plumber chuckled. "I'd keep the bathroom door closed, but the space is too small."

Mild irritation crossed Brandon's face. "It suits me."

"After being at Casa de Serenidad for a few days you might change your mind." The plumber shook his head and pulled his cap down over his forehead. "I was dead set against enlarging our bath until we went on vacation and the hotel had a bathroom where I couldn't stand flat-footed and touch the walls. Two days after I got back I was in our bath tearing out the walls."

"That's not about to happen here," Brandon said. "I plan to be back in here in three days."

The older man adjusted the mask. "I'd better get back to work and see if I can make that happen."

Accepting the plumber's statement as a good sign, Brandon picked up the box loaded with his kitchen appliances and went to the door. He didn't want his mother or Mrs. Poole carrying anything down his stairs; plus he didn't want his mother getting any more ideas about decorating.

The front door opened just as he reached the entrance of the restaurant where he was stacking the donations. His mother and Mrs. Poole came in the door he'd left unlocked for them.

"Good morning, Mama, Mrs. Poole." The women had been best friends for as long as Brandon could remember. Both were self-assured and sensible enough not to let Mrs. Poole's husband's millions interfere with what mattered: their friendship.

"Hello, Brandon," Mrs. Poole greeted him. She

wore a patient smile and a celery-colored pantsuit that complemented her fair complexion and red hair.

"Good morning, Brandon." His mother glanced at Amanda. "Did I ever tell you I had morning sickness with Brandon during my entire pregnancy?"

Amanda's lips twitched. "No, I don't think so. In fact, I'm almost positive you always said what a joy it was each time you were pregnant."

Ruth turned to her middle child. "Perhaps in my old age I forgot."

Brandon chuckled, then enveloped his mother in a bear hug, kissing her on the cheek. "I love you, too."

"Then you'll think about getting married and working on getting me some grandchildren," she said as she hugged him back just as fiercely.

Brandon could feel the noose around his neck tightening. It had been months since his mother had mentioned grandchildren. It would have been too insensitive to do so around Luke's wife, who couldn't have children. Whatever the reason, Ruth had given him some slack until now, but it was over.

"My place couldn't accommodate a family." He picked up a box. "Who's driving?"

"I am." Amanda pulled her keys from a brown-checkered Louis Vuitton bag shaped like a bowling bag. It probably cost close to a thousand dollars. Sierra had one just like it.

A bumping sound came from above. Frowning, Brandon peered up. "I hope he's finished before the lunch crowd starts coming in."

"Perhaps I should go up there and see how it's progressing," Ruth said.

Brandon put down the box and placed himself in front of his mother. "There's nothing to see."

"In that case, why are you so anxious that I not go upstairs?" she said reasonably.

While he was trying to think of an answer, he heard someone behind him. *Saved.*

"Good morning, Ruth, Amanda," Mr. Montgomery said.

The women returned the greeting. "I was just coming up to see your progress," Ruth told him.

"Glad I saved you the trip," the plumber said.

Brandon tensed. "What does that mean?"

"I was right. All the pipes in the bathroom need replacing."

Brandon wondered how long it could take to yank out some pipes and replace them. "So a week. Max."

"No, son. It was more involved than I thought." Mr. Montgomery clapped Brandon on the shoulder, making particles of dust fly up. "Try two."

Faith personally escorted Phoenix Grayson into her office, where a stylish mix of traditional furniture and antiques created an elegant setting. The two had first met at the bridal shower Amanda Poole had given Phoenix. Morgan's fiancée might not have any relatives nearby, but marrying into such a well-respected and beloved family had given her instant entry into the wide circle of the Graysons' family and friends.

"Please have a seat." Faith indicated one of the matching side chairs covered with rose silk damask fabric in a little alcove of her office. On the table between them was a fresh bouquet of flowers, hot water for tea, coffee, and an assortment of cookies and pastries. "I have refreshments, if you'd like."

"You're a lifesaver." Phoenix chose an iced Danish and sat down. "We didn't have time for breakfast. These looked so good the other day."

Faith had a pretty good idea why Phoenix and Morgan had missed breakfast. "You didn't eat one?"

Phoenix delicately licked icing from the corner of her mouth. "Catherine and I both declined. Poor Brandon had to share with us when we came to check on him. You know how he is."

That she did. "He likes to see everyone well fed and happy."

Finishing off the Danish, Phoenix reached for the coffeepot. "He's going to make a wonderful father and husband."

Faith's heart winced. "Yes."

Phoenix's attention snapped back to Faith. Tiny lines radiated across her brow.

"Thank you for seeing me on such short notice," Faith quickly said. She didn't like the way the other woman was studying her. Phoenix was an artist and saw things others might miss.

"It's no problem. You were one of the few women at the wedding who didn't look as if she wanted my quick demise." Phoenix sipped her coffee. "But since I love Morgan so much, I understand and forgive them."

Faith's lips twitched. "I might have known Morgan would choose a woman who speaks her mind."

"Not always." She relaxed back in her chair. "Now, what's this about a business deal?"

Faith was thrown off by the cryptic words, but she quickly recovered. "Every show you've had has sold out. Just recently you started having limited-edition pieces, but here again you've kept the numbers small and varied. They're snapped up as fast as they become available. None have appeared for sale afterward, at least that I'm aware of."

"That's probably because the art community is aware of my husband's passion for my work," Phoenix said. "If a piece did show up, he'd probably buy it."

That was an understatement. "He purchased the only known sculptures you and your mentor did together. It's been speculated that they've tripled in value, although no one has seen them since Morgan purchased them." Faith laced her hands together as a brief shadow crossed Phoenix's face. Initially there had been whispers of a scandal surrounding the pieces, but after Phoenix burst onto the art world as its newest star, the sculptures became a hot commodity.

"As I said, he's very passionate about my work."

"After seeing your sculptures, I agree. That leads

me to what I propose." Faith leaned forward. "Casa de Serenidad is a five-star hotel. Our guests pay a high price to stay here, and I'd like to think that our service is the best in the country. Santa Fe is known for its beautiful scenery and also its art. The Sangre de Cristo Mountains can be seen from many of the rooms. I propose to bring that art into the hotel as well. I'd like to start with sculptures by Phoenix."

Phoenix slowly set down her cup and saucer. "You want to commission me to do pieces for the hotel rooms?"

"Considering we have fifty rooms and the cost of your work, I might have a difficult time getting my family to go along with that decorating expense," Faith said. "What I'd like to do is display two or three of your sculptures in the lobby, in a protective glass case and insured, of course. If the guests like it, I'd want to place your pieces in the executive suites. Later, I propose to contact other artists and display their work as well."

Phoenix leaned back in her chair. "I'm sorry, Faith; my work is not for rent."

"No," Faith hastened to explain. "I'm aware of that. I thought you might consider loaning out one of your sculptures, similar to patrons loaning their art pieces to museums."

"The museum is nonprofit," Phoenix came back.

"I'll gladly make a donation to your favorite charity for the privilege." Faith pressed her point. "This will be the talk of the hotel and art world."

"You're already booked solid. Why should you want to do this?" Phoenix asked.

Faith hadn't expected this to be easy. "Art should be shared and appreciated. Many of the guests come to relax, but there are those also who come for business and who won't get the chance to set foot inside the museums or the art galleries. This way they'll leave Santa Fe being exposed to a great artist who happens to be a woman and African-American."

"And Casa de Serenidad distinguishes itself even more in the hotel industry," Phoenix mused.

"There is that, but it's not my main purpose."

Phoenix glanced around the office. "You have several Arthello Beck and Frank Frazier paintings as well as sculptures by Rudley and others. Obviously you enjoy art. I'm aware that some have made the transition, but other artists in your collection are still alive. Why not them, or did you ask and they turned you down?"

Phoenix was smart and cautious. Morgan wouldn't have married a woman who couldn't think for herself. "I've not asked another artist. Your work speaks to people. It hits people on a visceral, a gut level. *Together*, the sculpture of a man and woman sitting side by side on the grass, her head on his shoulder, his arm around her waist, speaks eloquently of love. The gray in their hair makes it even more powerful. Their love will last a lifetime."

Phoenix's face softened. "I started working on the

piece the week after Morgan and I were married. True love can last forever."

Although the love lives of her family seemed to refute that statement, more than anything Faith wanted to believe that love lasted. "You're fortunate to have found each other."

"Yes, we are. You've answered all my questions, but I'm still not sure," Phoenix said slowly.

"Just think about it, and let me know in a couple of weeks," Faith said. "If you say no, I'm going to ask another artist."

"You're not giving up."

Faith smiled. "The McBrides are a stubborn bunch."

"So are the Graysons, and I thank God for it." Phoenix stood and extended her hand. "Thanks for the refreshments. I'll think about what you said."

Faith clasped the unexpectedly strong, calloused hand in hers. "Please do, and thank you for coming. I'll see you out."

"There's no need. I can find my way." Phoenix went to the door and stopped. "We're having a few friends over Sunday evening around six. Why don't you come by?"

Faith was touched by the invitation and saddened that she couldn't accept. "Every ballroom is booked for that night. I need to be on hand."

"What if I told you Brandon has promised to stop by?"

Caught off guard, Faith's eyes widened a fraction. She hadn't thrown Phoenix off. "You must have been very persuasive. He almost never leaves his restaurant during business hours."

"He felt sorry for our guests if Morgan had to grill," Phoenix said with mild amusement.

"He would. I really wish I could drop by, but I can't."

"If things change, please know you're welcome." Phoenix reached for the doorknob. "Are you a gambling woman?"

Faith frowned. "Not really."

"Too bad. I hear since I hadn't participated in the pot for a blowout bachelorette party and married Morgan, the pot didn't dissolve. It now applies to any Grayson male," Phoenix explained. "I thought you might want to pay the thirty dollars and toss your name in the pot."

Faith had already put her name in, but she didn't want anyone to know. "Brandon and I are just friends."

"Of course you are." Phoenix finally opened the door. "Think about the invitation. If you come, you'll get a chance to see more of my work."

Again Faith was caught off guard by the unprecedented offer. "That's quite an enticement."

"Just like certain men." Phoenix studied Faith for a long moment.

Worry caused Faith's stomach to clench. She didn't want Brandon to even think she was interested in him. "Phoenix, Brandon is going through a lot now. An unfounded rumor might make it worse."

"I understand better than most about keeping secrets," Phoenix said softly. "But I have learned that the Grayson men are special and worth fighting for. Waiting too long could prove disastrous. Good-bye."

"Good-bye, Phoenix." Faith watched Phoenix walk away, then closed the door. The other woman would keep her secret, but she'd also given Faith a warning that she was going to heed.

Time to put Phase One into action.

Sitting behind her desk, Faith picked up the phone and dialed. After being passed through a succession of people, she was finally connected.

"Faith, how are you?" asked a deep, sexy voice that merely hinted at the magnificent owner.

"Hello, Blade. I need a huge favor." You didn't waste the time of a man like Blade Navarone.

"Name it," came the quick reply.

Faith relaxed back in her chair and did just that.

# 7

Brandon wasn't a happy man. He wasn't the kind to take it out on his employees. They understood as much, but they still gave him his space as he worked like a man possessed in the kitchen that night. When he was worried about anything or wanted to think, he cooked and cooked and cooked.

At the moment, he was putting the finishing touches on tequila-flamed mangoes. The baked mangoes spread with brown sugar were waiting on the serving cart along with two huge bowls of home-made ice cream enriched with sweetened condensed milk.

Pouring the heated tequila over the mangoes, Brandon firmly kept his mind on the process and not the destruction of his bathroom. As he'd told his staff, personal problems should never interfere with a guest having a perfect dining experience. He lit the dish with a long match. Flames swooped upward.

"It's ready," Brandon told the waiting waiter. He'd

often flambéed at the table, but tonight he wasn't in any mood to be on the floor.

"Looks good, Brandon." Luis pushed the cart from the kitchen, the flames on the mangoes six inches high. By the time he reached the table they would be a flickering flame.

"Thanks," Brandon replied absently, his attention already on the sea bass he was searing. He flipped the meat over, then slid it onto a plate and garnished it with parsley. Waiting hands picked up the dish and headed for the stainless-steel swinging doors.

"Brandon, the man I just served the flambé to asked to see the chef. Table eight."

Never looking up, Brandon stirred the vegetable mix of fresh green beans, baby carrots, broccoli florets, and new potatoes. "What about?"

"He didn't say."

Brandon scooped up the vegetables onto two plates. "Is he with a woman?" As a rule, men didn't order flambé desserts, and table eight was secluded and usually reserved for a couple wanting to be alone.

"Yes. I think I've seen her in here before." Luis shook his head. "Haven't seen the man, though. I'd remember him. He's courteous, but there's something about his eyes that makes you not want to turn your back."

"I'll protect you," Marlive said as she passed with her order.

Luis threw her an affronted look. "I can take care of myself."

Good-natured bickering away from the customers was an everyday occurrence at the restaurant, so Brandon ignored the two. The man might want to complain or thank the chef, but the bottom line was probably to impress his date. "Please tell him I'm busy and will come out as soon as I can."

Luis hesitated.

"Problem?" Brandon asked, a stack of white plates with a red cactus painted in the center in his hands.

"No," the waiter said, and left.

Brandon set the plates within easy reach of the three industrial stoves and checked the monitor to see which dishes were next. Rare Angus T-bones.

"He wants to see you now."

Brandon didn't like pushy guests, but he'd learned long ago they were unavoidable. "Tell him I'm busy; then see to your other guests. You don't have time to be his personal messenger."

A mixture of relief and dread crossed the young man's face. Again the young man hesitated. Brandon wasn't used to his staff not immediately following direct orders. Concern drew his brows together.

Marlive breezed back in and sighed dreamily. "Luis, I'll take table eight."

Brandon didn't have to think long to know the reason. Marlive might be happily married, but she was fond of saying that as long as she had blood running through her veins she was going to appreciate good-looking men.

Luis looked as if he was considering Marlive's offer, then glanced at Brandon. "I can handle it."

"Oh, well," Marlive said. "Faith said to tell you hello."

"Faith's here?" Brandon asked, surprised. That morning at breakfast she'd said she'd be busy.

Marlive sighed dramatically again. "She's with the gorgeous hunk at table eight."

"What?"

Brandon's hard expression whipped the dreamy expression from Marlive's face. "I saw her and went over to speak, Brandon. That's all. I'm happy here."

Realizing she had misunderstood the reason for his reaction, Brandon chose to reassure without explaining. "I know you're loyal." He studied the orders on the monitor and decided it wasn't anything his staff couldn't handle. Untying his apron, he hung it up and washed his hands. "I'll be on the floor."

Brandon was concerned about Faith. Was the man she was with the reason she wanted to know how to get a man? The thought disturbed him.

He hit the double steel swinging doors with more force than intended. With each step he worked to lessen the tension in his body and face. He set the limits at his restaurant. If he expected his staff to follow him, he had to be a good leader and do as he said. One of the many things his older brothers had taught him.

He greeted regulars as well as those he didn't

recognize as he made his way to the table, the one usually meant for lovers. His tenseness returned.

He saw them before they saw him, which was probably because both their arms were on the table as they leaned across it as if they couldn't stand to be separated.

"You wanted to see me?"

Faith jumped and straightened. The man with her slowly turned, his gaze sharp and assessing. Brandon recalled Luis's words and thought them apt. There was something lethal about this man Faith was with.

"Hello, Faith. I didn't expect to see you tonight," Brandon said mildly.

"I was talked into it." She sent her dinner companion a sweet smile. "I'm glad he did. Dinner was wonderful."

"Then why did you want to see me?" Brandon asked, his voice tight despite his attempt for it to be casual.

"*I* wanted to see you," the deep voice said.

"Brandon, meet Blade Navarone," she introduced them.

Brandon couldn't help the start of surprise. Blade Navarone was reported to be one of the richest men in the country. He and Brandon's cousin Daniel Falcon were friendly business rivals until Daniel married Madelyn Taggart and sold many of his companies in order to stay home with their son. The man who had been waiting to snap them up was Blade Navarone, an enigma. He'd come out of nowhere about fifteen years ago and proceeded to make a fortune.

"Welcome to the Red Cactus," Brandon finally greeted Blade. "What brings you to Santa Fe?"

Blade reached his large, manicured hand across the table. Faith instantly put hers in his. "A man doesn't need a reason to visit a beautiful and desirable woman."

Faith tucked her head. "Blade."

Brandon had the strangest urge to snatch Faith up. She didn't have the experience to deal with a man like Blade. "I wasn't aware that you two knew each other."

"You know all of Faith's acquaintances?" Blade asked, still holding Faith's hand.

Brandon knew a challenge when he heard it. "The important ones."

"Brandon," Faith scolded him while acting like a teenager on her first date.

Dark eyebrows rose; eyes blacker than any midnight narrowed and darkened even more. "It seems not all of them."

"Why did you want to see me?" Brandon asked impatiently.

Releasing Faith's hand, Blade leaned back in the chair, making it look small. He was a big man, but with muscles, not fat. "To hire you."

Of all the reasons Brandon expected, that was the last one. "No, thank you."

"You haven't heard my offer yet," Blade said in a way that implied most people had a price and he usually found what it was.

"I'm chef and owner. This is more than a restaurant to me." Brandon slanted a look at Faith. "She should have told you."

"I did," Faith said. "Since you're so fond of trying to steal Henrí, I thought it might be good to see the tables reversed."

"Since I'm staying with you, I promised not to." Brandon had no idea why he phrased the words so suggestively.

Faith flushed.

"As a guest at the hotel," Blade said. "Faith wouldn't turn her back on a friend."

"I've never heard her or her brothers mention you before," Brandon said, aware his comment was just as challenging and baiting as Blade's had been earlier.

"She hasn't mentioned your name, either. Well, we've kept you long enough." Removing his wallet, Blade placed enough money on the table to cover the meal three times over. It was an outrageous tip, one that would send Luis, a college student, into a fit of glee. It was a tip guaranteed to impress a woman.

Standing, Blade held Faith's chair. Brandon's annoyance increased when he saw that Blade was two inches taller than him. "Good night."

"Good night, Brandon," Faith said.

Brandon didn't like it that Faith was leaving with the man, but there was little he could do about it.

• • •

Faith waited until she was in the backseat of the Mercedes before she clapped her hands in joy. "Thank you, Blade. You were magnificent."

"You're sure this is what you want?"

"Yes," Faith answered without hesitation as the chauffeur pulled away from the curb.

Blade took her hand. His was rough with callouses. "Love can hurt."

Faith's hand covered his. She ached for him, but they had promised themselves that they would never speak of the past. "It doesn't have to. I'll take the chance of winning Brandon's love."

The sides of Blade's sensuous mouth lifted slightly, as if unfamiliar with a smile. "You were always stubborn."

"Determined."

He nodded. "I've made arrangements for all that you asked. I'll be unavailable for the next couple of weeks."

"Going after another company?" she asked as the car pulled up in front of her hotel.

"In a manner of speaking." Opening the door, he emerged, then reached back to help her out.

Faith noticed the chauffeur had gotten out as well, his gaze constantly searching the area. If she hadn't known, she would have never guessed that the tailored black jacket hid a 9mm, just as Blade's jacket hid his. Neither would be caught off guard again.

Memories for the reason behind their caution tugged at her heart and almost brought tears to her eyes. One look at Blade's determined face and she knew he wouldn't want her sympathy now any more than he had then. She hugged him and was unsurprised to feel his hands briefly touch her, then fall. At least he had allowed that little bit of warmth. He hadn't accepted even that much in the past.

He stepped back. He couldn't move past the tragic and senseless deaths of those he loved more than his own life. He didn't want comfort. Revenge certainly hadn't helped. Faith wondered what would heal him and make him the laughing, caring man she'd once known. "Thank you."

"I would do more. Good-bye, Faith." He stepped back into the car. After the chauffeur took one last look, he got in and drove away.

"God, please help him." Turning, Faith went into the hotel.


Phone in hand, Brandon paced. Neither Cameron nor Duncan answered his cell. There was another man who would have the answers he wanted. The answering machine clicked on and Brandon barely kept from throwing the phone against the wall.

"Daniel Falcon." Then the tiny voice of a child said something like "Da-yel Junjer." There was a giggle followed by the deeper laughter of a man.

Brandon scowled. When it came to his son, Daniel was putty in the little boy's hands. Brandon deactivated the phone and admitted they all were. Next to Morgan and Phoenix at their wedding, Daniel Junior had been the star attraction. Brandon didn't know anything about children, but Felicia and John Henry, proud grandparents that they were, were quick to point out that their very advanced fifteen-month-old only grandchild had been walking since he was eight months and now had a four-word vocabulary, could swim and turn on the computer.

Brandon glanced at the clock. Nine forty. He gave up. His brothers as well as his cousins and their extended family, the Taggarts, didn't answer the phone after eight thirty. They might not be available, but the computer was available 24-7.

He'd check on things downstairs, then turn on the computer in his main office on the first floor. He was halfway out the door when another thought struck. He dialed the hotel.

"Casa de Serenidad, House of Serenity. Good evening; may I help you?"

"Is Ms. McBride in?"

"Who's calling, please?"

He hesitated. He didn't want Faith thinking he was checking up on her. At the same time, he didn't want Blade to take advantage of her. "A guest."

"Your room number, sir?"

"Never mind." Frustrated, Brandon hung up the

phone. He'd do a run-through downstairs, then drive over to the hotel and check. No man was taking advantage of Faith.

Faith was smiling as she strolled through the lobby of the hotel. Her plan was working. She'd just gotten off the phone with one of the hotel operators. Janice had been concerned because a man who said he was a guest had called asking for her. When Janice had asked for his room number he'd hung up.

Faith hugged her notepad closer to her chest. It had to have been Brandon, checking on her. He cared. She hadn't missed that brief flare of anger and challenge in his eyes. Still smiling, she briefly closed her eyes. When she opened them, Brandon stood a short distance away.

He looked as surprised as she must have looked. He stepped back as if to leave. She quickly went to him. "Is everything all right at the restaurant?"

"You working?" he asked.

Faith decided to let him evade the question. "Yes."

"Your date left already?"

"He has a business meeting early in the morning and had to fly back," she answered.

"Too bad," Brandon said, but he didn't sound like he meant it.

"What are you doing here?" she asked, unable to hold back the question any longer. "And don't try to evade me this time."

"Blade left before I got his card," Brandon told her. "I have a buddy who might like the job offer, that's all. Uh, I guess I'd better get back to the restaurant."

She didn't believe him. "You're sure that's the only reason?"

"What other reason could there be?" he asked. "Night."

Faith watched his long-legged stride carry him away. The earlier happiness she'd felt faded. Brandon had come to check on her, but it had been as a friend, not as a man who was interested in her. Only time would tell if he could see her differently. Unfortunately, time was something she didn't have.

The Women's League was a charitable support network that helped the needy men and women of Santa Fe. The league was in its fifth year and had received numerous awards for helping the citizens of the city. Two yearly events, the Bachelors Auction and the Kitchen Cooking Show and Extravaganza, were the most anticipated.

Cooking classes were popular attractions in Santa Fe, but Brandon took the classes one step further by opening the show up to anyone and auctioning off new kitchen items he'd secured from various manufacturers. All the proceeds went to the Women's League. It had been easy to secure a classroom in one of the culinary schools.

"Ladies and gentlemen, tonight we're going to prepare Cornish hens, spring peas, romaine salad with honey-lime vinaigrette, and honey cheesecake with blueberry sauce for dessert. Finally, we'll select a wine appropriate for the meal," Brandon said, indicating several wines nearby. "Once we've dined, we'll have the silent auction for the articles on the tables near me, many of which are absolutely necessary for any good cook." The appliances from his home would be given to families in need.

"If I'm the top bidder, will you come over and give personal instructions?" Elizabeth asked.

The crowd broke into shouts of laughter. "I'll be happy to give *cooking* instruction to the highest bidder," Brandon told her.

Several women in the audience got up to go to the silent auction table and place additional bids. "That's it, ladies," Ruth said from beside Brandon. "You're helping others, and there's no better cook than Brandon."

Brandon barely kept the pleasant expression on his face as more women went to the long tables several feet away to write down bids. He just hoped the highest bidder was happily married.

"I may not cook, but I'd be happy to come over and sample a meal cooked by the next to the highest bidder," Pierce said from across the room.

Brandon tipped his head slightly in thanks for his brother showing up and for throwing himself on the pyre as even more women went to the table. But Brandon knew there was another reason behind Pierce's sacrifice. Carmella had flown out that afternoon, so Pierce was in the market for another woman.

"Men in the audience, I know you can cook." Sierra came to stand beside Brandon. "Surely you aren't going to let the women have all the great appliances?"

Ed Peters, sixty, balding, and owner of a small print shop, came to his feet. "If a man wins, will you cook for him?"

"Not unless you sign a waiver releasing me from any medical bills or loss of wages due to illness." She sent Ed a teasing smile.

The men hooted, then made their way to the thirty-odd appliances, from smoothie makers, to stainless-steel cookware, to a fifteen-piece forged cutlery set. "If you'll have a seat, we'll proceed," Brandon said.

The audience went back to their seats. Just as Brandon was about to begin the demonstration, the door in the back opened and in came Faith. She wasn't alone.

The tall, lean man dressed in a suit and tie didn't have the presence or the dangerous looks of Blade. Brandon pegged him as a successful businessman.

Aware that his mike was on, Brandon refrained from asking Sierra for her take on the man. Besides Luke and perhaps Morgan, their sister was the best at reading a person. Brandon caught the interested gleam in her eyes. He'd seen it a hundred times. It meant the man had money and Sierra was going to do her best to interest him in Santa Fe real estate before the night was over. That answered one question Brandon had and left a lot more unanswered.

"Brandon, we're ready when you are."

Brandon didn't dare look at his mother. She read her children too easily. He didn't want her to get the wrong idea as to why he was worried about Faith.

"I've already prepared the meals for us to enjoy. Let's see how it's done." He picked up the Cornish hen. "Seasoning is vital and the key. Because the hen is so small, it's easy to overcook. There's nothing worse than dry chicken." He picked up a crystal shaker. "You want spice in your life, you need it in food as well."

"I couldn't agree more."

The distinctive voice had come from the back. Brandon's hand clenched. It had come from the man with Faith. It was going to be a long demonstration.

Faith was the center of attraction. Rather, Holt Durant, her date and dinner guest, was. He was almost as popular as Brandon and Pierce. And that was saying a lot.

Faith's meal grew cold as she was interrupted time and time again to introduce Holt to another woman. That he had grown up in England and had a British accent added to his charm and allure. He was gracious to each woman and deftly sidestepped personal questions. Blade had chosen Faith's next man well.

Elizabeth finally moved away after obtaining no

more information than the woman before her. Faith picked up her fork only to put it down again when she saw Sierra coming toward her. She leaned over to whisper one word in Holt's ear. Sierra possessed something many of the women who had stopped by their table hadn't: a sharp intelligence and a keen knack for obtaining information.

"Trouble," Faith whispered.

Holt followed the direction of her gaze. His handsome face eased into a grin that said it was the kind of trouble he liked. He rose, his smile broadening. He hadn't stood for any of the other women. Faith knew the gesture wasn't lost on anyone.

"Hello, Faith. Glad to see you here again this year." Sierra switched her attention to Holt and extended her hand. "I don't think we've met. Sierra Grayson."

"Holt Durant." He took the slim hand in his and continued to hold it long past what would be considered appropriate.

"Hello, Mr. Durant." Lightly Sierra pulled her hand free. "Please sit and enjoy the meal. My brother is an excellent cook."

"Please call me Holt," he said, finally taking his seat. "The meal is superb. Faith said it would be."

"Perhaps while you're here you'll get a chance to visit his restaurant, the Red Cactus."

"I'm flying back to Denver tonight."

"I see. Our loss. Don't let me keep you from your meal. Enjoy."

"Bye, Sierra."

Faith kicked Holt underneath the table when he continued to stare after Sierra. He started as if coming out of a trance. Horror washed across his face. "Blade will have my hide if I mess this up."

"Not if you redeem yourself," Faith said.

Holt scooted his chair closer. "Consider it done."

# 8

Sierra pulled her chair out and sat at the table with Brandon and Pierce. Luke and Morgan had dropped by with their wives to help with the silent auction and then left before dinner, to no one's surprise. "That was a bust," Sierra said.

"What do you mean?" Brandon asked. Thankfully, his mother was sitting with Amanda Poole and the other officers of the Women's League, so he could freely ask questions.

"I recognized the name, if not the face." She took a bite of romaine salad. "He's a Denver developer. He's slated to break ground in another month on a twenty-five-hundred-acre community that will eventually have almost three thousand residents. The sprawling residential project will take ten to fifteen years to develop. He's not about to take on anything else. He's flying back to Denver tonight."

Pierce stopped eating. "Then he'll need good financial guidance. I'll make sure I give him my card before he leaves, just in case he ever finds he needs to make a change."

Brandon wasn't surprised by his brother's words. Pierce played hard, but he was also a shrewd businessman. "Good riddance."

"Why would you say that?" Sierra asked.

"He looked unsavory to me," Brandon answered slowly.

Sierra cut into her chicken. "That's what makes him so appealing to women."

Brandon snorted. "Then it's a good thing Blade Navarone went back to wherever he came from last night." All he'd learned on the computer was how wealthy the man was.

"Blade Navarone was in Santa Fe?" Sierra and Pierce asked in unison.

"You know him?" Brandon asked, shocked.

"Not personally, but who in real estate doesn't know *of* Blade Navarone?" Sierra leaned toward her brother. "He's amassed an obscene fortune and is still going strong. Navarone Resorts and Spas are spectacular and scattered around the world. They are just one of the properties he owns. He keeps a low profile, but he's been the financial backer behind countless developments."

"If I could secure a tenth of his assets to manage, it would double my income. Where did you see him?" Pierce asked.

They weren't telling Brandon anything he didn't know. "He was at the restaurant last night with Faith."

Brandon looked across the room at Faith and Holt. They didn't have to sit so close to each other. She was almost in his lap. "Now she's with this other guy."

Sierra whistled. "Well, way to go, Faith. I didn't think she dated very much. Seems what they say about the quiet ones is true. She's certainly making up for lost time with a bang."

Brandon frowned. "Faith doesn't know anything about handling men."

"You might be wrong about that, brother dear." Sierra glanced over her shoulder at Faith and her date. "To have nabbed dates with two wealthy men the same week, I'd say she knew something."

Brandon didn't care what Sierra thought. Faith was like a baby chick in the henhouse with a fox. She was too innocent and trusting. He'd expect Duncan or Cameron to keep an eye on Sierra if she got herself in a situation she might not be able to handle; not that there were many men Sierra couldn't handle. He couldn't say the same for Faith. She hadn't been turning down dates as Sierra had since she was in junior high.

As people began to leave, Brandon and Pierce carried the women's purchases to their cars. Every time he came inside, Brandon would search for Faith. She wasn't difficult to locate, since she and her date were always surrounded by several women.

As long as the women weren't after him, that was fine with Brandon. Under different circumstances, he might have thanked Holt.

Finally, they were down to the last of the items. Pierce grabbed the top-of-the-line mixer that belonged to long-legged Carolyn Davis, a jewelry designer. She'd paid twice the retail cost. However, by doing so she'd guaranteed Pierce would come over for a meal. From the interested look on Pierce's face, he was looking forward to becoming better acquainted with her.

"I'll take this one."

"Thank you, Pierce," Carolyn said, her moist red lips curving beguilingly. "I don't think there's room in my car. Do you mind following me home?"

Carolyn's doting father owned a foreign-car dealership. She changed cars every six months. At the moment she was driving a red convertible baby Benz that would have ample space for the mixer.

"Not at all. Good night, Brandon," Pierce said.

"Good night." Brandon watched the two leave. Pierce might date a lot of women, but he did so responsibly. Carolyn would be disappointed if she expected more than conversation tonight.

Some men weren't so disciplined.

Brandon's hard gaze cut to Holt. He might plan to leave tonight, but what time? Troubled, Brandon picked up the last item of the silent auction, a set of cast-iron cookware. Faith had been the high bidder, as she had been the year before. Somehow whatever she won always ended up back at the Women's League pantry to go to a needy family. She was a good woman. Too good to let some man use her.

Brandon started toward her. Apparently the women had given up. For once she and her date were alone. "Faith. Here's the set of cookware."

"I'll take that." Holt extended his hands and looked down at Faith. "Perhaps you'll cook me a meal."

"It'll be my pleasure," Faith said.

Brandon handed over the large box, inordinately pleased that for a moment Holt had to shift to balance the heavy weight. "What time is your flight out tonight?"

"A couple of hours," he answered. "But there's an important reason for me to return. In fact, you couldn't keep me away."

Faith momentarily tucked her head. "You're so gallant, Holt."

"How can any man be otherwise around you?" Holt said softly.

Brandon snorted. He hadn't heard such lame crap since high school. Faith's startled gaze met his. She looked away, but not before he saw the flush of embarrassment on her cheeks. Belatedly he realized that she thought his derision was due to disagreeing with Holt.

"I think we'll be going," Faith said quietly. "Good night."

Tight-lipped, Holt glared. "You might be a great chef, but your manners need work."

Before Brandon could think of a way to explain, they walked away. He was left staring after them. Not for anything in the world would he hurt Faith, but that was just what he had done.

Chefs, the great ones, learned patience early. Brandon had always prided himself on that attribute until tonight. He found himself checking his watch every few minutes as he cleaned up his work area.

"Is everything all right at the restaurant?" his mother asked.

Against his wishes, as she always did each year after his cooking demonstration, she had stayed to help him clean up. He was thankful that he was cleaning the stove while his mother worked on the counter behind him and couldn't see his reaction. He slid the cleaning pad over the black glass surface before answering, "Great. Michelle called a bit ago and said everything is going well."

"It's about time you let her do the job you hired her for," his mother said. "I don't see why you made her manager if you're always there. You need to take more time off."

"I took off tonight." It was an old argument. "Almost finished here, then I can walk you to your car."

Her sigh was long-suffering. "Are you going back to the restaurant?"

"Yes." He glanced at his watch. They'd closed five

minutes ago. He had a competent staff, but he liked seeing for himself that all was well.

He hadn't taken any consecutive days off since the restaurant opened, except for the out-of-town weddings of his cousins and Luke. And if Brandon did take time off, he always did a walk-through before going to his apartment upstairs. Tonight would be no different. However, first he planned on seeing Faith to apologize.

"Finished." Ruth placed her cleaning supplies in the carry-all on the counter next to the built-in cook-top.

"Same here. Thanks for helping." Brandon put his cleaning supplies inside the carryall and picked it up. "You must be tired. You've been working for two months to get ready for tonight."

His mother fell into step beside him. She was tall and slender, and her head came to his shoulder. "It paid off. Thanks to the hard work of a lot of people that included you and my other children."

"You know we didn't mind." Locking the front door of the cooking school, he took her arm. Except for her 4×4 and his vintage Porsche, the well-lit parking lot was empty.

Taking out her keys, Ruth stopped by the door of her vehicle. "If you had a wife, you'd be going home with her instead of back to the restaurant."

"Mama." His mother always worked the conversation back to marriage. "I'm happy the way things are."

Unlocking the door, she climbed in. "You see how fast your brothers left. You could have what they have."

"I'm happy, Mama," he repeated.

She cupped the strong line of his jaw. "Then why haven't you smiled in the last thirty minutes?" She dropped her hand and started the engine before he could answer. "Good night, Brandon."

She wasn't going to cry, Faith promised herself, and she planned on keeping that promise no matter how much her heart ached and her eyes stung. She had to face reality. Brandon would never think of her as a desirable woman.

She swallowed the lump in her throat that threatened to choke her. He hadn't meant his reaction to Holt to be cruel; he just saw her differently. And he always would. Why shouldn't he?

She put down the schedule she'd been working on. Her thoughts were too scattered to think clearly.

*Brandon doesn't think I'm desirable.*

She felt moisture pool in her eyes and dashed the tears away. She had other things to be thankful for in life. One disappointment wasn't so bad.

The knock on her door caused her to glance up. Her brow puckered. The staff always called before coming. She glanced at the clock as the knock came again. 10:09 P.M.

Getting up from the desk, she went to the door

and looked through the peephole. The most beautiful man in the world stared back at her. She jerked her head away as if he could see her.

He knocked again, this time more persistently. "Faith, please open up."

Unconsciously she took a step back. She'd never been very good at hiding her emotions. As much as he'd hurt her, seeing how much pain he'd caused her would wound him deeply. Brandon cared about people. She didn't want to distress him.

"Faith, please. I saw your shadow through the curtain."

She bit her lip. She'd forgotten to pull the heavy draperies over the sheers when she returned.

"All right, just listen."

*Please, just go away,* she wanted to say, but was afraid if she opened her mouth the tears would flow like rain.

"You know I would never do anything to hurt you."

*I don't want your pity.*

"We're good friends."

*And I should be grateful for that, but I wanted more.*

"That's why when Holt was trying to run a line on you I got angry."

Her head came up. "What?" She wasn't sure if she mouthed the word or said it aloud. She moved closer to the door.

"You're too trusting and gullible."

Her eyes narrowed. She didn't like being called gullible. A gullible woman didn't manage a hotel that continually received a five-star rating.

"How can anyone be otherwise around you?" he mimicked Holt, then snorted again. "He was conning you."

*Conning me.* Unlocking the door, she swung it open. "So no man can give me a compliment and mean it?"

Brandon's mouth opened, gaped. His gaze made an unhurried trip from her head to her toes.

Belatedly Faith remembered she was in her robe and nightgown, this one black silk. At the end of the day she always took a nice long bath and put on loungewear or her sleepers. She checked the impulse to step back inside when Brandon continued to stare at her.

She might not have much experience with men, but Brandon's altered breathing stiffened her spine. She dared to ask, "Am I so hideous a man can't desire me?"

Brandon gulped, then finally managed to drag his gaze up from the flare of her hips, the full thrust of her breasts, to her outraged face. "May-maybe we should talk about this later."

She danced with joy inside. "You were the one banging on my door. Let's talk now."

His unsteady hand swiped across his face. "All right. I'll wait here until you get dressed."

"Oh, Brandon," she said with just enough pique to

throw him off. "I'm not getting dressed just to get undressed again."

His chest shuddered with the breath he blew out. *Wonderful.*

"If you don't start talking, this door is closing in five seconds. One. Two. Thre—"

"I just don't want you to get in over your head," he said quickly. "You could have just as many dates as any other woman if you wanted to. You're just more sensible."

"Maybe I'm tired of being sensible," she challenged.

This time he was the one who stepped closer, close enough for her to feel the heat of his body. "You get that nonsense out of your head about attracting a man. Some men aren't to be trusted."

To her horror and embarrassment, Faith felt her nipples harden, her breasts grow heavy. She folded her arms across her chest. It was definitely time to end this. "Blade and Holt aren't two of them. Good night, Brandon." Unfolding her arms, she turned to go inside.

Brandon laid his hand gently on her shoulder to stop her. "I just want what's best for you."

Desire and heat built quickly. It was all she could do not to walk into his arms and lift her lips to his. "I know that, but I'm a big girl. Literally and figuratively."

Irritation crossed his face. "Age doesn't matter and there's nothing wrong with your figure."

"Oh, Brandon," she said, almost giving in to the urge. "If you think that, then why don't you teach me how to tell my prince from the frogs out there?"

"Because. Because . . ." His other hand came up to rest on her other shoulder. He stared down at her.

*Kiss me,* she thought. *Just kiss me.*

Frowning, he stepped back. "Because it's idiotic."

Frustration and unfulfilled desire welled within Faith. "Then fine. Good night, Brandon." The door closed with a sharp click. "Just you wait, Brandon Grayson. I'll show you," she whispered.

Brandon slammed the door to his hotel room, pulling off clothes as he went. Pausing only long enough to sit on the commode top to remove his boots, he stripped off his jeans and Jockeys and stepped into the shower. He turned it on full blast.

Cold water sloshed over his heated skin. He took the punishment gladly. He was definitely losing it. Celibacy was taking its toll on him.

Eyes shut tightly, his hands propped on the tiled wall, he bowed his head and let the water slosh over him. He tried to keep his mind blank but found it impossible. The tempting picture of Faith kept intruding. The nightgown had shown him every lush, desirable curve. He might have been able to keep it together if he hadn't touched her.

Her skin had felt like warm velvet. She smelled of some exotic flower. Her bare lips had beckoned. For a wild moment he would have given anything to have been able to gently press his mouth against hers.

He turned on the two remaining jets, letting the water hammer him. He never had this problem before. He didn't lust after his friends.

His hands flexed. He straightened and let the water blast his face and roll down to the lower part of his body, which throbbed and ached for release that wasn't going to come. He threw back his head and laughed, a ragged sound, at the last thought, then sobered.

He might remain single, but he was turning into a randy old goat. One thing for certain, he was staying away from Faith until he got whatever it was under control.

Wednesday afternoon Faith moved to Phase Two of Get Brandon. Phase One had not been without its setbacks, but at least Brandon now saw her as a desirable woman. At least she thought he did. She wanted to shout every time she recalled the flash of desire in his eyes, his uneven breathing. She'd gone to sleep aching for him and wondered if he had had as much trouble falling asleep as she had.

She hadn't been able to test her theory since Tuesday night. He'd been gone when she went by his room this next morning to ask him to breakfast.

Flicking on her turn signal, Faith pulled into the parking lot of the realtor's office where Sierra worked.

Picking up the bakery box, Faith climbed out of her Lexus and went inside the single-story building. She stopped at the receptionist's desk. "Sierra Grayson, please."

The dark-haired receptionist looked up from a stack of papers. "Is she expecting you?"

"Yes. Faith McBride." She'd called that morning.

The receptionist picked up the phone and dialed. "Ms. McBride to see you, Ms. Grayson. I'll send her right in." She replaced the receiver. "You can go in. It's the last door at the end of the corridor to the right."

"Thank you." Faith continued down the well-lit hallway lined with the pictures of realtors and their awards and accolades. She wasn't surprised to see that Sierra's accomplishments took up a good portion of the wall. Stopping at the last door, she knocked softly.

"Come in, Faith."

Faith drew in a deep, calming breath and opened the door. Sierra came around a beautifully carved antique desk with a computer on one end and almost every surface covered with papers. "Thank you for seeing me," Faith said.

Sierra's gaze flickered to the box in Faith's hand. "I'm a sucker for pastries."

Faith offered the box. She'd stacked the odds in her favor by offering to bring them. "Your secret is safe."

"Please have a seat." Waving Faith to a comfortable chair at a small glass-topped table, Sierra placed the box on top, then went to a hutch and returned with napkins, paper plates, and two bottles of orange juice. "Always prepared."

"I've worked through enough meals to understand." Faith accepted a raspberry Danish from the box. "Thanks."

Sierra picked up a croissant and bit. "Yum. Still warm. Whatever it is you want, unless it's illegal, I'm in."

Faith blinked. "What gave me away?"

Sierra laughed, then opened her orange juice. "These." She indicated the box. "Not that I'm above being bribed, but Morgan being an officer of the court and Luke an ex–FBI agent, I certainly hope what you want is legal in all fifty states. This is the first time you've visited and you bring my weakness. How did you know?"

"Brandon mentioned you ate the only croissant."

"I noticed there were three inside today. Good thinking." Sierra took a sip of juice. "So, what's up?"

"I want you to teach me how to dress a bit more . . ." Faith faltered.

"Flattering?" Sierra asked.

Faith nodded and glanced down at her beige slacks and long white blouse. "You always look fantastic and fashionable. I realize we're different sizes, but I was hoping you might be able to guide me."

Sierra took another sip of juice, then set the bottle down on the table. "Only if we agree on one thing:

it's not the size; it's the woman that makes the difference. Until you believe that, have faith in yourself, what you wear won't make any difference."

"That might take a bit of doing." Faith twisted the bottle in her nervous hands. She had self-confidence in her ability as a businesswoman, but not as a woman who could tempt a man.

"Is there anything about you that works differently because you're not Twiggy?" Sierra asked a bit impatiently.

"No."

"Right the first time." Sierra pushed her plate away. "You're intelligent, have great managerial skills and superior work ethics—all of which have helped take Casa de Serenidad to the top. If you think you're less, then others will, too."

Something about the fierceness in Sierra's voice told Faith she had been harshly judged by others. "You wouldn't, would you?"

"Wasn't allowed." Sierra chose a croissant. "I can't believe it was in the McBride family, either."

"Not in business, but I've never dated very much," Faith confessed.

"Well, then you're certainly making up for lost time. Blade Navarone *and* Holt Durant all in one week and it's only Wednesday."

"They're just friends," Faith said slowly.

"You picked two doozies." Sierra made a face. "Getting to Blade is about as easy as having an audience with the president. I've tried."

"I wish I could promise an introduction." Faith bit her lower lip. "I can't."

"In that case . . ." Sierra stood and tossed her plate and empty bottle in the chrome wastebasket.

Faith's head fell. She'd chosen Sierra because of her style and also because she wanted to be her friend. Now that wasn't going to happen.

"I'm busy until this afternoon around five. We could meet here at six and go to one of my favorite boutiques in my car."

Faith's head lifted abruptly. "You're going to help me even though I can't introduce you to Blade?"

"If you betrayed Blade's trust, you'd betray mine. That's not the type of person I want to spend any time around," Sierra said frankly.

Faith came to her feet. She should have known that Sierra would have as much integrity as Brandon. "Thank you."

Sierra folded her arms and studied Faith. "If I asked you who the lucky man is, would you tell me?"

"No."

Sierra's arms dropped to her sides. "Thought not. See you at six."

"Won't the store be closing then?"

"I know the owner. She'll stay open for me."

Faith looked at the beautiful aqua and pink designer suit that fit Sierra like a dream and knew it cost dearly. Faith didn't doubt her statement for a moment. Too many times to count, she herself had made exceptions to rules for good repeat customers. "See you at six." Opening the door, Faith left.

Shopping had never been the fun outing to Faith it was to many women. There was nothing guaranteed to ruin her day and deflate her ego quicker than trying on outfit after outfit that didn't fit or finding a darling one that didn't come in her size. She'd been disappointed too many times. Following Sierra into Impressions, Faith hoped her luck was about to change.

"Hello, Sierra," a voluptuous saleslady in a pretty pink suit with a short skirt greeted her.

"Hello, Dot. This is Faith McBride, a friend of mine. She's looking to add a few pieces to her wardrobe."

"Hello, Faith," Dot said. "You've certainly come to the right store." She waved her hand to the room to the right. "Are you looking for sexy, casual, dressy? Do you want comfort or style?"

"I'm not sure. I have a date tonight."

Sierra whistled. "You certainly aren't losing any time."

Faith flushed. "I've lost enough, don't you think?"

"I'll say," Sierra answered.

"Is it possible to combine style and comfort with sexy?" Faith asked.

"At Impressions we specialize in doing the impossible," Dot said. "Isn't that right, Sierra?"

A gleam entered Sierra's dark eyes. "I have a weakness for designer clothes and want them as soon as they hit the runway. If it's on this planet, Dot can get it for me."

"Pretty designer clothes don't come in my size," Faith said a bit wistfully.

"Wrong." Sierra took her by the arm. "And I know just where we'll start looking."

# 9

There probably wasn't a man alive who hadn't gotten on the wrong side of a woman, Brandon thought. Things like that happened. Some women might not forgive a man, but Faith wasn't the type to carry a grudge. She'd be over her pique soon. He just wished she'd get the crazy notion out of her head that she needed to attract some guy. If his strange behavior was any indication, she didn't have anything to worry about.

"Brandon, Sierra is at the family table." Elaine walked up to the long stainless-steel counter on which orders were placed. "She wants Caesar salad, fried catfish, and a baked potato all the way."

He glanced at the monitor. "Tell her it will be about ten minutes."

"Will do." Elaine shook her pretty head. "I wish I had her style, looks, and metabolism."

"Take her chips and salsa in the meantime." He put the finishing touches on a platter of chicken *flautas*.

"Doing it now along with her diet cola." Elaine picked up the waiting bowl on the warmer. "She asked you to please save her a slice of carrot cake for dessert."

Brandon paused in spooning refried beans onto the plate. *Faith likes diet cola with her high-caloric desserts, too.*

"You all right, Brandon?" Luis asked.

Brandon glanced up. The waiter already had one order on the tray and was waiting for the other one. "Yes."

He quickly finished, then went to the refrigerator to set aside Sierra's dessert. There were two slices left. Faith hadn't eaten her carrot cake the other night. She'd blackmailed him, but she'd also come through for him.

Taking one of the slices of cake, he slid it into a white box and placed it back in the refrigerator. Perhaps the peace offering would get them back on an even footing. He didn't like it that they were uneasy around each other.

"Brandon?"

He turned at the sound of Elaine's voice. "Yes."

"Sierra wants you to come and tell her how the bathroom is going," Elaine said, then ducked back out of the kitchen.

There was absolute quiet in the kitchen for three full seconds. Only Sierra would think nothing of pulling the tiger's tail. "Michelle, I'm going out and talk to my baby sister about living dangerously."

"Better her than me," came Michelle's answer as she headed out the swinging doors with a tray of food.

Removing his apron, Brandon followed. Automatically his gaze swept over the room. The bustle of the waiters, the clatter of flatware against dishes, the hum of conversation, the southwestern decor, always put him in a better mood.

Moving easily, he went to the family table, a booth near the back. His family had been close growing up. Breakfast had been a mad affair with all of them at the table, lunch had been hit-and-miss after they started working, but they usually gathered around the table again for dinner. He'd wanted that same connection in his restaurant—where problems were discussed and, if not solved, you always knew your family was behind you.

"What if a pipe in the ceiling broke over your converted closet?" He slid into the booth facing Sierra.

Horror widened her eyes. The chip midway to her mouth paused, then continued. "You and Morgan always did play dirty."

Brandon relaxed back against the leather cushion. "How did the date last night with Mr. Peters go?"

Sierra laughed. "He was so cute. He made us strawberry smoothies and we danced."

"He's sixty if he's a day. That must have been some sight."

"It was." Sierra picked up her diet cola. "You get

out of cooking for Faith. She sent the set of cast-iron cookware to the Women's League yesterday."

"She always donates what she purchased," he said, propping his elbows on the table. "I don't think I can ever recall her cooking anything when I was over at her house all those years with Cameron."

"Here you go." Elaine set the plate of food on the table, then withdrew.

"Now she doesn't have to. With twenty-four-hour room service I certainly wouldn't cook." Sierra reached for her fork. "If they could build a house without a kitchen, it would suit me." Sierra could cook but chose not to.

"On the other hand, I need one. The only way I can get by living at the hotel is that when I come early to let Mr. Montgomery in I can experiment with dishes and start on the desserts before the crew comes in."

"How is the bath going?" She pushed her salad aside and started in on her baked potato and fried catfish.

"Glacial slow." Brandon slumped in his seat. "Seems the pipes are special. He had to order new ones. We might be looking at adding more days to his two-weeks estimate."

"Sorry. But at least the time will be spent in luxurious surroundings."

Brandon grimaced. "I'd rather be in my place." He looked at her almost empty plate. "You ready for your dessert?"

She shook her head. "I think I might take it with me."

"I'll get it." He rose to his feet. "You and Faith have the last two pieces."

"Faith?"

"Yeah, I thought I'd take her a slice," he explained. "She never did get hers the other night."

"You might want to wait and give it to her tomorrow." Sierra reached for the Gucci billfold that matched her croc handbag and placed a large tip on the table. Brandon never allowed any family member to pay.

"Why?"

Sierra glanced up. "Because she and her date are dining at the Pueblo as we speak."

Faith had racked her brain all evening on the best way to let Brandon find out she was having dinner with Shane Elliot, an associate of Blade's. It didn't do any good to wear the attention-getting black halter dress with turquoise piping and matching chandelier turquoise earrings and necklace if Brandon didn't see her. And it didn't look as if he would.

She'd been with Shane for almost an hour and, while he was a charming dinner companion, she'd learned little more than his name. She wasn't even sure what he did for a living, only that he would be in Santa Fe for two days to "escort" her anyplace she wished. He wasn't handsome, but there was an edge, an intensity, about him that would draw and intrigue most women.

Halfway through her medallion beef cooked to perfection, she glanced up. Her heart fluttered. Her problem was solved.

Discreetly she leaned over the small, intimate table in a quiet corner of the elegant restaurant and whispered, "Brandon's here."

Shane smiled like a cat in front of a birdcage with an open door. His large manicured hand covered her free one. "How jealous do you want to make him?"

She shook her head. "I don't want him jealous."

"You're sure?" He lifted her hand and kissed the inside of her wrist.

Faith's intake of breath was sharp. She jerked her hand back.

"You all right, Faith?" Brandon asked, towering over them.

Faith swallowed, then moistened her lips. Shane had done that on purpose. Blade had warned her that he was unpredictable. "Hello, Brandon. What are you doing here?"

"I think you know the answer to that," he said; his voice carried an edge she hadn't heard before.

It was one thing to want Brandon to think of her as desirable, quite another for him to treat her as brainless and in need of his macho protection. "I'm fine, as you can see."

Brandon's hard gaze drilled into Shane. "I don't think we've met."

After a long, tense moment Shane momentarily lifted his gaze and said, "No, we haven't," then went back to his rare prime rib.

Faith saw the swift change in Brandon's face and knew if she didn't act quickly, one of the men might do something stupid. She recalled that Blade had said Shane could be dangerous as well. "Excuse me," she said, standing.

Shane lazily unfolded himself and came to his feet as well. "Certainly, but only for a moment or I'll get lonely."

Throwing Shane a "behave yourself" look, she took Brandon's arm and led him outside into the patio. Lights flickered in the lanterns. Flames danced in the kiva fireplace. "What are you doing?"

"When did you meet him?"

"Brandon, that is none of your concern."

"That might be if you hadn't asked me to help you—"

Her hand covered his mouth. She knew it was a mistake immediately when his warm breath licked her skin; his firm lips enticed, making her wish she could replace her hand with her lips. She jerked her hand away. "I'd rather we not talk about that."

"You're going to get in trouble if you keep this up."

Her chin lifted. "As I said, it's about time and I can handle it. Thank you for your concern, but I need to return to my guest and you have a restaurant to run." With her head held high and her knees shaking, she returned to her table.

Shane stood and reached for her chair. "Should I kiss you on the back of your neck?"

Faith gritted a smile. "Do so at your own risk."

Chuckling, he took his seat. "I almost feel sorry for him."

Entering the door of the Red Cactus, Brandon admitted that he had crossed the line . . . again. The fault wasn't his . . . not entirely. He just wasn't meant to live a celibate life. Why else would he react so strongly every time Faith touched him? Weaving his way through the tables, he decided it was time to begin dating again.

He spotted Elizabeth Jackson with her younger sister, Willie, and started toward them. Elizabeth was sophisticated enough not to become emotionally involved in a relationship. It would just be two consenting adults enjoying each other for as long as it lasted.

"Hello, ladies. Is everything all right?"

"Hello, Brandon," they said, watching him as if wishing he were on the menu.

"Looks like you're ready for dessert. Please let your server know that it's on the house," he said, his gaze lingering on Elizabeth.

"That's so sweet of you, Brandon," Elizabeth cooed.

"I was just thinking the same thing about you," he said.

A slow smile crossed Elizabeth's face. Propping her arms on the table, she leaned over, causing her ample breasts to threaten to spill out of her scoop-necked top. "I hadn't thought you noticed."

"I noticed. Would you like to go out sometime?" There was no sense in waiting.

"When?" Elizabeth asked, excitement in her voice.

"Tomorrow night . . . if you don't mind dining here again. Say around eight." He'd had more first dates than he could count at the Red Cactus.

"I'll be here."

"I'll be waiting." Brandon strolled away, wishing he were thinking more of the coming date with Elizabeth than what Faith and her date were doing.

She'd looked different, softer somehow, and every bit as enticing in the dress as she had in the silk night-gown. Both drew his attention to her full breasts and made his hands and mouth ache to touch, to taste. Brandon stopped. If that man touched her, he would— His fists clenched. There was nothing he could do. The thought wasn't comforting as he continued to the kitchen.

The next night Faith didn't try very hard to talk Shane out of taking her to dinner at the Red Cactus. She'd chosen another of the new outfits Sierra had helped her select. This time it was a sheer blue multi-colored printed top that bared one shoulder, and linen capri pants.

She felt a little flirtatious in the Gypsy-inspired creation and heeled sandals until as she and Shane were on their way to be seated she saw Brandon and Elizabeth sitting side by side in one of the booths.

Faith's heart stopped, then pounded furiously in her chest. For a moment she was afraid she'd faint. She was unable to take her eyes from them. Their shoulders touched. Their heads were so close together their breaths probably mingled.

Her time was up. Misery almost took her to her knees.

"Faith?"

"Shane. I-I'd like to leave," she managed to say.

Shane followed the direction of her gaze and cursed softly under his breath. His hand moved from Faith's waist to curve around her shoulder. "We've changed our minds," he said to the hostess, then whispered to Faith, "Hold your head up."

Somehow she managed to do so. And then wished she hadn't. Brandon chose that inopportune moment to look up. Their gazes met. Afraid he'd see the anguish in her face, she turned away, burrowing closer to Shane as she allowed him to steer her outside.

"Cry if you must, but it won't change one thing."

Her throat and eyes stung. "I don't guess you've ever lost anyone you loved."

Shane's eyes, a startling gray, chilled her. "No, and I don't plan to."

Taking her arm, he helped her into the black luxury sedan. Getting in the driver's seat, he started the motor. "I'll take you back."

"Thank you," she managed. "I'm sorry to have wasted your time."

"Helping a friend is never a waste of time," he said as he pulled into the narrow, congested street.

"Blade," she said, more as a statement than a question.

"That's a man who has been to hell and fought his way back." Shane zipped around a car, reminding her of Cameron, who claimed he wasn't an impatient driver as much as he was one who didn't like wasting time getting to where he was going.

"How did you meet Blade?" she asked.

"You wouldn't want to know." Shane pulled up in front of the hotel, exited the car, and came around to the passenger side.

Faith got out of the car when the door opened and studied the man standing in front of her. Like Brandon, his shoulders were wide, his body muscular. But there the similarities ended. Brandon's eyes were warm, caring. She couldn't begin to imagine the secrets behind Shane's unblinking stare. It was small wonder he and Blade were friends. Both had secrets that would probably break lesser men.

"Sometimes talking helps."

A flicker of surprise crossed Shane's face. His hand lifted, one long calloused finger brushed her hair back. "Blade said you were a pushover."

Her chin lifted defiantly. "I'm not."

His hand fell. His face became shuttered once more. "Rio is up tomorrow night. Your friend should be careful. Rio doesn't have my sense of humor."

Faith wondered if she had imagined the tenderness. "It won't be necessary. Brandon has another woman in his life now."

"So?"

"He's not the type of man to play around. It's over," she said, the words difficult to utter aloud. "Thank you."

"So you're giving up?" There was no mistaking the derision in his voice.

"I can't compete against Elizabeth."

"Why? You've got everything she's got."

"Twice as much," Faith said, trying to be flippant and failing miserably.

"I guess Blade was wrong about you. Good night."

"Wait!" she cried. "What do you mean?"

He stopped at the driver's side of the car. "He said you were the most courageous woman he'd ever met. Never known Blade to be wrong, but there's a first time for everything." Opening the door, Shane climbed inside and drove off.

Faith went inside the hotel, speaking to the valet

attendant and doorman as she passed. Risking her life was one thing; her heart, quite another.

It wasn't going to happen.

Five minutes after joining Elizabeth in the booth, Brandon knew the spark he'd hoped to stoke into a roaring flame wasn't going to happen. He'd stayed because it was the gentlemanly thing to do and counted the minutes until he could leave.

"Why don't you come over to my place after you've closed?" she said, snuggling closer.

"Not tonight." He glanced around the restaurant and saw Faith. He tensed. For a long time they stared at each other; then she turned, snuggling up to the guy she'd been with the night before.

"Brandon, what's the matter?"

"Nothing." He watched them leave. Faith probably didn't want him interfering again.

"That about sums it up," Elizabeth said.

His attention came back to Elizabeth. "What?"

"You're about as interested in me as I am in that cactus in the corner."

He didn't know what to say, so he remained silent.

"What I can't understand is why you asked me out."

He'd always prided himself on honesty. "Because I was hoping it would click."

"Me, too," Elizabeth said. "But I've been in enough one-sided relationships not to want to be in another one."

"Sorry," he said. "You're a beautiful and desirable woman."

She shook her head of auburn curls. "Neither of which seems to help me get and keep a man." She tilted her head to one side. "Perhaps I should hire your mother."

Brandon winced. "Please, don't joke about that."

"I'm not," she said. "I'm ready to get married."

Brandon stiffened; his eyes bugged.

Elizabeth went into peals of laughter. "You should see your face." She sobered. "But I won't settle for less than a man who's crazy about me."

"You'll find him," Brandon told her.

"I know. In the meantime, you owe me dinner." She picked up the menu. "Iceberg salad with blue cheese dressing, filet of beef tenderloin with portobello mushrooms, asparagus spears, chocolate cheesecake, and a bottle of your best chardonnay."

Brandon's tense shoulders relaxed against the back of the leather booth. "You're making me pay."

Closing the menu, she placed it on the table. "If I can't get the man, I can at least tell all the women who are going to ask me tomorrow that I had a fabulous meal," she joked.

"That you can." He stood. "I'll go put your order in."

"You're coming back, aren't you?" she asked a bit anxiously.

Brandon didn't have to look around to know they

had drawn the attention of several customers, mostly women. "You couldn't keep me away."

He was halfway to the kitchen before he recalled one of Faith's dates saying the same thing. Brandon scowled.

Somehow Faith managed to keep the tears at bay for the two hours it took her to conduct business for the hotel. Now, as she sat on the padded wooden bench in her private courtyard, tears pooled, then rolled down her cheeks.

When she and the landscape designer had worked together to create the lush flowering garden Faith had foolishly thought that one day she might share the sight with Brandon. That wouldn't happen now. Faith sniffed, then brushed a tear away with the soggy tissue in her hand. It would take more than bringing out Brandon's protective instincts or a new wardrobe to get him to take a romantic interest in her.

"Faith?"

She jerked around to see Brandon at the gate. She'd been so caught up in her misery that she hadn't heard the gate open. Straightening her spine, she wiped her eyes. "Brandon."

He crossed to her, his eyes narrow as he studied her face. "Did that guy get out of line?"

"No. Sad movie." Sometimes lies were best for all concerned. "You're home early."

He hunkered down in front of her. "Guess neither of our dates worked out."

"There's always the next time." But for her there would not be a next time. Her days of trying to make Brandon see her as a desirable woman were over. Dating others only made her ache for him more.

His black eyes narrowed. "I suppose you want to get married like Elizabeth."

Faith's sharp intake of breath hissed through the air. "She asked you to marry her?"

Shock crossed his face. "No. She just told me she wanted to get married and is looking for a man who'll be crazy about her."

"That's what every woman wants," Faith said, unable to keep the ache and loneliness out of her voice.

"So, that's what this is all about." Brandon came to his feet. "You're looking for a husband, too."

"No," she told him. "That would be hoping for too much."

Frowning, he sat beside her. "Why?"

She might tell Shane, but she didn't want Brandon comparing her to other women. "Too busy. I'd settle for a man I could trust to be faithful and caring."

"Why should you have to settle?" he asked, annoyance in his voice.

"It's just the way it has to be."

Brandon stared at her a long time. "No, it isn't. You win."

"Win what?" she asked, completely baffled.

"I'll teach you how to get a man."

Once she would have given anything to have Brandon's undivided attention. Now she couldn't imagine anything worse than to be around him and know he could never be hers. The ache would be so much worse when he was gone, and the pretense would break her heart. "I've changed my mind. I apologize for putting you in that position."

"I said I'd do it, and I will," he said a bit adamantly. "You deserve to be happy. I might not want to settle down now, but I will one day, so I understand."

*Yes, and it won't be me.* Faith felt tears well up in her eyes again. She stood. "All that crying has given me a headache. I'd better go take something."

He came to his feet as well. "Do you really have a headache or are you putting me off?"

"I really have a headache," she answered truthfully, and went to her door. "Good night, Brandon."

"Night." He brushed strands of her hair behind her ear, causing her to shiver, a marked contrast to when Shane had done the same thing.

"You're cold." His hand went to her forehead. "It's eighty degrees tonight. I hope you're not catching anything."

*Nothing that your love wouldn't cure.* "I just have a headache. Good night." On impulse she kissed Brandon on the cheek. It might be her last opportunity to do so. Opening the door, she escaped inside.

Brandon stared at the closed door and flexed his hand; the impact of the shiver that had raced through him lingered. *Why Faith?* The question had no more than formed before he had his answer. She was safe. She wasn't looking to drag him to the altar, so he could fantasize about her. Catherine wasn't the only one in the family who could figure things out.

Faith was the kind of woman a man could depend on, could trust with his innermost thoughts. A woman like that deserved a man to love her completely.

Brandon started walking slowly back to his room. He didn't like seeing Faith unhappy. He'd always had a special affinity for Cameron's little sister, probably another reason that his body reacted to hers so strongly. Trouble was, as he'd seen this week, Faith could be as stubborn as Sierra, and that was saying a lot. He'd just have to take things into his own hands the way he had for Faith's dances in high school.

Brandon had never understood why boys, then men, didn't ask her out or, if they did, didn't continue to ask her out. Apparently the men she'd dated this week were out of the picture.

He was caught between happy they were gone and angry with them for leaving. Faith was great just the way she was. She didn't need to change to attract men.

What she *did* need was for her confidence to be boosted. He was just the man to teach her. As for the little blips, he'd just have to live with them. Faith's happiness was important. Somehow he'd get Faith to let him help her or go down trying.

# 10

The next morning Faith had just fastened the chandelier earrings on her ears when she heard a knock at the door. She'd decided that there was no reason to let the new clothes or jewelry go to waste. She almost felt sexy with the brush of cool metal against the sides of her face.

She had to admit as she gazed at her reflection in the full-length mirror in her bedroom that the open lightweight sage cardigan over an oyster embroidered dress formed a layered look that suited her better than the pieces she usually picked out for the same effect. Sierra knew clothes.

The knock came again. Picking up her leather-bound notebook, Faith left to answer the door. She was meeting with the supervisor of housekeeping in fifteen minutes at the entrance of the courtyard. Lonnie was early, but Faith didn't mind. Their monthly meetings were often lengthy.

The smile and greeting Faith intended never

materialized. Her eyes rounded in shocked surprise. "Brandon. It's seven thirty!"

"Good morning. I'm early because I wanted to catch you before you left."

"Is there a problem with your room?" she questioned, trying to figure out what was going on.

He propped his hand on the door frame; a grin tugged the corner of his sexy mouth. "I *can* get up when it's important."

Now she understood. "You're meeting Mr. Montgomery this morning at your place."

That whipped the grin from his face. "He's out of town on family business. At the rate he's going, it'll be three weeks before he's finished."

Once that would have given her immense joy; now it meant she would have to endure the continued heartache of having Brandon around and knowing he'd never be hers. "Perhaps not." Stepping onto the small concrete porch with big clay pots of variegated vines and pink geraniums and begonias on either side, she closed the door.

"I thought we'd have breakfast together. At least I can enjoy Henri's cooking if I can't steal him away from you," he teased.

"I commend you on your restraint," she said drolly.

"You should," he said. "How about it?"

"I have an appointment with the head of housekeeping. I thought you were her." She started up the flagstone path toward the rustic gate.

Brandon fell into step beside her and took her arm. "I'll wait for you. Then, if you have time, you can go with me to my place to look at the damage in my bathroom and tell me which fixtures I should buy."

Opening the gate for them, he let her pass through, then caught her arm again. Her skin tingled, heated beneath his fingertips. "I'm sorry, Brandon. We'll be at it at least two hours, probably more."

"Do you have plans for lunch or dinner? We could do it then."

She stopped. "Brandon, I know what you're doing."

"I never thought you were stupid or the kind of woman to give up."

She hugged the leather-bound notebook closer to her chest. "In some things no, but others—"

"In nothing," he said, cutting her off. "Whenever you can make it to the Red Cactus is fine. We close at twelve on Saturday night."

"We have several events tonight," she told him. "Two might last past that time."

"If you can't make it, I'll expect to see you at breakfast in the morning. Since you like to get an early start, we'll meet at eight." His tone broached no argument.

Her lips curved upward. "Getting up early two mornings in a row. My, my. I'm honored."

"Friends do that."

Faith barely kept the smile on her face. "Yes, they do. I see Lonnie waiting for me. Enjoy your breakfast."

"I will. Sierra won't be there to swipe my croissant." Like a young kid or a man who didn't want to take his eyes off a woman he cared about, he walked backward. "See you when you can." With a wave, he turned and continued up the path whistling, with his hands in the pockets of his jeans.

She bit her lip. "Brandon, don't do this to me, please," she whispered. Swallowing the lump in her throat, she tried to smile and went to meet the waiting supervisor, making a mental note to call Brandon later on and cancel for breakfast tomorrow.

Brandon had a problem. As he drove to Morgan and Phoenix's house Sunday afternoon, he wasn't sure how he was going to solve it. Faith hadn't taken him up on his invitation to breakfast, lunch, dinner, or anything in between. After leaving messages all afternoon Friday, he'd finally managed to track her down late Saturday evening. She'd told him she was swamped, asked for a rain check, and hung up, leaving Brandon listening to a dial tone.

Thoroughly at a loss, he turned into the gated community where his older brothers and their mother lived. Well, Luke still had a home in the subdivision, but he and Catherine preferred the mountain cabin where they'd met. Brandon suspected it was because the place held a lot of good memories for them, but Catherine could also keep an eye on her pet wolf hybrid. Catherine could stand toe-to-toe with any man and not flinch. Faith was proving to be just as strong.

Women had played hard-to-get before and kept him dangling, but Brandon had a feeling that Faith wasn't playing games. She was avoiding him. He wasn't going to allow that. He just hadn't figured out how he was going to overcome her resistance. From the way things were going, maybe she should be teaching him how to handle women.

He pulled into the driveway of Morgan's Mediterranean-style home with white brick and red-tiled roof and parked beside a black Lexus SUV he didn't recognize. Probably someone who had just dropped by, he thought as he got out of his sports car. The cookout was an hour away. At least it wasn't his mother.

Opening the passenger door, he picked up two stainless-steel pans of beef, chicken, and links heavily wrapped in cellophane. He'd started cooking the meat on the grill at his restaurant to cut down on the cooking time and ensure that it wasn't over- or undercooked. Morgan's skills on the grill were hit-and-miss. Phoenix was learning. Brandon was happier when he handled the cooking.

No one wanted to chance ruining the cookout to thank the Santa Fe Council for the Arts for welcoming Phoenix with open arms. Morgan and their mother might be members of the council, but learning Phoenix had contributed heavily to the sculptures attributed solely as the work of her mentor could have ruined her credibility. Morgan had worked tirelessly to ensure that hadn't happened. Brandon balanced the containers and rang the doorbell.

Morgan opened the door. "Hi, come on in. Anything else in the car?"

"Salads and baked beans." Brandon stepped into the artful entry. Since Morgan's marriage to Phoenix it now held *Unbowed,* a one-third-life-size statue of a woman with tears on her cheeks but a radiant smile on her face. The figure made him pause and remember the tears he'd seen on Faith's face, tears he'd caused. He didn't like how that made him feel.

Morgan noticed the direction of his brother's gaze. "Although I've seen it a hundred times, it still gets to me, too. Especially when I know how close I came to losing her."

"She loves you too much to have stayed away," Brandon said.

"I tell myself that now, but when she was in New York getting ready for her first opening I spent a lot of restless nights." His hand reverently touched the face of the statue.

"She's where she belongs." Brandon might not want to get married, but he was happy for his brother. "Although why you married a woman who loses track of time in her studio and forgets to cook I can't imagine," Brandon teased in a voice loud enough to carry.

"Because she has other qualities I value more," Morgan said just as loudly.

"I'll bet." Laughing, Brandon stepped into the great room and came to an abrupt halt. Faith stood beside Phoenix near the bust of Morgan. From the surprised look on Faith's face, she hadn't expected to see him any more than he had her.

"Hi, Brandon," Phoenix greeted him. "You know Faith, of course."

"I'm beginning to wonder." He came farther into the room. "Hi, Faith."

"Hello, Brandon." She moistened her lips and spoke to Phoenix. "I don't want to keep you any longer from getting ready for your guests. We'll talk later."

Phoenix put her hand on Faith's arm to stop her. "They won't be here for a while yet."

"Honey, where should I put these salads?" Morgan spoke from the entrance to the great room. Each arm circled a large stainless-steel bowl.

Phoenix shook her head. "To say my husband is lost in the kitchen is an understatement. Faith, I know you didn't come to work, but could you please help me?"

"Of course." There was no hesitation.

Phoenix removed the bowl of potato salad from Morgan's grasp and gave it to Faith, then took the bowl containing field greens. "Brandon, please come into the kitchen and we can put what you don't want on the grill in the refrigerator. Then, too, you can talk Faith into staying."

"No, I have to get back," Faith protested.

"I'm sure you have competent staff members. The kitchen is this way," Phoenix said.

Faith threw a helpless look at the front door, then slowly followed Phoenix.

Brandon and Morgan exchanged puzzled looks. Brandon placed the heavy tray of meat on the leather hassock. "Guess being married to you cured Phoenix of her shyness."

The frown on Morgan's face didn't clear. "I hadn't thought so until now. But what do I know? I'm just the man who's crazy about her."

"You think you know a woman and then, wham, she pulls a three-sixty turn on you." Brandon shook his head.

"Any woman in particular you're talking about?" Morgan asked mildly.

Brandon didn't keep secrets from his family, but neither was he about to discuss Faith's request. "All women are the same."

Morgan picked up the containers of meat. "If I thought you really believed that, you'd have me worried. Come on. Let's get this meat on the grill."

Faith didn't know how it happened, but thirty minutes after Brandon arrived she was still at the house. Phoenix always had one more request: please take the men a glass of raspberry tea, do you mind slicing tomatoes for the cucumber salad, could you please take the bouquet of flowers out of the refrigerator and put them in a vase?

If Faith hadn't been so worried that Brandon would come inside and press her for the reason she had been avoiding him, and he was smart enough to know she had been, she would have enjoyed the time with Phoenix. As it was, Faith kept one eye on the back door leading outside and the other on what she was doing.

"The flowers look beautiful."

Faith set the white long-stemmed gladiolus in the center of the kitchen table. "I couldn't very well mess them up."

"That's debatable." Phoenix studied the oblong table for eight. "Everything looks ready to me. What do you think?"

Faith's practiced gaze swept the table with its colorful yellow and blue swirl dinnerware, flatware, the side dishes and desserts. "All you need is the meat."

"I'll go see if any of it is ready." Phoenix headed for the back door.

"I should be going," Faith said.

Phoenix stopped. "Could you please wait until I get back in case the doorbell rings?"

"Phoenix, I really have to get back."

"I know, but considering that along with the arts council members we've invited several artists, it might be a good idea to stay and speak with them about your vision to display works of art in your hotel."

Faith hesitated. She'd always put the hotel's welfare ahead of any personal considerations. "Just for a little while."

Phoenix was out the back door in nothing flat. Through the half-glass door Faith saw her walk to Morgan and curve her arm around his waist. He did the same to her.

*To love and be loved. What must that feel like?* Faith mused. She was afraid she'd never know.

She turned away to fuss unnecessarily with the flowers. She didn't want Brandon to see her looking at him with the longing that was becoming more difficult at certain times to hide.

A bump sounded on the door. She looked around. Brandon stared back at her with a platter of meat in his hands. Forgetting she'd been trying to avoid him. She rushed to open the door.

"Thanks. Where does Phoenix want this?"

"There." Faith indicated a spot near the head of the laden table. "There's a lot of food here."

"She'll need it. I've fed this group before." He set the platter in the space provided beside the plates, napkins, and flatware. "Phoenix said you're thinking about staying."

She glanced away. "Just for a bit."

"Would you stay longer if I wasn't here?"

Her head whipped back around. The lie hovered on the tip of her tongue, but she didn't want her feelings for him to take away any more of the honesty that had always been there between them. "I'm not sure."

"Fair enough." Folding his arms, he leaned back against the counter. "Mind telling me what I did wrong?"

"Oh, Brandon, you know as well as I do." She shoved an impatient hand through her hair. "It's embarrassing to think of what I asked you."

"So put it out of your mind." He straightened and stared down at her. "Good friends are hard to find."

"Yes, they are," she said, then was relieved to hear the doorbell. "Phoenix asked me to answer the door for her."

"Send them out on the patio. I'll check the food."

Faith continued to the front door. She'd stay for a little while, and then she was leaving.

Monday morning Brandon dragged on his jeans, then stuffed his crisp white shirt into the waistband. Faith had managed to avoid him at the cookout. Sitting on the bed, he pulled on his boots, then stood. If he wasn't a strong man, Faith might give him a complex.

Standing, he shoved his billfold into his hip pocket and the change into his front. Today was going to be different. One way or another, they were going to spend some time together, and he knew just the way to accomplish his goal. A quick glance at his watch confirmed that he was on schedule. Grabbing his keys, he was out the door.

He found Faith just where the night desk clerk had

told him she'd be. He shook his head. She worked too hard. The coffee had probably grown cold, the iced orange juice watery, the food cold. "Good morning. Mind if I join you?"

"Brandon," she said, a little startled. The long earrings danced in her ears.

"Good morning. You don't usually wear those, do you?" He flicked the dangling turquoise stones. He'd noticed them yesterday as well.

"No." Her voice sounded a bit breathless.

"You should. They're pretty." He closed his hand on the top of the iron chair. "May I?"

"Please. I'm sorry." She laid the notebook aside.

A middle-aged waiter with a warm smile appeared almost instantly with a glass of orange juice and one of water. "Good morning, Mr. Grayson. Your usual?"

"Yes. Thank you, Troy." Brandon picked up the large glass and gulped half of it down.

Faith folded her hands and placed them on the black mesh surface of the table. "You're turning into a morning person."

"Don't tell anyone."

The waiter served Belgian waffles sprinkled with cinnamon and powdered sugar, crisp apple-cured bacon, pan sausage, and scrambled eggs, picked up Faith's cold plate of food, and replaced her coffee, juice, and plate with wheat toast, scrambled eggs, and crisp bacon.

"Thank you," Faith and Brandon said.

Brandon nodded toward her plate. "Does that happen often?"

"A bit." She picked up her fork.

Faith took care of everyone, but who took care of her? "What are you working on?"

"A business venture." She picked up her juice. "Nothing makes Henrí happier than people enjoying his food."

"We have that in common." Brandon cut into his two waffles, which were three inches high. "By the way, I know you changed subjects."

She sipped her juice, then picked up her fork. "You were always perceptive."

*Had she always been stubborn?* Brandon cut another wedge of waffles. "How did it go with the artists?"

"Ralph Dawkins and Deloris Juarez agreed to let the hotel display their work," she told him, excitement in her voice. "Of course, they consented after Phoenix said she was thinking of offering her sculptures."

"Dawkins was flirting with you," Brandon accused, the image still having the power to annoy him. The artist had cornered Faith, making outrageous compliments on her eyes, saying they resembled pools of dark chocolate, and asking her to sit for him.

Faith beamed. "He was, wasn't he?"

Brandon put his fork down. "That man is a known womanizer."

Her dark brow arched. "Brandon, isn't that like the pot calling the kettle black?"

"There is no way you can compare him to me," Brandon denied, his voice rising. "I don't lead women on just to get them—"

"Brandon, I was teasing," Faith said. "I turned down his offer to do my portrait."

"Dawkins does landscapes."

Faith munched on her toast. "That's why he said it would be such an honor for me."

"That guy is full of it."

"Perhaps. Perhaps not." She picked up her juice. "How is the bathroom going?"

Brandon could see it coming. Faith falling for the bull Dawkins was going to feed her. Not if he had anything to say about it, and he knew the perfect way to keep her busy. "I'm thinking about having it remodeled."

"You are? I thought you were just getting new fixtures, since you're anxious to have it done."

"After growing accustomed to the spaciousness of the bath in my hotel room, I've decided to remodel mine the same way," he explained, warming to his story. "You and a designer worked together, didn't you?"

"Yes."

Although she'd already said as much, Cameron had mentioned that Faith had a hand in every phase of the extensive renovations the hotel had gone through three years before. "I know you're busy, but would you mind coming over this morning and giving me your opinion?" He placed his fork on his empty plate. "If Mama hears that I'm redoing the bath, she'll have that decorator from Albuquerque here in nothing flat."

"She's single, I suppose," Faith said.

Brandon thought he heard annoyance in her voice. He expected as much. Faith knew how he felt about being pushed into marriage. "She owns her own design studio and has won numerous awards." He didn't have to work too hard to look put upon. "Save me."

The smile started in her dark eyes, then spread to her face. She picked up a crisp slice of bacon. "I might."

"Name your price and it's yours," he declared, feeling victory within his grasp.

Her smile wavered for a moment and he knew she was thinking about attracting men. "I haven't had lobster and steak in a while."

"What time should I expect you?" He'd give much more to see her keep that smile on her pretty face and be happy.

"If you're going to remodel the bath, I probably should come over this morning," she said thoughtfully. "I could see the space you have to work with, then offer suggestions."

"I knew you wouldn't let me down. Eat up, and then we can walk over." He finished off his juice.

She laid her bacon aside. "We could leave no—"

"No. We're not moving until your plate is empty,"

he said adamantly. "You have to take better care of yourself."

Her eyebrow rose at his statement, but she didn't comment, just picked up her fork and began to eat.

Definitely stubborn, he thought, *and* she didn't like being told what to do. He grinned.

Faith stood inside Brandon's bathroom while he and Mr. Montgomery waited outside. To her immediate left was the white commode, the glass-front medicine cabinet, a seven-foot wall showing exposed pipes. In front was a small shower.

The men had stayed outside to let her have an unimpeded view of the bath and because it was too small for the three of them to fit in comfortably. She didn't see how Brandon had stood such a cramped space for five years.

"What do you think?" Brandon asked.

She spoke without turning. "That I'm glad you're not claustrophobic, and the redo is about thirty years past due."

Mr. Montgomery chuckled. "Faith always was smart."

Brandon might have disagreed if he hadn't begun to grow accustomed to the spacious bath in his hotel room. In that he'd been truthful. "You'd agree because it means more money."

Mr. Montgomery didn't even try to deny it. "You'll thank me and Faith when it's finished."

"Excuse me." Coming out of the bath, she opened the closet door next to the bath. "You're saved. You can take the connecting wall out and extend the bath."

"Where will my clothes go?"

"In the new closet, which will be in the nook next to it, where you have a floor lamp that serves no purpose but which would look great—with a new lamp shade—next to the sofa." She closed the door.

"I know you just wanted to do the bath, but if I were you I'd think about later replacing the kitchen cabinet doors. The solid cherry cabinets glazed chocolate are beautiful but plain. I'd recommend using the same solid cherry glazed chocolate in the bathroom with detailed doors to make the rooms flow. The glass medicine cabinet goes. Instead, I'd put a decorative mirror in its place with sconces on either side. For storage I suggest a hardwood cherry chest with a built-in ceramic sink. You could also use about five or six canned lights. The results would be striking."

"I was thinking just tile and paint," Brandon said, a bit worried.

"That, too. I'd consider wallpaper if I didn't know how some men dislike it on principle." She looked from the bathroom to the kitchen. "I'm thinking black and nickel to complement your kitchen countertop. Just a touch of creamy beige to tie in the cabinets."

Brandon's eyes grew wider with each statement.

She patted his cheek. "You'll love it. I promise."

"I guess," he said slowly. "Mr. Montgomery, how long will it take to do all that?"

"The pipes came in. I can get a couple of helpers and tear out everything today. I know a carpenter who just finished a job and I can get him in here today if he's still free. If what you want is in stock, and with my added crew and his, working together, we're looking at five days," Mr. Montgomery said.

"I could pick up a few samples and bring them tonight when we meet for dinner," Faith offered. "But it would be best if you saw them in natural light."

Brandon brushed his hand over his face. "You're busy with the hotel. Maybe I should just get the pipes fixed and let it go."

Faith took his arm and pulled him into the bathroom. "This is too small, Brandon."

They stood inches apart. She could smell his woodsy cologne, feel the heat of his body. Each time she inhaled she drew his scent into her. The desire that was never far surfaced. Moistening her lips, she stepped out of the room. Brandon was slower to follow, his brows furrowed.

"What do you think, Mr. Montgomery?" she asked. She didn't like the way Brandon was looking at her.

"You have the eye." He put his hands on his lean hips. "But if you're uncertain, Brandon, you can always ask your mother."

"No," Brandon said quickly. "And don't you tell her." He turned to Faith. "I'd appreciate it if you'd pick up those samples. Mr. Montgomery, I guess you can start tearing out that wall and call the carpenter. Should I expect more dust?"

"Afraid so. Might as well get started." The older man reached into the closet and grabbed an armload of clothes.

Faith lifted her arms to do the same. "No. You've done enough." Brandon reached past her and grabbed several pairs of jeans. "I'll see you tonight."

Faith could argue and waste time or visit the stores where she'd shopped for her own home. "I'll let you know what I come up with. Bye."

"Whatever you pick will be fine." He went back for another load.

After one last look Faith left. She was going to help Brandon remodel his bath that he'd most likely share with the woman he would marry and she was going to do it with no regrets.

Brandon was going to be stood up again. It was almost closing time and Faith still hadn't shown. Late that afternoon she'd called to say she had several samples for him to look over and would "try" to make it before closing. Since he didn't see how you could mess up granite and nickel, he was going to choose whatever she'd picked out.

At least Mr. Montgomery was on schedule. Brandon's bath was a shell; the joining wall connecting his closet was gone, as were his kitchen cabinet doors. The carpenter had been available and had started that morning.

Luckily, Brandon had been able to get Sierra's maid to come over and give the place a thorough cleaning. Sierra, of course, had been able to tell him where to get a rolling clothes rack. Why anyone needed all those clothes she, Pierce, and Morgan had was beyond him.

"I'm locking the door, Brandon." Michelle passed on the way to the front. A few diners remained.

"Give it a few minutes. I'm expecting someone."

"You got it," Michelle said as she veered toward the bar where Julian was emptying the till.

"Brandon, you have a phone call," yelled Luis from the back of the restaurant.

"Transfer it to my cell." Just as Brandon pulled his cell phone out, it rang. "Hello."

"Brandon, I won't be able to make it," came Faith's rushed voice.

"You all right?"

"No. An engagement party for fifty turned into seventy-five and of course the bride's mother thought it would be a snap to accommodate them with food and specially prepared desserts."

He'd had that happen to him more times than he cared to remember. "Is there anything I can do?"

"A number of things come to mind, but none of them legal."

Brandon's lips twitched. He eased into a chair and waved to the last of the diners as they made their way to the front door. "I can imagine."

"Henrí is fit to be tied. He had to make twenty-five additional individual caramel-cranberry nut tarts. Luckily, the entrée was salmon à la Ballou and we had enough salmon on hand. The Garriety sisters came through with flowers for the additional tables. Dinner was an hour late. Things have settled, but I don't want to leave until the last of the party is out the door," she said. "Mrs. Applegate is singing our praises now, but we both know how quickly her tune can change. Especially when I present her with the additional bill."

That he did. "I understand. Don't worry about the samples. I'll go tomorrow before we open. I guess I'll ask Sierra if she can go with me. She has great taste, but she doesn't think of cost if she likes an item."

"I have the samples. We can meet for breakfast in the morning."

"Thanks, Faith. I owe you. What time?"

"Eight? I have a full day tomorrow."

She had a full day every day and still took time for him. "Eight it is. See you then."

"Night, Brandon."

"Good night, Faith." He disconnected the phone and went to lock the front door. He was on his way back when it hit him that, as usual, while Faith was making sure the engagement party went smoothly she probably hadn't taken time to eat. Before he had taken two steps farther he knew he was going to fix that.

It was eleven fifty-three when Faith said goodbye to Mr. and Mrs. Applegate in the front lobby. She'd been on her feet five straight hours. All she wanted to do was take a long soak in the tub and go to bed.

She waved to the two night clerks at the front desk. She opened her mouth to bid them good night and yawned instead. "Excuse me. Good night."

Tricia, a leggy blonde with big green eyes, came around the counter and handed her a note. "Mr. Grayson left this for you."

From the awed expression on Tricia's face, Brandon had made another conquest. "Thank you." Continuing on, Faith removed the note from the sealed envelope:

> *Since you couldn't come to the Red Cactus, I'm bringing it to you. Grilled shrimp and olive bread salad waiting. Conquistador Suite.*
>
> *Brandon*

He could be so sweet at times and so dense. But then he was a man.

Her lips curved; then she sobered. She'd heard her mother say those very words so many times while she was growing up. Faith had always believed her mother said them with loving affection. She'd been wrong.

Faith wondered if her mother thought the same thing of the movie producer she'd married. Or did she regret her decision to divorce a man to whom she was once his entire life? A divorce that was as painful for their children. Life offered no guarantees. Love didn't always last. If the McBride curse had taught Faith one thing, it was that hard lesson.

She paused and looked at the light shining through the sheer curtains in Brandon's room. You couldn't tell your heart who to love or not to love.

No matter what the future held, her love for Brandon wouldn't change, wouldn't fade. There wasn't a shred of doubt in her mind.

Avoiding Brandon wouldn't change how she felt. She only had to recall the pain in Blade's tortured eyes to know she didn't want to live with regrets as he did.

Suddenly she wasn't so tired. Since she'd agreed to help Brandon with his bath, there wouldn't be any way to avoid seeing him. And she was tired of trying. Going to her room, she refreshed her makeup, spritzed on perfume. Gathering up the shopping bag of samples for the bathroom, she was out the door. Her heart raced as she knocked on his door.

It opened almost immediately. Her breath snagged. Brandon wore black jeans and a T-shirt that delineated his roped muscles. Her hands itched to slowly peel the cotton material off and run her hands, then her mouth, over his hard chest.

"Hi. Glad you could come. Here, let me take those." Lifting the bags, he stepped back.

Trying to get her mind off his body and on a safe topic, she stepped into his room. "Hi. You're right. I didn't get a chance to eat."

"Thought so. Have a seat on the patio and prop your feet up. I'll bring the food out." He placed the bags on the coffee table, then went to the small refrigerator. Faded denim cupped his rear.

Faith's gaze lingered on the impressive sight. Tight.

He easily rose with two covered bowls. "You're supposed to be sitting down."

"I'm fine." She was taking every opportunity to look at and enjoy him. She wasn't running away from her feelings any longer.

"It won't take me but a second to toss this." He added the shrimp to the salad ingredients and gently tossed. "Things go all right with the engagement party?"

"The father of the bride almost had a coronary when I presented him with the additional bill, but after giving his wife the eye, he handed me his credit card."

Brandon filled a chilled salad bowl, placed it on a tray with two bottles of water chilling in the ice bucket, flatware, and a cloth napkin. "I can imagine. Patio or sofa?"

"Patio." She definitely needed the air.

"Lead the way."

Faith sighed inwardly in regret. She'd much rather he go first so she could get another view of his nice butt. She yawned. Perhaps sleepiness was making her horny.

Brandon nudged her with his shoulder to get her moving. "Get going before you fall asleep on your feet."

She went to the patio, pleased and surprised to see a candle flickering, a flower from the garden in a bud vase. "This is nice."

"You deserve more, but this was all I could come up with on short notice." Setting the tray on the glass-topped table with one hand, he pulled out her chair with the other. "Sit and eat."

She did as he requested. "This is delicious. I don't usually eat this late."

"I gathered as much." He stretched out his long legs and linked his fingers over his flat abdomen. "When did you eat last?"

"Not since breakfast. You'd think, as little as I eat, I'd be smaller."

He frowned. "You're you."

She stopped eating. "I beg your pardon?"

He sat up and braced his arms on the table. "I can't imagine you looking any other way."

Faith didn't know if she should take his statement as a compliment or really start on the diet she'd been putting off for years.

"When I look at you, I see a caring, loving woman. I see a woman of substance."

Her heart swelled. "Thank you."

He twisted in his seat as if a bit embarrassed.

"Let's go look at those samples." Picking up her bowl, she went inside and sat on the floral sofa. "Please put everything on the table and I'll go over it with you."

Brandon sat beside her, his thigh brushing against hers, causing her skin to tingle. She wished she had thought to bring her water.

Setting the woven tray containing issues of the *Santa Fean* magazines aside, Brandon emptied the bags on the table. "I thought there would be more."

She swallowed a bite of salad before speaking. "Too much becomes confusing. You want something sleek and uncluttered. Open the book on the tab and you'll see the doors with the detailing. I checked with the carpenter. He can stain them to match your existing cabinets."

She went on to explain the marble tile, point out pictures of the nickel fixtures, the showerhead, the mirror she'd picked out. "The effect will be stunning."

He stared at her. "This took more than a few minutes."

"I wanted it to be right." She wouldn't be selfish.

"Thank you."

His eyes were midnight black and beautiful and much too tempting. Faith set her half-finished salad on the table. "I'm stuffed. I'd better go to my room before I fall asleep and you have to carry me."

"I wouldn't mind. I've done so in the past. Remember?"

She'd never forget. She'd been the envy of every girl at the sophomore dance. "It rained and I was afraid I'd get my new pink satin shoes dirty. You were gallant. My Prince Charming."

"We had a lot of fun that night."

"Yes, we did." Just as they had at her junior and senior proms. But she'd never been able to get him to play the saxophone for her again. "You still play the sax?"

He frowned, then shook his head. "Nah. I'd rather spend the time in the kitchen."

"Pity." She came to her feet and went to the door. "Night, Brandon, and thanks."

"I'll walk you to your door."

Faith would have argued if she thought it would do any good. They were quiet on the short walk to her place. Opening the door, she turned. "Thanks again."

"My pleasure." He brushed back a strand of hair from her cheek. "I'll see you at eight."

Air fluttered over her lips. Longing swept through her. "You still want to meet for breakfast?"

"Yes. We can see the samples in natural light, as you suggested."

"All right. I'll see you in the morning."

"Night."

Faith thoroughly enjoyed herself at breakfast. Afterward she went with Brandon to his place. Mr. Montgomery and the carpenter, Mr. Radford, were waiting for them. She'd quickly gone over the samples she and Brandon had chosen and told them her vision for the bathroom, new closet, and kitchen cabinets.

The men nodded and made notes as they talked. Occasionally Faith would ask Brandon if he had any questions or objections, but he always deferred to her opinion. "I'm in your hands." He rubbed his chin and looked around his room. "If you think of anything else that will update this place, let me know."

"Well, there were a few things," she began, and didn't finish until ten minutes later.

Mr. Montgomery shook his gray head. "Never met a woman yet who wasn't ready to decorate."

"That's because men are too busy with other things and it's natural for a woman to want to beautify their surroundings," Faith said. "Men can become complacent. They only notice if they aren't pleased or if their routine is changed." An imp of mischief beamed in her eyes. "Like a pipe bursting in a bathroom."

"I don't like change," Brandon admitted.

"So I noticed," Mr. Montgomery said deadpan.

Faith's lips twitched. "I'd better be going. Mr. Montgomery, you have my cell if you or Mr. Radford have a question about anything. However, I've already checked and everything I want is in stock at the store I indicated."

"I don't anticipate any problems, but I'll call if I have any," Mr. Montgomery said. "I want to finish the pipes, and while I'm doing that Mack can start on the closet with the built-ins you indicated."

"I should get a good portion of it done today," Mr. Radford said.

"Sierra will be impressed," Brandon joked.

"That she will." Faith picked up her purse. "See you tonight, Brandon. Good-bye, Mr. Montgomery. Mr. Radford."

"Bye, Faith."

"Good-bye, Ms. McBride."

"Until tonight."

Waving, she went to the door and opened it. Just as she was closing it she heard Mr. Montgomery say in a quiet voice, "Faith is going to make some man a fine wife." She paused as long as she could without being obvious, but she was unable to hear Brandon's reply.

# 12

It was after eleven that night when Brandon waved good-bye to Michelle and looked down the street for Faith. The desk clerk had called five minutes ago to say she was on her way.

Late that afternoon Faith had called to say she was putting out fires again and asked if the kitchen would still be open when she finished. He'd reminded her that one of the perks of being the owner was that for him the kitchen never closed. She'd laughed, a warm, infectious sound, and told him to keep the light burning in the window.

Even now, remembering her laugh made him smile. Then he saw her coming toward him on the almost deserted street and the expression on his face turned to disapproval. He quickly went to meet her. "You shouldn't have walked. Why didn't you drive or call me to pick you up?"

"Because I'm perfectly capable of taking care of

myself," Faith said, hooking her arm through his. "Now, stop being macho. I'm starved."

He'd never understand why women disliked being told what to do even when it was in their best interest. He opened the door to the restaurant. "These streets can be dangerous at night. I'm just concerned."

"Noted and I appreciate it. I'll fake him out with a left. Now, where's the food?"

Knowing he had hit a blank wall, Brandon seated her at the family table near the back of the restaurant and kitchen. "I'll be back."

She scooted out of the booth. "Can I help?"

"Yes, by sitting down and relaxing. I'll be back before you know it."

Continuing to the kitchen, he prepared their food, put everything on a large tray, and grabbed a tray deck on the way out.

Faith stood on seeing him. The moment he settled the tray on the deck, she began helping him put the food on the table. "This smells divine."

"It will taste even better."

"That's what I like about you, Brandon. Your modesty." She reclaimed her seat.

He grinned and slid into the booth across from her. Faith wasn't afraid of putting him in his place. He liked that about her. Bowing his head, he blessed their food. "All the fires put out?"

"Thank goodness." She bit into the steak, chewed,

savored it with a small moan of delight. "You have a right to brag."

Brandon didn't expect his body to harden at the sound of Faith's moan. Or to have the urge to draw the same sounds from her body again but for an entirely different reason.

"What's the matter?" she asked, staring at him.

*I keep wanting to make love to you.* "Just thinking."

She continued to stare at him a long time, as if she didn't believe him. "How was your day?"

He slowly blew out a relieved breath, grateful that at least for the time being he wasn't in danger of losing it . . . if she didn't make any more moaning sounds. "Busy. Just the way I like it. There's always a tourist who thinks the chile peppers here are the same as they're used to at home when they're ten times hotter," he told her. "I felt sorry for one guy trying to impress his family. You could almost see steam coming out of his mouth. He downed the milk Marlive gave him to douse the fire in nothing flat."

"When I went to visit Mother in New York, she took me a Mexican restaurant. The food was so bland I couldn't eat it." She dunked her lobster in butter. "The seafood was infinitely better." She threw him a look. "But not as good as this."

"How is your mother?"

Sadness washed over her face. "I don't know. She seemed happy when I was there. I mean, she laughed a lot, but I have this feeling lately when we talk on the phone that everything might not be going well in her marriage. Daddy certainly isn't happy."

"I'm sorry. It's always sad when a marriage doesn't work. It goes double when children are involved," Brandon said. "Your parents always made me feel welcome."

Faith placed her fork on her plate. "They are great parents. I always thought they would be together forever. What I wonder about is, would they have broken up if there hadn't been a McBride curse?"

He frowned. "I don't understand."

"Did Mother use it as an excuse to leave us?" she said softly. "Did she give up because she thought there wasn't any hope of things getting better?"

Brandon's hand covered hers. "Whatever the reason, the results are the same. Your mother loves you and your brothers."

Faith moved her hand from beneath his and picked up her fork. "I know. I just feel sorry for Daddy."

"Love doesn't always work." Brandon turned contemplative. "Even when it does, there's no guarantee that you'll be together always. Losing my father was a blow to all of us."

This time Faith was the one who reached out to take his hand. "He would be so proud of your mother and how his children turned out."

"I'd certainly like to think so. Although I'm not so sure how he'd feel about her trying to marry us off."

She withdrew her hand, hoping he hadn't felt her sudden tension. "How is the remodeling?"

"It's shaping up. Before we leave, you can take a look." He cut into his rare steak. "Maybe you can take a peek at my bedroom and let me know if you can come up with any suggestions for it." He smiled sheepishly. "I think the Conquistador Suite is spoiling me."

She clasped her hands together. "That's exactly the kind of accolades we like to hear. Putting the artwork of nationally known artists in the lobby, then later in guests' rooms, will only make their stay more enjoyable and memorable."

"When do you plan on starting?"

"I'm shooting for a month from now." She cut into her steak. "It's going to be so exciting. I'm lining up media and people in the art community to attend the unveiling. Phoenix hasn't told me definitely if she plans to exhibit, but I think she will. Hopefully, she'll let me know by the end of the week."

"When she does, you'll want my cousin Daniel and aunt Felicia to attend. They have one of the finest collections of African-American and Native American artwork in the country. Many of the pieces are of museum quality," Brandon said. "Then there is all the money they donate to art each year. They're highly respected."

"Tell me something I don't know. They're on my must-invite list, but it remains to be seen if they'll show," Faith said, disappointment in her voice.

He twisted his head to one side. "You didn't even think of asking me to put in a word for you, did you? Just like you didn't ask me to talk to Phoenix for you."

She frowned at him as if he'd stated the obvious. "I wouldn't impose on our friendship that way."

"You're not. If I can help you in any way, I'd like to. You certainly send me business."

She waved his words aside. "You deserve the referrals." She savored the last bite of steak. "With superb food like this, the Red Cactus deserves to be patronized."

"So does Casa de Serenidad," Brandon said. "When you have the date firmed, let me know and I'll call Daniel and Aunt Felicia. If possible, one or both will be here."

"Thank you, Brandon."

"You certainly came through for me when I was in need." He tried not to think of the other need she could help with and hoped he succeeded.

An hour and a half later, Brandon locked the restaurant's double red doors. It seemed natural for him to link his fingers with hers. "Do you want to get the car or walk?"

"Walk," she said; not for anything would she give up the chance to hold hands with Brandon. She embraced the tingles that raced up her arm.

They continued in companionable silence to the hotel. Brandon's hand moved to her waist as they entered the lobby. The night clerks waved, then went about their business. Arriving at her door, she unlocked it and turned. "I had a wonderful time."

"So did I." He stared down at her; then his finger brushed down her cheek. Her skin was velvet soft. It seemed the most natural thing to lower his head and kiss her.

The first touch of her warm mouth against his jolted his senses. He gathered her closer, his arms tightening as he deepened the kiss, learning the sweet essence of her mouth. Fire licked along his bloodstream. The desire he had tried to suppress flared. His hand cupped her breast; his thumb grazed her taut nipple. She moaned, thrusting her breast against his hand.

The needy sound snapped him out of the sensual haze. Shocked, he lifted his head and stared down at Faith, watching her eyelashes flutter open.

He opened his mouth to apologize, to say he didn't know what had come over him, but gazing at her moist lips, parted and waiting for his mouth, he couldn't utter the lie. He wanted nothing more than to keep on kissing her. And, from the ache in his lower body, he wouldn't stop at kissing. He lowered his forehead to hers so he couldn't see the open desire in her eyes, eyes that made his body tighten even more.

"Brandon."

There was such total wonder in that one word. No woman had ever said his name with such tenderness before, such honest need. No woman had ever tested his control as much as Faith. She felt wonderful in his arms. Her breasts pressed invitingly against his chest. He'd like nothing better than to run his hand under her blouse and press his hand to her naked flesh. His hands flexed. He drew in one shuddering breath, then another.

Finally, he lifted his head. "I'm not sure what is happening here."

She smiled at him as if she knew all the secrets of the universe. The back of her hand brushed tenderly across his cheek. "I'm sure you'll figure it out. Good night, Brandon."

Brandon stared at the closed door. Women. Why didn't they ever act the way they were supposed to?

Faith closed the door, then twirled in circles until she was dizzy and plopped down on the sofa. *Brandon wants me.* There was no mistaking the kiss that was tender and hot, or the hard bulge poking her. She laughed, too excited to be embarrassed. She'd dreamed of this moment for too long.

"Brandon," she whispered his name, then closed her eyes and laid her head back on the blue chenille upholstered sofa, only to bound up and do a good imitation of Tina Turner performing "Proud Mary" on the way to her bedroom.

After a few more Tina moves, Faith went to the tall French-inspired secretary and opened her bound wish book. A pink ribbon marked the spot where she'd written: *Operation Get Brandon.* She wasn't foolish enough to think a kiss was a slam dunk. Especially since he was obviously having a difficult time seeing them as anything other than friends. She'd just have to show him differently.

Brandon thought of skipping breakfast and going directly to the restaurant, but that would have been the coward's way. If he took a little longer to shower and get dressed, flipped through the newspaper that was delivered daily, which he almost never got around to reading, then took a leisurely stroll to the restaurant, it would just be coincidental. Then he stepped onto the patio and saw Faith.

She wore a loose-fitting pale blue striped cotton jacket and pants. The wind played with the hair he'd dreamed had grazed his chest as she dropped sweet kisses on his chest. His heartbeat quickened, desire unfurled like a flower kissed by the gentle rays of the sun.

Momentarily both hands palmed his face. *Mercy.* Now he was getting poetic. In high school, he'd discounted the tale that doing without sex could drive you crazy. Now he wasn't so sure. Perhaps there was some truth to it after all. He was certainly having problems.

Across the courtyard Faith looked up, waved, then went back to the papers laid out on the table in front of her. Brandon stared. That was it! A wave! Images of them naked and driving each other to the edge of sanity had kept him awake half the night, and she acted as if nothing had happened. He didn't know whether to be pleased or affronted.

One thing for certain: he couldn't stand there like a dummy all day. He stuffed his hands into his pockets and tried for cool. "Morning, Faith."

"Hi, Brandon." She shoved a manila folder under his nose while the waiter placed orange juice and water on the table.

"Good morning, Mr. Grayson. Monsieur Fountain said he has crepes that will make your taste buds weep with pleasure."

"I can attest to that," Faith said.

He'd like to do the same to her. Brandon cleared his throat. "That will be fine."

"Right away." The waiter withdrew.

"I thought for your place we'd keep it simple and use the brownish color of the cabinets as the third color." She pointed to the schematic drawing. "You'll see the seating area of the living room is pulled together and defined by grouping the furniture that is now scattered around the room. You'll be able to use the sofa and chairs you have by covering them with slipcovers in oyster cotton duck. If you're not partial to the old headboard, you could build around it to give you space for all the books and other articles you have in your place. What do you think?"

*That you smell like my fantasy, taste like a forbidden dream, and you're driving me crazy.*

"Here you are," the waiter said.

Faith and Brandon reached for the folder at the same time. Electricity arced between them. His gaze cut to hers, but she was already looking through another folder. "Thanks," he managed, his voice rough.

"Look those over at your leisure." She stuffed the papers into a zipped case. "If you'll excuse me, I have meetings." She stood. "Enjoy your breakfast. Bye."

"Faith?"

She turned back to him, her expression one of infinite patience. She wasn't fighting the need to reach out and draw him into her arms, press her lips to his, the way he was fighting her. Brandon's spine stiffened. No woman had ever gotten the best of him. He could be as nonchalant as she was.

"Where do you think I could buy the slipcovers?"

"The addresses and phone numbers of all the stores are listed in the folder. That particular store is located around the corner from the Red Cactus," she told him. "Anything else?"

Nothing that he'd admit to. "Not that I can think of."

"If you do, you know where to find me." She continued inside the hotel.

Brandon's brow arched. Had he heard a hint of sexual challenge in her voice or was it wishful thinking?

Faith didn't walk; she floated to her office. In the bright light of day Brandon still wanted her. Oh, he'd tried to be cool, but she could tell. An imp of a smile touched her lips as she entered her office and took a seat behind her desk. It was a good thing she had more practice hiding her feelings, or she might have succumbed to the heat simmering in his dark eyes and invited him back to her room.

"You naughty woman," she said aloud, then laughed.

The knock on her door caused her to clamp her hand over her mouth. She didn't have any appointments until ten. *Maybe it's Brandon.* She moistened her lips, straightened her jacket, patted her hair. "Come in."

The door opened and the last person in the world she expected entered. "Good morning, Faith; do you have a moment?"

Faith shot up from her seat and rounded her desk. "Yes, of course, Mrs. Grayson. Good morning."

A pleasant expression on her face, Brandon's mother entered the office. She wore a white organza blouse and a black and white woven full skirt. She looked elegant and a bit intimidating. "I know I don't have an appointment, but this is important."

Faith's heart clenched. His mother wanted Faith to help some other woman entrap Brandon. "Please have a seat. Would you like coffee? Tea?"

Ruth settled gracefully in the chair in front of the desk. Despite being in her sixties, she remained a beautiful woman, with midnight black hair, high cheekbones, and ramrod posture. "No, thank you. Please sit down."

Her hands moist, Faith retook her seat and waited for her dreams to come to a crashing end.

"As you might have guessed, this is about Brandon."

Faith flinched in spite of herself. Inside she screamed that she could love Brandon better than any woman Ruth might have picked out. "Yes, ma'am."

"This is rather awkward," she began, folding her hands in her lap. "Brandon would be upset with me if he knew I was here."

Faith said the only truth she could. "Brandon knows you love him."

"But that doesn't mean he always agrees with what I have to say." Ruth leaned back in her chair and glanced around the room. "This is a lovely room. Your art collection is impressive."

"Thank you. What about Brandon?" Faith asked, hoping she wasn't being too obvious or pushy. She genuinely admired and respected Mrs. Grayson. "This couldn't be about another birthday party," she joked.

"No, this is about his living quarters. They need a woman's touch, just as his life does."

*No! No! No!* Faith thought. The award-winning designer from Albuquerque wasn't going to get her hands on Brandon's body *or* his apartment. "I'm not sure what I have to do with this."

"You have such style and class, and you and Brandon have always been such close friends for so many years, I thought he might listen to you."

"That he should get married?" Faith cried in disbelief.

Ruth lifted a brow. "Do you have anything against marriage?"

Faith twisted uneasily in her seat. "No. I just thought . . ."

"Thought what?" Ruth asked.

*That I had more time.* "Nothing." She took two slow, deep breaths. "Brandon and I are friends, but no one could ever persuade him to do something he didn't want to do, especially in this case."

Ruth sighed, her straight shoulders seeming to slump. "You're right, of course. My children think for themselves." She stood. "Sorry to waste your time and, more important, impose on your friendship with Brandon. I beg your forgiveness. He wouldn't thank you for trying to steer him toward marriage."

Truer words had never been spoken. Faith came to her feet. "You came here out of love. There's nothing to apologize for."

"You were always so sweet and gracious," Ruth said. "It's nice knowing you haven't changed."

"Thank you."

Ruth walked to the door. "You were gone by the time I arrived at the cookout at Morgan and Phoenix's house, but I understand Phoenix might join you in a venture to display her work and that of other artists at the hotel."

"Yes. I'm excited about it. Two other artists have

also agreed, but I want to lead off with Phoenix's work first," Faith told her. "Her work moves me."

Ruth nodded in understanding. "Her talent is great. So is Catherine's. The Master of Breath and God have blessed and honored me with two wonderful daughters-in-law, as I prayed they would."

Faith's happiness faded a bit. She couldn't write a book or sculpt and she certainly didn't have any other discernible talent. "They're both nationally acclaimed."

"Talent lies in many areas." Ruth stared at Faith intently. "Each one of us is given a gift. We just have to search within ourselves to find out what it is. You've already found yours."

Faith's eyes widened. "I have?"

"Like Brandon, you're a nurturer. Your happiness comes from making others happy." Ruth opened the door. "I know it isn't necessary, but thanks for being Brandon's friend. Good day."

"Good-bye, Mrs. Grayson." Faith closed the door. Brandon's mother might not have picked her for him, but his mother thought well of her. That meant a lot. But Mrs. Grayson's visit also meant she was working to marry Brandon off to the designer. Faith had to move faster to—

The door in front of her opened abruptly. Brandon, his eyes wide, rushed in, closing the door behind him. "What did Mama want?"

He was so handsome he made Faith's heart turn

over. And if his mother had her way, he'd marry another woman.

"Faith, what did she want?"

"For me to help her with the plans for you to get married," she answered, watching shocked horror spread across Brandon's face, mirroring exactly what she felt inside.

# 13

Brandon plopped into the same chair his mother had sat in, dug his elbows into his thighs, and placed his face in his hands. "Why? Why?"

Faith knelt in front of him. "Because she loves you."

"Maybe she could love me a little less," he said from behind his hands.

"For some people love doesn't work that way," she said softly. "They only know one way to love, and that's with all their heart."

His hands moved. He stared down at Faith, who was too close and too tempting. For a crazy moment he considered putting his hand behind her head and bringing her closer, then fastening his mouth to hers to see how long they could kiss without coming up for air. Instead he sat back. "What else did she say?"

Faith came upright and moved behind her desk. It was safer. She might be tempted to reach out to him and comfort him with her mouth, her body. "I think you're right about the Albuquerque designer. Your mother thinks your place—and you—need a woman's touch."

He scowled, then brightened. "I got you." Was it his imagination or did she flinch? "What's the matter?"

"Nothing." She moved the folders on her desk aside. "I thought you had gone."

He frowned. "I was on my way when I saw Mama. I thought she was looking for me until she went in the opposite direction from the rooms," he explained. "I saw her come in here and I waited. I might have known she wasn't here to visit me. She had on her power clothes. On those rare occasions when she dresses up, she means business. She's relentless."

"She wants what's best for you."

"What's best for me is not a wife." He rose to his feet and rounded the desk, placing the folder she had given him on top of her desk. "Can you take off anytime today or tomorrow to help me with this?"

"You're going to show your mother you don't need a wife."

He shot her a look. "It's scary how you know what I'm thinking sometimes."

"That was easy," she told him. "You don't like being pushed into anything."

"Who does?"

"No one, I guess." She checked her appointment book. "I've got an opening at two this afternoon. I can meet you at the House of Décor."

"I'll pick you up. That way we'll shave time and you can grab a bite to eat."

"How do you know lunch wasn't already on the schedule?"

"Because in the time I've been here it never is." He picked up the folder and went to the door. "You're not going to skip lunch just to help me. You aren't the only one who can tell what a person is thinking."

"Oh, really."

The expression on her face made him frown. It was pure woman, pure challenge. Neither was what he was used to from Faith.

She opened the folder in front of her. "I'll be at the front waiting for you."

"See you then." Brandon left the hotel beginning to think Faith might make him reevaluate what he *thought* he knew about women.

Faith walked out of the hotel just as Brandon pulled up at the curve. Both were five minutes early. Faith felt a little punch when Brandon hopped out of the fire engine red Porsche convertible without benefit of opening his door. She had seen him do that dozens of time when she assumed he was in too much of a hurry to open the door for his dates. Never in her wildest dreams had she ever thought she'd see him do it for her.

"Hi," he said. "I thought I'd have to wait."

"Hi, yourself. I try to be punctual."

Nodding to the valet, he took her arm and steered

her to his car. "You should tell that to Sierra. She keeps everyone except her clients waiting."

"I don't think anyone would get very far trying to tell Sierra anything." Faith got into the low-slung car when Brandon opened the door, forever thankful that Cameron loved sports cars as well and she was used to getting in and out of them gracefully.

Brandon closed the door and rounded the car to get in the driver's seat. "I'll put the top up."

"If you're doing it on my account, don't bother." She pulled a light blue loose-weave linen scarf over her head. She'd heard her brothers complain countless times about the women they'd dated who worried about their hair. "What is the sense of a convertible if you have to drive with the top up?"

He grinned. "I don't know why I expect the usual from you."

"Beats me."

Chuckling, he pulled into traffic, then sobered. "I don't like shopping."

She settled back in the car, enjoying being with Brandon and feeling the wind in her face. "That's not exactly true."

"I have no reason to lie," he said, darting in front of a slow-moving SUV with an out-of-state plate.

"If we were going to Williams-Sonoma, Chef's, or a similar store you would have been there fifteen minutes early," she said.

Shaking his head, he parked in front of the store. "Remind me never to play cards with you."

"So noted." Opening her door, she met him halfway. He was frowning. "You can be gallant another time. We're on a tight schedule, remember?" Ignoring the frown on his face, she hooked her arm with his and entered the store.

The sleek two-story store carried everything the home needed, from doormats, to linen, to furniture. There were plates, glasses, and flatware but not a piece of cookware in sight on the many shelves. The colors ranged from soothing earth tones to bold reds and purples.

"Why don't I let you pick out what you like and just pay the bill?" he said, resisting her tug on his arm to pull him farther into the brightly lit store.

"Because you'll be the one living there." She tugged harder. "I want you to be happy."

He moved up a couple of steps. "I like my room at the hotel."

She released his arm and stepped in front of him. Time to play dirty. "It's me or Albuquerque Slim."

"You've seen her?"

"No, of course not."

"Then why did you call her Albuquerque Slim?"

Because his mother had chosen women with shapes as beautiful and as alluring as their faces. "Just a matter of speech. What's it to be?"

He stared at her a long time, then took her arm and walked farther into the store. "I'm going to call Cameron and ask if he knows he has a sadistic sister."

"It got you moving, didn't it?" she said. "Janet, the manager, is coming this way. I worked with her to do my place. Try not to be grumpy."

"Faith, it's good seeing you again," the manager said, her gaze going to Brandon and staying. "How do you do?"

"Fine, thank you," Brandon mumbled.

Faith considered elbowing him in the side but let it go, since Janet was a pretty divorcée and he hadn't gone all stupid and tried to flirt like her day manager had when he'd met Janet. "Janet Hill, please meet Brandon Grayson. Brandon is redoing his place."

Janet's light brown eyes lit up. "Brandon Grayson, owner of the Red Cactus? The food there is divine."

Brandon finally smiled. "Yes. We try."

Faith rolled her eyes. A modest Brandon? Who would have thought it?

Janet moved to his side, taking his arm. "We'll endeavor to show you the same great service and hospitality I've always been shown at your restaurant. Do you have any idea of what you want, or would you just like for me to show you around?"

Brandon looked at Faith. "I'm in Faith's hands."

And in Janet's clutches. "We'll start with slipcovers in oyster for the sofa and chair, then an area rug, perhaps throw pillows," Faith said.

"I don't like throw pillows," Brandon said, shaking his head vehemently.

"A lot of men don't," Janet said in a sweet voice, smiling up at Brandon as if she was trying to figure out how to work the conversation around to a personal level.

"The sofa in your hotel suite has pillows," Faith reminded him. "You like that room."

"You're at Casa de Serenidad?" Janet inquired.

Brandon explained and ended by saying, "I should be moving back to my place by the end of the week."

"Then you'll want everything by then." She smiled invitingly up at him. "I'll personally guarantee to see that any purchases are delivered by Friday afternoon."

"That's great." Brandon turned to Faith. "Isn't that great?"

"Fabulous." If Janet thought she was going to roll over Faith, she was mistaken. "Brandon, why don't we get started? We're on a tight schedule." Looping her arm through his, Faith put on her most charming smile. "I know where everything is, Janet. We'll call if we need help, but the store is so well laid out, with so much to choose from, the difficult part will be deciding."

Janet slowly withdrew her arm and stared at Faith, trying, Faith knew, to determine if she had been warned off or Faith was simply telling the truth. The door behind them opened and another couple came in. "I'll let you browse. Excuse me."

"You're sure we won't need her to help find things?" Brandon asked.

"Positive," Faith said. "Now, let's do some

shopping." Ignoring Brandon's groan, she headed toward the linen department.

"To Mission Impossible completion." Brandon reached across the booth at the Red Cactus and touched his glass of cola to Faith's glass of diet cola.

"The completion of Mission Impossible," she said, sipping her drink.

Brandon took a sip, then set his glass aside. "I can't believe we're finished."

"Shopping is simple if you're able to focus on what you need and the colors involved." She set her glass aside and glanced at her watch. "I have to run."

"You haven't eaten," he protested.

"I'll grab a bite later." She slid out of the booth, dragging her purse with her.

He slid out of the booth and scowled down at her. "I thought you had time to eat."

"I don't remember saying that. Good-bye, Brandon," Faith said, turning to leave.

Brandon stepped in front of her. "Helping me could have waited," he said.

"We both know it couldn't." She glanced at her watch. "Now, please step aside or I'll have to practice my sneaky left hook on you."

Slowly he moved aside. "This isn't funny. You need to be a little selfish sometimes."

"Don't pout. It causes wrinkles. Bye, Brandon."

Brandon's eyes narrowed as he watched Faith

leave. At least it started out that way. He wasn't sure how his gaze dropped to her hips, then lower, wishing she didn't have on pants, so he could see her legs.

Seconds later it hit him what he was doing and he looked around to see if anyone had caught him scoping out Faith. He didn't know if he was relieved or not to see Pierce and Sierra heading in his direction. The food Brandon had ordered for him and Faith arrived the same time as his sister and brother.

"Hi, Brandon." Sierra slid into the booth and pulled the flour tortillas and meat for fajitas in front of her. "This is what I call service. But what is Pierce going to eat?"

"Why, his portion of course." Pierce slid in beside her and pulled the sampler plate of chicken quesadillas, steak nachos, and chicken *flautas* to him. "Hurry and say the blessings. I'm hungry."

Sierra did as requested. "Since there's lipstick on this glass, either your dishwasher is malfunctioning or you weren't expecting us."

"How astute." Brandon slid into the other side of the booth.

Pierce swallowed, then cocked a brow. "Astute. My, my. Who have you been hanging around late—" He lowered the quesadilla. "You're dating?"

Sierra stopped piling sour cream, *pico de gallo*, and guacamole on top of her strips of beef. "Who is she?"

Brandon propped both arms on the table. "I'm not dating."

"Whose lipstick is that?" Sierra demanded.

"Faith's," Brandon answered, waiting for the questions and accusations.

"What a relief." As Luis passed, Sierra ordered a diet cola for her and regular for Pierce, then took a sizable bite out of her fajita.

"I knew you were made of sterner stuff." Pierce finished the quesadilla and reached for the nachos. "This is good. I haven't eaten since breakfast and have appointments lined up until late this afternoon."

"Same here. I won't make it home until late. I might drop back by for a to-go box tonight," Sierra said.

Brandon stared from one to the other. "You aren't worried about Faith?"

Both waved his words aside. "You and Faith have known each other forever. If the spark was there, it would have ignited by now," Pierce said, stealing a bite of Sierra's Mexican rice while she wasn't looking.

Brandon twisted in his seat. It wasn't a spark. More like spontaneous combustion.

"Faith is obviously after another man." Sierra slapped Pierce's hand when he tried to get another spoonful of rice.

"Faith has given up on that idea," Brandon said, wondering why the idea pleased him so much.

"Says who?" Sierra dipped her nacho chip into spicy hot red and green salsa.

"She told me. We're friends." *Kissing friends, and I'm going to do my best to see that it doesn't happen again.*

"Here you are." Luis placed the drinks on the table. His mouth twitched on seeing Pierce and Sierra eating the food prepared for Brandon and Faith. "You want anything, boss?"

"Maybe later. You might bring another bowl of rice and salsa before the children start to fight over it, too," Brandon said, his thoughts straying to Faith. He was unable to get over the worry that she might be hungry.

"Sierra always did have a difficult time sharing." Pierce swooped in for another bite. "How is the bathroom going?"

For the first time Brandon didn't feel like butting his head against the wall. He realized in large part that was due to Faith's help. "Should be finished by the weekend. I decided to spruce up the whole apartment a bit."

Sierra put down the glass she had just picked up. "You let Mother call the decorator in Albuquerque?"

"You think I'm suicidal?" Brandon retorted. "But she'd like nothing better. I thwarted her plans. Faith is helping me."

"What colors?" Pierce and Sierra asked almost simultaneously.

"Black and nickel in the bath with shades of brown to blend with the glazed cherry cabinets in the kitchen and bath. The area rug in the living room is ecru, a shade darker than the oyster slipcovers, the scooped chairs a soft patina, and the throw pillows a bold stripe of all the colors to tie everything in."

Pierce and Sierra looked at each other, then banged on their ears with the palms of their hands as if they were hard of hearing.

"Glad I could be your after-dinner entertainment," Brandon said with a wry twist of his mouth.

"Brandon, you know if it doesn't involve cooking, you could care less about colors." Sierra pushed her empty plate away. "Your apartment is a mishmash of styles and colors. I don't want to be a traitor, but Mama had a point. You do need a decorator."

"Did." He folded his arms and sat back. "I have Faith."

Pierce picked up his glass. "Let's toast Faith. Brandon's secret weapon."

Glasses were raised. "To Faith, my secret weapon," Brandon repeated. He couldn't help but think about the other secret he and Faith shared.

Faith had a nonstop day. She preferred those to doing paperwork or other duties in her office. Her feet and body were tired, but she felt good as she slowly strolled the lighted paved path bordered by colorful flowers leading to her room.

She liked being in the thick of things, working alongside her staff to ensure their guests enjoyed their stay or seeing that the event planned went off without a hitch. Their guests probably never thought of all the manpower and hours of planning involved, and that was all right with Faith. Their satisfaction was what mattered.

Despite it being a little past nine at night and knowing the Red Cactus remained open until ten, she glanced at Brandon's room. It was dark. She hadn't expected him to be home, yet she was disappointed all the same. Time was running out on her. She had three days, and then he'd be gone forever.

With one last look, she opened the wooden gate to her place and came to a complete halt, her mouth open.

"Dinner is served, Ms. McBride, compliments of Brandon Grayson," a waiter in a white dinner jacket said. He stood by a small table draped with a white tablecloth. Twin tapers flickered. A small bouquet of white gardenias lay by the plate.

Another waiter, similarly dressed, offered her his arm. "If you'll have a seat, we'll serve."

Her legs shook as she walked to the table. There were two chairs. "Is Brandon coming?"

"Brandon is unsure of his schedule, but we have strict orders not to leave until you've eaten." Releasing her arm, he pulled out a chair.

Faith sat. The waiter placed the napkin in her lap, then lifted the silver dome. Wisps of smoke rose from the grilled salmon served with raspberry vinaigrette, green beans amandine, and field greens. "How did you know when to expect me so the food would be hot?"

"You'll have to ask Brandon." The waiter lifted a bottle of vintage wine and a sixteen-ounce bottle of diet cola. "Which one would you prefer?"

"The wine." She felt a little daring. If Brandon dropped by, and she hoped he would, she could always claim it was the wine that made her jump his bones.

She picked up her fork, then put it down as a horrible thought came to her. "Have you done this before? Met women with dinner, I mean?"

"My first."

"Me, too."

Warmth spread through her. Her fingers touched the creamy white blossoms. Had Brandon remembered he'd given her gardenia corsages when he took her to her dances in high school? "Brandon is really thoughtful. I skipped lunch today to help him."

"He mentioned that," the one who had seated her said. "Your salmon is getting cold."

She picked up her fork again. "You really have orders for me to eat?"

Both men nodded.

"And if I don't?"

"Let's just say we'd rather not find out," one said.

Faith easily recalled the last flash of anger she'd seen on Brandon's face. Another thought hit her. "Has he eaten?"

To his credit, the waiter's expression didn't change. "I'm not sure, Ms. McBride."

She could call and check or simply enjoy the wonderful surprise and plan a surprise of her own. She began to eat and heard twin sighs of relief from the waiters.

# 14

With his one hand in his pocket and two fingers of his other hand crooked around the clothes hanger holding jeans and a shirt under a plastic cleaner bag, Brandon waved the doorman away and opened the heavy glass door of Casa de Serenidad. Nodding to the desk clerks, he continued to his room.

The day had been one that, as a restaurateur, he loved. The restaurant had become increasingly busy as the afternoon progressed. The wait time had averaged thirty minutes by six and hit forty minutes by seven thirty. In his business waits were unavoidable.

You couldn't rush a diner, but since Brandon himself hated waiting, he and his staff of chefs and cooks did their best to get orders out quickly and correctly without sacrificing quality. After all, it didn't do any good to rush food that was sent back by the customer.

From all accounts from the part-time waiters he'd sent to serve Faith, she'd enjoyed her meal and the wine. The timing had been perfect, but he'd been prepared to send another freshly prepared dinner if the first one had grown cold. Going down the walk, he stared at the gate leading to her place.

Twin lights burned on posts on either side of the wooden door. It was well after eleven. She was probably asleep. He resisted the urge to go see for himself. Being alone with Faith at night was asking for trouble.

Unlocking his door, he went inside. He had just hung up his clothes when he heard a knock on the door. He didn't need two guesses to know who it was. He hesitated, then went to answer the door. There wasn't a woman born he couldn't resist. He controlled his emotions.

He frowned on seeing an unfamiliar member of the hotel's staff. "Yes?"

"Good evening, Mr. Grayson; this is for you. Good night."

Brandon was so surprised by the letter that the man was several feet away before he remembered he hadn't tipped him. "Wait." Sliding his hand into his pocket, he handed the man a bill. "Thank you."

"Thank *you*."

Opening the letter, Brandon entered his room. It was an invitation to dinner from Faith. The menu caused his taste buds to do a happy dance and remind him that he hadn't had time to eat since breakfast. He considered not going, then quickly dismissed the idea. After all she'd done to help him, it would be rude and ungrateful not to accept. Shoving his key back in his pocket, he headed for her place. He'd eat enough to be courteous, then leave.

"You can do this, Brandon." Taking a deep breath, he knocked.

"Come in."

Blowing out a breath, he opened the door and knew he was in trouble. Numerous candles illuminated the room, and in the center was Faith in something silky and black that flowed over her full figure and made his body hum.

"Thank you for dinner. Now it's my turn." She waved him to a seat at a table by the window. "Have you eaten?"

"No."

Her smile was radiant. "You will now. Please have a seat."

Brandon thought that was a good idea, since there was no way to hide his response. Crossing the room, he pulled out a chair for her. "Thank you. You didn't have to do this."

She looked up at him over her shoulder. "Yes, I did."

Her face was close to his, her scent of orange blossom curled around him like a silken rope. Breath shuddered over his lips. His hand clenched on the chair instead of reaching out and grabbing Faith.

"Please eat. I don't cook often, but Henrí gave me some pointers." She turned away to serve Brandon.

*Saved in the nick of time.* Brandon took his seat across from her.

"Since I know how much you like pastries, Henrí and I thought you wouldn't be able to resist salmon wrapped in phyllo."

What he might not be able to resist was Faith. After saying grace, he tried to keep his attention on the salmon wrapped in delicate paper-thin layers of golden-brown pastry. The taste was crunchy and delicious. He remembered Faith's lips tasted sweet and even more delicious.

"There's more, if you want it," she said.

Brandon's traitorous body stirred. He wanted more of her; he just couldn't have it. "This is wonderful. I appreciate you going to all this trouble for me." His voice sounded rough, strained.

"For dessert, there are cherry-apricot turnovers." Propping her elbows on the table, she laced her fingers and placed her chin on top. "I must admit I might indulge with you."

He'd like to indulge all right, but not with dessert. He cleared his throat. "This might be all I can handle. Thank you."

"One little bite, please." She came to her feet. "I'll go get it."

Brandon practiced taking deep breaths, but when Faith returned to place the luscious dessert on the table he realized it wasn't doing any good. "Please have a seat."

"Not until you take a bite."

Hoping she'd move away, Brandon did as requested. She didn't.

"Few things taste as delicious, don't you agree?"

He could think of one. He pushed the dessert across the table. "Please eat the rest."

With an indulgent smile, she retook her seat and picked up her fork. With her first bite he realized his mistake. The tiny moan started deep in her throat and slowly worked its way over her lips. "Low in calories, irresistible, and addictive. What can beat it?"

Brandon didn't want to think about the answer. He lurched to his feet. "Thanks for dinner. Good night."

"We haven't discussed when we'll get together to finish your apartment," she protested.

"We can do it at breakfast."

Her expression downcast, she came to her feet. "I guess you didn't enjoy my meal as much as I did yours. I'm sorry."

"I did," he quickly told her.

"Yes. Then why can't you wait to leave?" She started past him.

"Faith," he began, then stopped, not knowing how to explain what was happening.

"Yes, Brandon?" She stopped even with him and waited.

He shook his head. "Nothing."

"Is everything all right at the restaurant?" She placed her hand on his arm and stared up into his face. "I'm feeling sorry for myself when you're having problems. Forgive me."

He closed his eyes. She was too close. Smelled too tempting.

She moved in closer, lifting her face, letting her hands rest on his chest. "How can I help?"

His heart hammered beneath her hands as need built and resistance weakened. He reached out to push her away and somehow brought her closer. All he had to do was lower his mouth just a little. She met him halfway.

One touch, one taste, was all it took. Fire erupted. Need rushed through them, sweeping away resistance.

Brandon didn't think; he just gathered Faith's voluptuous body closer to him, relearning the heady taste of her mouth while his hand swept up and down her back, the satin material sensitizing his skin. Nothing had ever excited him as much, driven him to take more and more and given the same intense pleasure.

His mouth nibbled, bit, then kissed her mouth, enjoying her little moans, her slight trembling. His hand moved around to close over her breast; his thumb flicked across the hard nipple. Her arms tightened around his neck.

Her need was as great as his, and as desperate. His lower body felt heavy and ached for release. He buried his mouth in the curve of her neck, the sound of his breathing hoarse and ragged. He had to have her. His hand gathered the material and lifted.

"Brandon."

The thready sound of his name rocked through him. It resonated with desire out of control and another emotion that had him drawing on all of his own control to pull back . . . complete trust. Releasing the caftan, he drew her flush against him, resisting the lure of her body, the desire he felt to lie down and explore every tempting inch with his hands, his mouth.

He groaned. Thoughts like that weren't going to help.

"Brandon?" This time there was uncertainty in her voice.

"Shh," he whispered. "Nothing is going to happen."

"Oh?"

He lifted his head and stared down at the top of hers. Surely he hadn't heard disappointment. "Faith?"

"Yes?"

Unsure of what to expect, he lifted her chin with his fingertips. In the flickering candlelight he couldn't see her eyes clearly enough to read her thoughts. "You all right?"

Her fingertips tenderly grazed his lower lip. "Yes."

He caught her hand in his, then stepped away. He released her hand as he turned and went to the door. "Good night."

"Good night. I'm glad you came by."

Brandon wasn't so sure he was. In his room he sat on the edge of the bed. Faith was proving to be too much of a temptation. Knowing why he was attracted to her wasn't helping him control the desire.

He thought about asking Catherine to help him,

then dismissed the idea. He would take care of this on his own. He'd simply stay away from Faith.

The note from Brandon was waiting for Faith when she passed the front desk the next morning. Even before she opened it, she knew he was canceling. Last night obviously had confused him even more than the first time they'd kissed.

He probably thought it was a fluke and wouldn't happen again. Being the decent, honest man he was, he might even be laboring under the misguided thought that he was taking advantage of their friendship. It would never enter his mind that she was in love with him.

Too logical.

Continuing to the patio, she ordered breakfast and considered her next move. She had to keep the heat on, and that meant they had to keep seeing each other or, at the very least, she had to keep thoughts of her on his mind.

Picking up her pen, she tapped it on her notebook. If Brandon wouldn't come to her, she'd go to him. Signaling the waiter, she put in a second order. If Brandon thought he could run from her, he was mistaken. She'd waited too long for him to realize she was a woman to let him dismiss what they were feeling.

She wasn't going to fool herself into thinking it was anything permanent. She'd caught him at a susceptible time when he was steering clear of women ... with the exception of Elizabeth. Faith didn't mind being the stand-in because no matter how much Brandon tried to avoid the idea of them being more than friends, and she was sure he had, he couldn't hold her, kiss her so sweetly, if he didn't feel an emotion deeper than lust.

He was not getting away from her.


Brandon had never run from a problem and it bothered him that he had done so now, but he didn't see any other way. Behind the desk in his office on the first floor, he worked on a list of supplies and tried not to think of Faith . . . an impossible task. He shoved his hand through his unbound hair. He'd rather wrestle a grizzly bear than hurt her, but he was afraid that was exactly what he'd done.

She trusted him to stop before things went too far; he wasn't so sure he could. She didn't seem bothered by the new direction their friendship had taken. In fact, she acted as if making steam come out of his ears was no big deal. He couldn't decide how he felt about her being so nonchalant.

Then another thought came: maybe she was under the misguided impression that the kisses were part of her training to tempt a man. The more he thought of it, the more it sounded reasonable. And if that was the case, she'd expect them to continue.

*He was a goner.*

The phone on his desk rang. He pounced on it. Anything to take his mind off Faith. "The Red Cactus."

"Morning, Brandon. Ready to start the day."

"I'll be right out, Mr. Montgomery." Standing, Brandon went to the front door and unlocked it. The plumber wasn't alone. "Faith," Brandon said in shock.

"Hi, Brandon. I thought I'd drop by and see how things are going, since I didn't have a chance to yesterday," she said. "Hope you don't mind."

"Of course he don't." Mr. Montgomery entered the restaurant, bringing Faith with him and heading for the stairs. "You're his decorator. Besides, you're not leaving until I see what smells so good in that box you've got."

Brandon followed. By the time he reached the apartment, Faith had disposable dessert plates, cups filled with Blue Mountain coffee, and orange juice waiting. "There's scones, fresh-baked croissants, cranberry-walnut and raisin-pecan bread with honey-butter and cream cheese. What would you like first, Brandon?"

*For you to leave.* This morning she wore an apricot-colored suit with a waist-length jacket and short skirt. Her hair was pulled atop her head, tendrils hanging on either side of her face, making a man think of pulling out the hairpins one by one, then burying his face in it.

"Make up your mind, son. I've got work to do," Mr. Montgomery admonished him.

"Anything will do," Brandon finally told her.

Faith put one of each on a plate and handed it to him. "You didn't eat very much last night."

His eyes narrowed, but she turned away. "Mr. Montgomery?"

"The nut bread." He held out his plate. She put a slice of each on his plate, then closed the lid.

"You didn't prepare anything for yourself?" Brandon said as Mr. Montgomery leaned against the counter to eat.

"I already had breakfast. Mind if I take a look at the bathroom?"

"Of course he don't," Mr. Montgomery said around a mouthful of bread. "If I do say so myself, I outdid myself."

She didn't move. "Brandon?"

He placed the plate on the counter. "I'll show you."

"You stay and eat. I know the way."

"That's a mighty sweet woman," Mr. Montgomery said as Faith entered the bedroom. "Heard she was dating some rich man. He's a lucky man if he marries Faith."

"She's not dating anyone," Brandon said with more force than necessary.

Mr. Montgomery's bushy eyebrows lifted. "How would you know?"

"I just know. Excuse me." Brandon went to join Faith. He found her hunkered down in front of the shower stall that was now big enough for three people. He didn't have to think too hard to imagine him stripping off her suit and them in the shower together. "What do you think?"

Slowly she turned. For a split second he thought he saw the same thought mirrored in her eyes. "He's done a wonderful job. When did you decide on a tub?"

*After you mentioned how much you liked to soak after a long day.* "Seemed like a good idea at the time."

She nodded. "The cabinets around your bed turned out well. You'll have room for your books. I didn't see any clothes, so the closet must be finished."

"Yesterday. I'll show you." He stepped away, then followed her as she left the bath and opened the folding closet doors.

"It's just as I imagined." Faith ran her hand over the center island with multiple compartments in solid cherry.

"I won't ever have to look for anything again." Everything had a place in the new walk-in closet, with his shirts and coats on low racks and his pants on taller ones. "I owe you a lot."

"It was my pleasure."

They stared at each other. Brandon wasn't aware of either of them moving, but suddenly she was directly in front of him.

"How did you like it, Faith?"

She jumped and stepped away. Brandon muttered under his breath.

"Better than my expectations, Mr. Montgomery," she said softly, not looking at Brandon.

He nodded. "I took pictures. If this doesn't get me and Mack more business, I don't know what will."

"In that case, you two should give me a cut or

discount your bill," Brandon said, trying to get the older man's attention off Faith.

"Funny, Brandon. Very funny. I'd better get started on laying that tile." The plumber left as quietly as he had come.

"You all right?"

She lifted her head. "Why do you keep asking me that?"

He stared at her. "Isn't it obvious?"

"If it was, I wouldn't ask."

He frowned. "You usually know what I'm thinking before I do."

"My crystal ball must be on the blink today." She stopped at the door. "They're delivering the rug and chairs tomorrow afternoon. They'll call first and you can call me. Good-bye."

It didn't make much sense, but he didn't want her to leave. She looked unbearably sad. He was the reason. "Faith. You know I only want what's best for you, don't you?"

"What you think is best for me may not be. If I don't see you tonight, I'll see you tomorrow." This time she didn't stop.

Outside the restaurant, Faith tightly shut her eyes. Wanting her was making Brandon miserable. She hadn't counted on that.

She could push the issue or let him figure out for himself that the change in their relationship shouldn't cause him to worry about her. He wouldn't hurt her any more than loving him all these years and knowing he'd never love her back the way she wanted him to had. But he wasn't aware she loved him, and she wasn't about to tell him. Deep in thought, she started back to the hotel.

# 15

Late Friday afternoon water gushed from the nickel-plated Roman faucet in the tub and the multiple showerheads in Brandon's bathroom. Black ceramic tile gleamed on the walls and beneath his booted feet.

"Am I good or am I good?" Mr. Montgomery asked the rhetorical question.

"Faith did this," Brandon said from beside the plumber.

"She had the idea." Mr. Montgomery folded his arms. "Which I turned into reality. A feat in itself. I thought she would be here."

"She's busy." Brandon shut off the water and left the bathroom. "I'll get your check."

"Wasn't she supposed to come by yesterday to fix up the living area? It looks the same, and the things they delivered are in a corner," Mr. Montgomery said, standing by Brandon's elbow as he sat at the kitchen table writing the check.

Brandon didn't bother answering. He and Faith had stayed out of each other's way since Wednesday, and that was how Brandon planned to keep things. There was no sense asking for trouble. "I'll get to it eventually. Good-bye, and thanks."

The plumber shoved the folded check into the pocket of his overalls. "I bet you can't wait to move back in here."

He'd thought the same, but now he wasn't so sure. "I'll walk you down. I need to get back to work. The dinner crowd is just starting to come in."

Mr. Montgomery looked around one last time. "This place doesn't look the same with the new cabinet doors and the curved counter around the existing island to give you more space to entertain. The hidden open shelving on the other side for all those cookbooks of yours was a stroke of genius. Mack did a good job. Faith knows her stuff."

"Yes, she does." Brandon opened the door leading downstairs. "Thanks again."

"I know when I'm being rushed." Leaving the apartment, Mr. Montgomery went down the stairs and stopped at the bottom. "You two have a tiff or something?"

The blunt question might seem rude from anyone else, but Mr. Montgomery always spoke his mind and he'd known Brandon and Faith since they were in grade school. Brandon knew he could play dumb and lengthen the unwanted conversation or answer. "Like I said, she's busy."

"That never stopped her before from helping you out." The older man pulled his cap down over his brushy brows. "If a woman went out of her way to help me, I think I'd find a way to thank her. Night, Brandon."

"Night."

Brandon toured the restaurant to check on the dinner guests, then went to the kitchen. Checking the monitor for the next order, he began preparing the fajita nachos. Staying away from Faith was best. He just wished he didn't have trouble believing it.

Brandon tried his best to close promptly at eleven so he could check out of the hotel when the chance of him seeing Faith wasn't as great, but it hadn't worked that way. Hands stuffed in his pockets, he continued down the street to the hotel. In the past he hadn't minded the short late-night walk. He'd even enjoyed the exercise, but tonight he was too tense.

He'd thought of checking out that morning, but yesterday afternoon Mr. Montgomery had encountered a problem with the water pressure. He'd given Brandon the dire news that most likely it wasn't coming from his end, but the possibility remained that, if it was, the plumber would have to go back in the wall, tear out the tile, and the water would be off again. Luckily that hadn't happened.

Brandon was ten feet inside the hotel when the one thing he dreaded became reality. Faith was standing with a group of people he didn't recognize. There was a moment that seemed to freeze in time when their eyes met, his breath caught, and the need he'd tried to deny so long came hurtling back.

Faith nodded her head slightly, then continued talking with the people she was with, turning her back slightly as she did. The gesture made his gut clench, but he realized it was no more than he deserved. She'd put his welfare above her own, and he'd repaid her by taking advantage of her, then turning his back on her.

His jaw clenched, he went to his room, pulled his duffel back from the top of the closet, and began shoving his things inside, berating himself as he did so. He should have never touched her. Now, he'd lost a friend. Worse, he'd hurt a good woman.

Dragging the bag from the bed, he went to the front desk and checked out, very much aware that Faith still stood nearby. The bill in his hand, he turned and looked straight at her. Lips that he'd dreamed about trembled, then firmed. Her chin lifted.

With a curt nod, he left, but each step away from her was more difficult than the one before, his mood more foul. He hadn't wanted it to end this way.

In his room over the restaurant, he tossed the bag on the bed. Everywhere he looked was a reminder of Faith. She'd put her stamp on his place just like she'd put her stamp on him.

To repay her, he'd left without the simple courtesy of thanking her. He knew the reason he had to steer clear of her. She didn't and, to a softhearted, generous woman like Faith, that had been like a slap in the face.

"Hell." He was out the door again.

*Brandon was gone.* He hadn't even said good-bye.

As soon as he'd left she'd excused herself from the group celebrating the retirement of a teacher and escaped to her room. On automatic, she'd prepared for bed, but she was too keyed up to sleep. She'd ended up outside looking at a full moon that appeared close enough to touch. It was a night for lovers. She would never have that pleasure. Misery swamped her.

She'd gambled and lost. At least in the past she'd had his friendship. Now she only had memories of his evocative kisses that made her body yearn for something deeper and wish for what might have been.

She'd said there'd be no regrets. At least she had gone after the man she loved. Perhaps the McBrides were truly cursed never to find happiness in a relationship.

Her head lowered. How had her brothers and father stood this pain that went soul deep, knowing that there was no ending in this lifetime?

She heard the creak of the gate and glanced up just as Brandon entered the courtyard. His face looked as tortured as she felt inside.

She wanted to tell him to leave, beg him to stay. The knot in her throat wouldn't let her do either.

"Faith." He rushed to her and knelt. "I'm a bastard for hurting you. I told myself I'd cut off my arm before I did that, but when it came down to it, I ran because if I didn't, I'd make love to you and hurt you even more."

Her heart pounded; her breath snagged. "What— what did you say?"

"I tried to fight it, but . . ." His head lowered then lifted. "I dream about you. I think about how sweet your mouth tastes, your soft skin, your scent that makes me want to kiss every inch of you. Call me a bastard. Slap my face, and tell me to never come near you again."

She launched herself into his arms. Brandon caught her, thinking she was attacking him, rightly so, until he felt her lips kissing his cheeks, his eyes, anyplace she could reach.

"You aren't mad?" he asked.

Sweet laughter was the answer. Then her mouth settled on his, her tongue darting inside his mouth to mate and tease with his. Brandon forgot about asking questions and pulled her to him, imitating and matching her ardor.

Then his hand discovered something else he'd known when he saw her, but he had been too concerned about her well-being for it to register. There was nothing but fragrant skin beneath the silky blue robe and gown. He tried to pull back. Faith nipped his ear and he shuddered.

Perhaps he could stop before it was too late. Picking her up, he almost ran inside. She was blowing in his ear, curling her tongue around his lobe. "Faith, wait a minute."

She bit him on the neck. He stumbled and set her on her feet in the living room. She jerked his shirt out of his pants. The air gushed through his lungs as if he'd run for miles. Warm, insistent hands roamed his chest, plucked at his nipples.

How had he ever thought he could stop? "Please help me."

She jerked his shirt open. Buttons popped. Her hot mouth replaced her hands. She took the hard point of his nipple between her teeth and flicked her tongue across it.

"You're killing me," he moaned.

Her head popped up; wonder and satisfaction gleamed in her eyes. "I am?"

He could only nod. The look in her eyes stole his voice and hardened his body.

"Oh, Brandon." She dipped her head again and went back to slowly driving him crazy.

He had two choices: be a bystander or be a participant. In the next instant she was back in his arms and he was heading for the bedroom. The covers turned back, the light of the full moon illuminated the pale sheets.

"I want to see you," he breathed.

"I want to see you, too." A dim light filled the room.

He gently kissed her on the lips, then slipped the robe off her shoulders. His unsteady fingers slipped beneath the spaghetti straps of her gown and ever so slowly eased them over her shoulders. The silk slithered to the floor. His breath stumbled as he looked his fill.

"Brandon?"

The uncertainty in her voice lifted his head. His hands cupped her face as he stared deep into her eyes. "You're the most beautiful sight I've ever seen."

"You must not look at yourself in the mirror," she said, then reached for his belt buckle.

He could have done it faster, but the sight of Faith unbuckling and unzipping heightened his arousal. Then her hand, by design or intention, grazed across his groin as she pushed his pants down. He groaned, his hands fisting as intense pleasure swept through him.

"Are you all right?"

"I will be." He plopped on the bed to take off his shirt and reach for his boots.

"Let me help." Faith straddled his legs, her beautiful backside to him, and grabbed his boot, pulled. He concentrated on breathing and maintaining control as one boot, then the other, slipped free.

"There." She faced him. "Where were we?"

He pulled her to him, his mouth fastening to the tempting sight of her full breast. His mouth laved the turgid point as his hands roamed her lush body. They swept up her back and down again to cup her hips. One hand continued downward until he discovered the very essence of her . . . and found her hot, damp, tight.

She gave a long, low moan of pleasure as her hands dived into his hair, pulling him closer. "Brandon."

His name on her lips heightened his need. He had to have her soon. Wrapping both hands around her, he scooted up in bed, then twisted so she was on the bottom. He needed to feel her full length against him, her body pressed against his, accepting his. The fit was as perfect as he'd known it would be.

He went back to what he found he couldn't get enough of: loving Faith. Each kiss was sweeter, each touch more arousing, than the last until he knew he had reached the breaking point.

"Faith, I have to know if you've made love before."

She squirmed against him, the hot junction against his throbbing manhood almost sending him over the edge. "Faith." Her name was a hoarse, desperate groan.

Heavy-lidded eyes opened. She stared at him a long time; then she twisted her head back and forth on the pillow. Brandon felt awe and pleasure with a good dose of fear. He didn't want to mess this up for her.

As if she read his thoughts, she reached out and cupped his cheek with her palm. "I trust you, Brandon."

He kissed her palm, then her mouth, thrusting his tongue deeply, drawing her once again into the sensual haze. Gathering her to him, he thrust, making them one. She stiffened beneath him. His hand reached between them to flick her sensitive nub. He stroked, once, twice, until she began to move, her hips lifting to meet his.

Removing his hand, he measured the length of her velvet sheath, again and again. Each time he brought them together the pleasure and passion built. Small moans grew in intensity.

Her legs locked around his waist; his hands cupped her hips. Each deep thrust brought them closer and closer to final completion until they both exploded in primal pleasure.

Still he couldn't let her go. He tightened his hold, burying his face on the side of her neck. Her body trembled as shock wave after shock wave swept over her.

When he was able to move, he rolled on his side, bringing her with him. Nothing had ever been as beautiful. "Are you all right?"

He felt her smile. " 'All right' couldn't begin to describe how wonderful I feel." She nuzzled his chest. "I'm glad I waited."

The pleasure Brandon felt turned to guilt. Women

didn't wait this long for nothing. They expected the man they gave their virginity to to marry them.

"Faith."

"Mmm."

She was falling asleep. He had to tell her now, when there could be no mistakes. It would be cruel to wait. "I intended to stop before we went this far. I should have stopped when I learned you were a virgin. 'I'm sorry' isn't enough, I know."

Brandon's words doused the sensual haze Faith was feeling. He was apologizing for the most beautiful thing that had ever happened to her. No jury would convict her if she did him in.

"We shouldn't have become lovers," he said.

*Lovers.* The word resonated in her brain; the warm feeling returned; she snuggled closer. Perhaps she wouldn't do him in just yet. She definitely had uses for him. She reached over and stroked him. He hardened instantly. The velvet texture amazed her. How could it be so soft, then so hard, and give so much pleasure?

"Faith, what are you doing?"

She laughed in spite of herself and moved on top of him. She had a lot of time to make up for. "Guess."

If you did something once and regretted it, that was understandable. Brandon wasn't sure what a second or third time meant . . . except he couldn't keep his hands off Faith if she was within reaching distance.

He stared down at her in sleep. She was on her stomach, a smile on her lips. She twisted his insides and made him happy to be a man, but it wouldn't last. And when it was over the one thing he dreaded would happen: he'd leave her with tears on her cheeks.

Unable to resist, he leaned down and kissed her.

"Brandon," she murmured, her eyes closed, her hand, even in sleep, reaching for him.

"Shh. I'm here." He caught her hand, sat on the side of the bed until her even breathing signaled she was asleep again. Slowly releasing her hand, he stood, dressed, and quickly left the room. This time he knew better than to linger.

In the courtyard, he looked at his watch and cursed softly under his breath. 3:15 A.M. He should have left hours ago. Heck. He shouldn't even be there. Now how was he going to leave without the desk clerk knowing what had happened? Brandon didn't want Faith to be gossiped about.

It wasn't likely he could scale the ten-foot wall surrounding the grounds, and although the Pueblo and the Mesa had outside doors, the main doors were most likely locked. There was no help for it. He'd have to sneak out . . . something he'd never done. But, then, he'd never been the first, either. Luke had made sure his brothers didn't take what couldn't be replaced. Brandon had always listened until now.

At the entrance to the lobby, Brandon breathed a

sigh of relief on seeing there wasn't anyone behind the counter. He quickly passed through, his luck holding out on seeing the night doorman at the opposite end taking a smoke break. Brandon didn't breathe easy until he was a block away. Another reason that it had to end: Faith's reputation was at stake. He'd done enough to hurt her.

Faith woke up by degrees. Contentment and happiness followed her into wakefulness. She smiled on feeling the slight soreness of her body, the protest of muscles as she remembered the cause: she and Brandon were lovers.

She hugged the knowledge to her, then reached over to touch him as she had so many times last night, loving the feel of his muscled warmth beneath her fingertips, awed that she could.

Instead, she felt only the cool bedsheet.

Her eyelids flew upward. Sitting up, she glanced around the room, then strained to hear if he was in the connecting bath or possibly in the kitchen. Silence. He was gone.

Before she could succumb to the loneliness nipping at her, she looked at the clock on the nightstand. 7:15 A.M. Some of the uneasiness disappeared. Of course he'd left. She had a loyal staff, but that didn't mean she wanted them to be privy to the knowledge that she and Brandon were lovers. He'd simply left to protect her reputation.

Perhaps there was a note. Not seeing one on the nightstand, she got out of bed ignoring her nakedness, to look on the floor in case it had somehow fallen. Lifting the bedcovers, she looked beneath the bed, shook the sheets. Nothing.

The wave of loneliness she had been struggling to keep at bay crept over her. She plopped on the side of the bed. In her erotic dreams they'd always made love, but on those occasions when she'd allowed herself to think of "afterward" she'd let herself imagine him holding her with love in his beautiful eyes or awakening her with a kiss or a breakfast tray with a rose.

Then another, more horrifying thought struck.

Perhaps she hadn't pleased him. Faith closed her eyes in abject misery. What was beautiful for her could have been mediocre for him. She jumped as the phone rang, then picked it up.

"Bra-hello," she quickly revised.

"Good morning, Ms. McBride. Are you all right?" asked Cynthia, a longtime operator for the hotel.

*No.* "Yes. Is there a problem?"

There was a slight hesitation before Cynthia said, "You had an appointment with Mr. Fountain thirty minutes ago. Since you're always punctual or call if you'll be late, we were concerned."

Faith's forehead momentarily dropped into the palm of her hand. The last thing she wanted to do was discuss the wine-tasting event menu with the executive chef. "Please tell Henrí I'll be there in twenty minutes."

"Mr. Fountain said he could reschedule if there was a problem."

Faith came to her feet. Henrí was as temperamental as they came. He didn't like to be kept waiting. For him to even suggest rescheduling was paramount to a leopard changing its spots. It just didn't happen. "Twenty minutes is fine."

"I'll tell him. Good-bye."

Faith hung up the phone with a new worry. This one about her executive chef.

Brandon didn't even attempt to go to bed. He showered, pulled on a pair of jeans and a shirt, then went to his office downstairs to work. His apartment was too much of a reminder of Faith. However, once behind his big mahogany desk, he soon discovered it wasn't so much a place as it was him.

She was with him wherever he went. Her softness, her quick smile, the heady knowledge in her incredible chocolate eyes that she turned him on, the intense pleasure of her body accepting his, the wonder in her beautiful face, her scream at climax, the tight clamp of her body around him, the lingering earthquakes.

Brandon's hand fisted on his desk. Images of Faith lingered, filling his mind and teasing his senses as no woman ever had.

And he'd left her to wake up alone.

That he'd done it to protect her reputation wouldn't

mean a thing to a sensitive woman like Faith, who gave everything to a man she trusted. Brandon looked at the phone as he had done since a little after six thirty that morning. It was seven.

She'd probably be waking up and reaching for him as she'd done so many times last night. This time he wouldn't be there to hold her, comfort her.

Brandon muttered under his breath, then picked up the phone only to put it down again. What could he say? "Thank you"? "How are you?" He certainly couldn't say he wished he was there with her, wished she wasn't the baby sister of his best friend. Wished that at times he didn't feel as if he'd been given a precious gift, then had it snatched away from him.

Brandon came to his feet and paced. If he was having this hard of a time dealing with him and Faith becoming lovers, how much worse was it for her? You couldn't fix this with flowers or dinner. There was only one way. Even as his hands began buttoning his shirt, he just hoped when he did see Faith he'd know what to say.

Grabbing his keys, he was out the door. In less than four minutes, he stepped onto the bricked entrance of Casa de Serenidad.

"Hello, Mr. Grayson. Welcome back." The greeting had barely left the valet's mouth before it was echoed by the doorman.

Brandon returned their cheerful greeting, trying to decide if they were any more effusive than before.

He was still deep in thought when he entered the lobby.

"Good morning, Mr. Grayson."

Brandon frowned as an attractive Hispanic woman in a little black suit stopped in front of him. He usually didn't forget women, but this time he drew a blank. "I'm sorry, I don't remember your name."

Laughing, she extended her slim manicured hand. "Esmeralda De la Vega, assistant manager. Faith is in a meeting with Henrí on the patio of the Mesa. She should be finished shortly."

Brandon politely shook her hand, trying to recall if he'd seen her at his party. He didn't remember seeing her during his stay at the hotel. The odds that she knew all the hotel's past guests weren't likely. Perhaps she had seen him and Faith having breakfast and surmised they were friends. He hoped that was all she knew.

"Thank you, but I don't want to disturb her," he said.

A slow smile spread across the woman's olive-skinned face. "I'm sure she won't mind. I'm going that way."

Brandon fell into step beside the slender dark-eyed woman, trying to decipher the little smile on her lips and hoping the answer he was coming up with wasn't the right one. The instant he stepped into the open patio, his gaze went to the table he and Faith always shared. She was there.

His body gladdened and yearned.

Completely forgetting the woman beside him, his attention centered on Faith. Her head was tilted to one side as she listened to Henrí. The little man was making gestures with his hands as he spoke. Brandon would have sworn that the executive chef commanded Faith's full attention. Seconds later he was proven wrong.

Abruptly her head lifted. Their gazes locked. Lips that had driven him crazy with desire parted slightly; eyes that he'd go to his grave remembering widened. The impact of her stare stunned him with its intensity.

He wanted her again. *Now.* He could feel the rush of blood through his veins, his breath quickening.

Faith's gaze went hot, her cheeks flushed, her body soft.

Henrí's gaze snapped in the direction Faith was staring. His eyes narrowed as he slowly looked from Brandon to Faith, his brow puckered, then cleared. There was no way any adult could miss the sensual heat and pull between them.

Brandon bit back a curse, then took Esmeralda's arm and propelled her across the patio. Faith was not going to be fodder for gossip in the employees' lounge. "Good morning, Faith, Henrí. Hope I'm not interrupting."

"I told him he wouldn't be," Esmeralda said when neither Faith nor Henrí spoke.

"So," Henrí drew out the word. "You have perhaps

found something else at Casa de Serenidad of interest?"

The color in Faith's cheeks deepened. "Good morning, Brandon."

Brandon's eyes hardened when he turned them on the other man. "I see you like living dangerously."

The chef's bushy eyebrow lifted. "Occasionally." He turned to Faith. "I'll finish this up and serve you the menu at dinner to sample." Gathering the papers, he stood and tucked them under his arm and stared at Brandon. "You're invited. Seven sharp. Good-bye."

"I need to be going as well. Bye." Esmeralda quickly took herself off.

Faith's hand fluttered to her hair, then back to her lap as if she didn't know what to do with herself. She had never been the nervous type. "I know you'll be busy this evening, Brandon."

Brandon resisted the urge to take her hand in his, to sit down. If he tried, his increasingly tight jeans would cut off the circulation to a vital part of his body. "Do you want me here tonight?"

"Yes."

The breathless word filled with desire went straight through him. Saturday nights were the busiest of the week, but he never thought of refusing. "See you then." Brandon turned to leave.

"You aren't staying for breakfast?"

Brandon glanced at her, then down meaningfully. A mixture of laughter and pleasure lit her eyes as she followed his gaze. Despite his discomfort, he found himself smiling. "Glad you find this funny, since it's your fault."

"I'd fix it if I could," she said in a voice that had dropped to a seductive purr.

Air hissed over his teeth. His unruly mind easily pictured all the ways Faith could remedy his problem—with her hands, her mouth, her body. "Faith," he groaned. "You're going to be the death of me."

"But what a way to go." Picking up her folder, she rose to her feet. Her gaze went from his head to the part of him that throbbed for her before she lifted her eyes. "See you tonight, Brandon."

His eyes glued to the saucy sway of her rounded hips, he vividly recalled caressing and stroking only hours earlier, he watched her walk away. There had been a promise, a brazen invitation, in her final words that he had every intention of resisting.

He'd come to assure himself that she was all right. He'd done that. He wasn't so sure the staff didn't suspect something was going on between him and Faith already. This was for her benefit. There would be no more hot, sweaty, incredible sex.

Slowly Brandon made his way back to the Red Cactus, hoping his body was up to the challenge.

# 16

Faith wanted to dance in the hallway, pump her fist, throw her arms wide, and spin in circles. With guests and hotel staff nearby, she could do none of those things. Yet.

The moment she closed her office door, she indulged in all four. He'd come. Brandon had come. He'd looked as unsure as she'd felt. Then Henrí had baited him and learned Brandon wasn't a man to push.

Sighing, she sat behind her desk. Brandon, of course, would want her reputation to remain unblemished. He'd blame himself if rumors of their affair leaked. He needn't have worried.

Henrí, who had been with her for five years, was like a second father and extremely loyal. Esmeralda, who had risen in the ranks after starting as a night clerk, was just as loyal. They wouldn't gossip, but Faith had to admit that she felt a certain thrill in others knowing Brandon found her sexy and wanted her despite her having some flesh on her bones.

She came from around her desk and headed for her room. She wanted to wear something spectacular that night that would keep Brandon's eyes on her. Stifling laughter, she continued to her room.

Thanks to Sierra again, Faith found the perfect outfit in less than fifteen minutes, and then she returned to work. She was crossing the lobby when a floral delivery came through the glass front door. She and every other woman there stared at the spectacular arrangement of birds of paradise mixed with roses, amaryllis, and hydrangeas to rise majestically before falling gracefully over the edge of an immense crystal vase.

"Delivery for Faith McBride."

Faith gasped.

Esmeralda, who was behind the desk, asked, "Do you want to sign?"

Faith rushed over to sign her name with fingers that refused to be steady. The flowers could be from Brandon or a grateful guest. "Thank you," she said, and handed the deliverywoman the tip Esmeralda gave her.

"Thanks. I don't think I've ever had a personal delivery this large." The robust woman touched the stem of the birds of paradise, then looked at Faith and hooked her thumb. "One for us."

Since the deliverywoman was a size larger than Faith, "us" probably meant "women of size." They usually weren't the ones men went after or sent immense floral bouquets to. Faith understood the expectant look on the deliverywoman's face. The flowers meant there was still hope for women who weren't the size of toothpicks. Faith's hands were shaking even more by the time she removed the card from the white envelope.

*If you change your mind, call.*
*Blade*

Faith couldn't hide the disappointment that knotted her stomach. "It's from an old friend," she told the waiting deliverywoman.

The robust woman looked at Faith with suspicion growing in her narrowed gaze. "Must be some friend."

Aware that the flowers had drawn guests and a few staff members, Faith slipped the card in the pocket of her light pink cardigan. "He is."

A slow smile started at the corner of the other woman's face. She nudged Faith with her shoulder. "Keeping it close to your chest, huh? If you ever get tired of your 'friend,' toss him my way."

Faith looked around the lobby as people began to move away. She received a wink from a couple of return guests, a nod of approval from another, a thumbs-up from a fourth. They all thought she was being coy. Far from it.

She'd desperately wanted the flowers to be from Brandon. Blade had made it ostentatious enough to get people's attention and make Brandon jealous. She'd call him later to say he'd have to settle for one out of two.

The arrangement was too big to fit on her desk without getting in the way of her computer screen. Nor would it fit on the small table in her office. She didn't have time to take it to her room. "I'll take care of the flowers later," she told Esmeralda, not noticing the white card at her feet as she moved away.

Saturday evening, the Red Cactus was as crowded as Brandon had ever seen it. In the past he never would have thought of leaving for five minutes, let alone the hour it would probably take for him and Faith to finish whatever dinner Henrí planned. There was no help for it.

Brandon glanced around the restaurant. Every table was occupied; the line to be seated was out the door and had been running close to fifty minutes up until an hour ago. The extra help he'd called in had cut the wait down to thirty minutes.

Satisfied that things were going well on the floor, he went to the kitchen. Three chefs worked over the stainless-steel stoves. Plates placed on the pass-through were quickly picked up. His staff moved with practiced ease around one another as they came and went.

"We got it, boss." Michelle passed him on the way to the freezer. "We won't know you're gone."

"Yes, we will." Luis grinned as he slid three platters of appetizers to a tray. "I say we take advantage of this and party hearty."

"I'm for that." Michelle passed him with two slices of chocolate cake covered with vanilla ice cream and chocolate syrup.

"You can all be replaced." Brandon moved aside for them to go through the swinging doors.

"But not tonight." Michelle was out the door with Luis behind her.

Brandon glanced at the clock and swiped his sweaty palm on his slacks. 6:43. He'd never been this nervous about a date. Technically, this wasn't a date, which somehow made him all the more nervous.

Michelle came back through the door, her naturally curly red hair in tight ringlets. "You'd better scoot. Sierra just popped in and asked you to stop by the table. Seems she has something hot to tell you."

"She probably sold another overpriced piece of real estate," he said, moving toward the door.

"If I had the money, I'd sure let her try. She is beautiful," called Antonio, who made the best tamales this side of heaven. He was happily married, with fifteen grandchildren.

"I'll tell Sophia you said as much," Brandon said, referring to the man's devoted wife, as he left the kitchen, earning an exaggerated groan from Antonio and laughter from the rest of the staff.

Brandon glanced at his watch and wondered if he would have time to get the box of chocolates he'd ordered by phone that afternoon without anyone seeing. His employees hadn't asked where he was going, and he hadn't volunteered the information.

They'd assumed it had to be important if he was taking off on a Saturday night. He could count on one hand the number of times that he'd done so.

Sierra was dunking a chip with one hand and making notes on her day planner with the other when he reached the booth. "What's the hot news?"

She glanced up, mischief dancing in her eyes. "You're never going to believe this, and I hate to tell you I told you so."

One side of his mouth kicked up. "Yeah, I can tell."

She laughed and closed the planner. "I confess. It's always a pleasure when men are proven wrong, and this time, in spades."

Brandon didn't even bother trying to think of what she was talking about. He glanced at his watch. "I hate to rush you, but I have an appointment in ten minutes."

His announcement whipped the humor from her face. "You're leaving? I thought you said you weren't dat—"

"I'm just going to help Faith with a menu selection," he said, cutting his sister off.

Sierra sat back in the booth and shook her dark head in amazement. "Talk about late bloomers."

He fought to keep from ducking his head and squirming. "We're just friends. I told you that."

"Seems she has a lot of them." Sierra picked up a nacho chip and dunked it in salsa.

Brandon went on full alert. His body tensed. "What's that supposed to mean?"

"I'll only tell you if you promise not to go over there acting all macho, as if she doesn't have a brain cell." Sierra narrowed her gaze. "I hate it when you and the others do that to me."

"Tell me," he said, his voice too soft.

She eyed him a few seconds longer. "Remember this is third- or maybe fourth-hand. I heard it from a client who is staying at Faith's hotel, who heard it from another guest, who heard it from who knows who else. I don't gossip, but I'll make an exception this time since you were so sure she was settled."

"Sierra, get to the point."

"Blade hasn't given up on Faith. He sent her a floral arrangement so big two men had to carry it into the hotel, with a note begging her to change her mind and marry him."

Faith had never been as angry in her life as she was now. Sitting at the dining table waiting for Brandon, she looked composed while she seethed inside. A guest—Faith was positive none of her staff would have violated her privacy—had found Blade's card, which she must have dropped, and told someone who told someone else who told who knows who until the note was embellished to the point that Blade would do anything to marry her.

Faith tsked and sipped her wine. She didn't care for herself, but she did for Blade. Dating was one thing, getting serious quite another. If news of their supposedly hot affair leaked to the media, she wasn't sure how he'd react. One thing she did know: he'd think of her safety first and her wishes later. He was not going to chance losing another person because of her close association with him. Any other time she might humor him, but not now.

The reason was coming toward her, his black eyes narrowed and hard. She waited until he took his seat in the leather chair across from her and the waiter discreetly withdrew.

"The rumor isn't true." She told him about her suspicions of a guest finding the card Blade sent. "He is just a friend."

"We're friends, too."

Heat flushed her cheek, but she held his gaze. "We're a lot more since last night, or did you forget?"

"I've forgotten nothing," Brandon said, his voice rough.

Her face softened. "Neither have I. But with the rumors flying all over the place I wanted you to know that, as outlandish as it may seem, you might be viewed by those gossiping as the other man."

His brow cocked. "So that's the reason we're in a cozy little alcove off the main dining room instead of on the patio?"

She blew out a breath. "Yes. I didn't think you'd enjoy your meal very much if we were the main attraction. Of course, I'll understand if you want to leave, because our being secluded together may generate more speculation and gossip."

He spread his napkin in his lap. "I'm staying."

Relief swept through her. "Here comes Henrí with the first course."

"Good evening, Mr. Grayson. Delighted to see you finally decided to show up." Henrí placed tuna tartar in front of them.

"I was only a few minutes late," Brandon defended himself.

Henrí stared down his long nose at Brandon. "There is never an excuse for keeping a lovely woman or an exquisitely prepared meal waiting." He straightened. "Various wines will be served to coax the flavor out of the dishes. Since your palate is hopefully more sophisticated, I've selected nonalcoholic beverages for you. We shall see."

Brandon gripped his fork as the chef left. "On closer acquaintance with Henrí, I think we both might be happier if he stayed in your employ."

"He's just protective of me, and very serious about his work." Faith placed her napkin in her lap.

"That's the only reason he's not wearing this appetizer."

Faith's mouth twitched. "I thank you for your restraint."

"You should. For now and earlier." His fork hovered over his food.

She studied Brandon's unyielding face. She wouldn't fool herself into thinking he was jealous. He was just being his usual protective self. "I do."

Brandon took his first bite. "Henrí had it wrong."

"About the meal?"

"About you," Brandon said. His eyes roamed over her face, her bare left shoulder, the swell of her breasts in the red halter evening dress. "You're the one who is exquisite."

Her lips trembled. "Brandon."

Panic filled his eyes. "Don't you dare do that or I really will leave."

"I wouldn't dream of it." She swallowed, swallowed again. "Tell me about the renovations."

He did just that as Henrí served them the five-course meal. They were waiting for dessert when the delivery arrived. Brandon stared at the orchid in the clear box and thought of snatching it up. It couldn't stand a chance when put up against the flower arrangement the other guy had sent.

"I ordered it early this morning. I'm sorry it's not bigger. I'll . . ." His voice trailed off as he worked up enough courage to look at her.

Tears glistened in her eyes. Removing the flowers, she grazed her fingertips against the creamy velvet petals as if it were the most delicate thing in the world.

That honor belonged to her incredible skin. He could visualize trailing the flower over the swell of her breasts, her quivering stomach, going lower, to the very essence of her, and his greedy mouth following its path.

"It's beautiful and absolutely perfect."

She'd just described herself. How was he going to

walk away from her? He didn't know how; he just knew he had to.

"*Voilà*." With a flourish, Henrí presented the desserts. "You will never taste anything better."

Brandon's gaze leaped from the key lime cheesecake with toasted nut crust to Faith's. Heat leaped between them. He read her thoughts as easily and as clearly as she probably read his. Henrí was wrong again. They already had.

Each other.


Faith complimented Henrí profusely on the food, the presentation, the choice of wines. Even as she said the words, she couldn't help looking over Henrí's shoulder to see Brandon, powerful and seductively handsome, leaving the restaurant. She couldn't wait until she had him naked again. Her heart sighed. Reluctantly, she reined in her lustful longings.

"As always, Henrí, everything was perfection." She reached out her hands to him.

He clasped her hands in his smaller ones, studying her. "Would it have been the same without Mr. Grayson?"

Her hands remained steady, but her pulse raced. "Sharing heightens the pleasure of anything, especially a magnificent meal."

The chef squeezed her hands, then released them. "True, and it's about time you realized that. You know what you Americans say about all work and no play."

"That I do. Now, if you'll excuse me, I need to get back to work."

He pulled a face. "What did I just say?"

"Work now so I can play later," she told him. She definitely had plans for the night.

"Then go. I'll see you at breakfast. You can be the first to try my new quiche."

Faith's plans for breakfast in bed with Brandon faded, but that was all she was willing to give up. "I might be later than usual."

"I'll see you when I see you."

"That works for me. Good night." Faith left the restaurant, busily formulating her plans to spend the night with Brandon.

Brandon waved good-bye to Michelle, the last person to leave the restaurant, then looked down the street toward Casa de Serenidad. He could be there in minutes. And if Faith was in her room they could be naked and in bed in nothing flat, doing all the things he remembered and all the things he'd fantasized about.

Michelle hooked the horn of her Volkswagen Beetle and waved as she passed. Brandon absently waved, took one last longing look toward Faith and a temptation that was becoming more difficult to resist with each breath, then turned to go back inside, hoping the image of Faith willing and wanton in his arms didn't haunt him, so he could sleep.

"Aren't you going to invite me in?"

He whirled. Faith was less than five feet away and closing the distance fast. "Where did you come from?"

"Back there." She pointed over her shoulder. "Can I come in? I thought tonight was as good a time as any to see your apartment."

What she said sounded reasonable, but with all the erotic thoughts he had been having of them making love, it would play hell with his determination to resist her.

Her smile faded when he didn't reply. "I'm sorry. I didn't think." Tucking her head, she started past him.

He caught her arm. His hand flexed. On its own accord, his thumb stroked the soft, warm skin beneath. "Didn't think what?"

She shook her head and remained silent.

"Faith." His other hand lifted her chin. Agony stared back at him. "Please tell me what you meant."

She swallowed. The words tumbled over her trembling lips. "That you'd have another woman waiting for you in your apartment."

The thought was so far-fetched, so idiotic, he couldn't wrap his mind around it. His mouth firmed. His hold tightened. "Is that your opinion of me? You think I'd make love to you one night and jump into bed with another woman the next?"

Down went her head again. "Maybe it wasn't as good for you."

His eyes widened. She'd blown the top of his head off.

Holding her arm firmly, he pulled her inside the

restaurant, slamming and locking the doors. Grabbing her arm again, he hurried up the stairs and into his room. He didn't release her until he had taken her into the bathroom and the walk-in closet before finally stopping in the middle of his bedroom. "Do you see another woman anywhere?"

She shook her head.

"I didn't hear you."

"No."

"That's right, and do you know why?" he barked out.

She started to shake her head, stopped, bit her lip, and said, "Because you wait longer between women?"

If she hadn't looked so miserable, so utterly lovely, he might have dragged her back downstairs and slammed the door with her on the outside.

Instead, he did something much worse. He told the truth. "Because you have managed to do what no other woman ever has . . . invade my thoughts and haunt my dreams. Because after loving you there isn't room to think of another woman. Because when I'm inside you, it's the most perfect moment of my life."

Utter joy started in Faith's eyes and spread until she glowed with happiness. Laughing, she launched herself into his arms, letting her kisses fall where they may. Weak fool that he was, Brandon caught her, swinging her around, letting her happiness sink into him and erase his anger.

Then she went in for the kill, wrapping her legs around him and fastening her mouth to his. Brandon went from warm to hot in warp speed. One arm curved under her hips, the other around her back. He tried to remember where they were in reference to the bed and couldn't.

It would take a man with more willpower than he possessed at the moment to break the kiss and look. It was pure blessed luck that the backs of his legs bumped the foot of the bed. He plopped down. With his hands free, he moved them both to her hips. He encountered bare flesh. Further investigation revealed a thong under the tiered skirt.

Faith had been right. She might kill him, but what a way to go. Reluctantly he broke the kiss, his mouth trailing down the curve of her chin to the lush swell of her breast. He nuzzled, then used his teeth to pull the single strap of her knit top lower on her shoulder to reveal more of the tempting flesh. But not enough.

Unable to wait a second longer, his teeth fastened on the pebbled nipple through the material. She whimpered. He wanted to. "Hold tight with your left arm." As soon as she did as he requested, he slowly pulled the strap off her right arm, his eyes watching the slow emergence of her breasts. "Magnificent."

Locking his arms around her waist, he went back to lovingly devouring her breasts, savoring them as he licked and suckled, driving them both closer to the point when they'd each want more, demand more.

Faith twisted against him, thrusting her breasts. "Brandon. Please."

Gathering her in his arms, he stood and made his

way to his dresser. Mercifully he found the condom on his first groping try, then made his way back to the bed. "Can you unbuckle my belt?"

She didn't have to be asked twice. She unbuckled and managed to shove his slacks over his hips. Her hand came back up to cup him, causing him to harden even more, his legs to tremble.

"Stop that."

She nipped his ear. "Can I later?"

He was counting on it. Hooking his finger in the band of her thong, he tried to pull it down, but the material proved difficult.

"I have lots," she said, nipping his bottom lip.

He snapped the waistband, then plopped on the bed. He kicked off his loafers, pants, and under-shorts. If he didn't get inside her soon, he was going to blow. He tore the wrapper on the condom.

"Can I do it?"

He was hanging on the edge of control by his fingernails. He didn't want to wait a second longer than necessary. He held it out to her.

She gave him a smile, took the condom, then stood and wiggled out of her tiered skirt. Brandon, already teetering on the edge, grabbed a fistful of bedding and gritted his teeth as she knelt in front of him. She picked him up in her hand and just stared. She started to lower her head.

"Faith." Her name was a desperate groan of warning.

She looked up at him through a sweep of dark

lashes. Her gaze held a promise that later she'd have her way.

Positioning the condom, she slowly rolled it down, smoothing it as she went, her lower lip tucked between her teeth as if getting it just right was the most important thing in the world. He was sure that for the rest of his life, when he saw her tuck her lip, he'd think of this moment. As soon as she reached the base, he reached for her, setting her on his lap and driving into her hot, moist center.

Sensations rocketed through him. From the rapt expression on Faith's face, she was experiencing the same wildly intense emotions. There had never been a woman his body and mind were so attuned to. Slowly he began to move, in and out, stroking, pumping, loving, until they shattered together.

His arms wrapped around her as if never wanting to let go. In the slow seconds that followed, as he held her limp body, he accepted the truth he had been trying to run from.

For as long as it lasted, he wanted Faith in his life, his bed.

Angling his head, he kissed the top of hers, the slope of her shoulder. "You want to shower?"

She lifted her head and smiled at him. He'd never seen anything so beguiling. "I'd rather make love again."

"I figured we'd do both."

# 17

"I think it looks absolutely perfect." Barefoot and wearing one of Brandon's black T-shirts, Faith curved her arm around his trim waist and surveyed the sitting area in the living room.

The large rectangular ecru-colored rug on the pine hardwood floor pulled the area together. To the left of the newly covered oyster-colored sofa was a large palm that would thrive from the light shining through the window directly behind it. The vivid green leaves stood out in the room in tones of beige and black.

Brandon kissed the top of her tousled head. "Thanks to you."

"I'm glad you like it." She glanced around, happy that she had been able to make his living space more comfortable and inviting, then said, "I especially like the shower."

Chuckling, he curved his arms around her waist. "Same here. We'll have to try the Roman tub next time. You can have your candy with champagne, if you'd like."

"I'd just like you."

"You can have me any way you want."

She shivered in anticipation. Brandon naked was truly an awesome sight, and so arousing. He wore only jeans now and was still impressive. Bronzed muscles rippled as his arms tightened around her. "It wasn't part of the original plans."

He shrugged. "It just came to me, or perhaps I envisioned you naked in it."

Her heart melted. Staring up at him, she couldn't imagine loving him any more. She palmed his cheek. "You first."

He kissed her palm. "I'll see what I can do. For now, we need to get you back home."

Faith pushed out of his arms. "Not yet."

Brandon put his hands on his hips. "Don't be stubborn."

She shook her head and glanced at the black case holding the tenor saxophone. She'd moved it from the far corner of the room and leaned it against the arm of the sofa. "It's early. I was hoping you'd play for me."

"I haven't played in years. The sound would probably hurt your ears. Besides, it's past one in the morning. We might escape gossip with having you back before two, but anything past that and it's a sure bet people will know what we've been doing," he said bluntly.

She folded her arms and lifted her chin. "I'm a grown woman."

"Yes, you are." His hot gaze roamed greedily over her body. "You're also the woman who was steamed to have her privacy invaded."

Her arms fell to her sides. "That's because I didn't want you to get the wrong impression."

He closed the distance between them, pulled her into his arms, and stared down into her mutinous face. "I don't want people to get the wrong impression about you. You're too sweet and softhearted not to be hurt."

She splayed her hands on his chest. "They'll think we made love, in any case."

"What they know and what they can prove are two different things." Catching her hand, he headed for the bedroom. "No one is going to gossip about my woman and, if they do, they'll be looking for a dentist or the nearest hospital."

Faith gasped and came to an abrupt halt.

Brandon stopped and stared back at her. "What's the matter now?"

"You . . . you called me your woman." She whispered the words as if to say them louder might negate their power and worth.

Lines radiated across Brandon's forehead. "I did?"

Afraid he'd retract his statement, she nodded.

He rubbed his chin, considered. "You're sure?"

Swallowing, her hands clenched, she nodded again.

"Well, then," he drawled. "Since I'm a man of my word it must be true."

"Oh, Brandon." She kissed him once before he pulled her arms from around him and shoved her into his bedroom.

"Behave and get dressed." The door closed on Faith, a dreamy expression on her face.

Hand in hand, Brandon and Faith strolled to the hotel. A few feet from the entrance, his hand moved to her elbow. The interested and approving gazes of the valet, the doorman, Esmeralda working the front desk, and a few guests followed them as they made their way past the entrance to the outside courtyard.

Brandon again linked his fingers with Faith's. She leaned her head on his shoulder. "I think the wide smile on my face might have given us away."

"Since, hopefully, I helped put that look on your face, I'll share the blame." He opened the wooden gate and they continued to her front door.

She unlocked the door and curved her arms around his neck. "How much time before they start thinking you-know-what?"

He kissed her nose. "Not enough for what you're thinking."

She nipped his chin and let her lower body sink against his. "Why don't we find out?"

"Behave." Pulling her arms down, he urged her inside, then stiffened on seeing the floral arrangement on the coffee table. The thing spread three feet if it was an inch and must have cost a small fortune. "So that's it."

"I thought about giving it away, but I didn't think it seemed right somehow." She shrugged. "The orchid you gave me is in my bedroom. It will be the last thing I see before I go to sleep and the first thing I see when I wake up."

His chest felt tight. "You're an amazing woman."

"That's because you're an amazing man." She rested her hands on his wide chest. "Henrí is preparing a new quiche dish for me in the morning. How about joining me?"

His hands bracketed her face; his thumb traced her lower lip. "I don't think Henrí likes me."

Her tongue grazed his thumb. "*I* do."

His restraint snapped. His mouth took hers in a long, deep kiss. When he lifted his head, they both were breathing heavily. "How about I meet you at nine? Afterward we can go for a drive, then attend the Summer Arts Festival. Perhaps you'll find another artist you'd like for the hotel."

"I'd like that."

One last kiss and he left. By the time he was two steps out the door he was whistling.


Faith had spent a day that she would never forget and it wasn't over yet. Breakfast with Brandon had been wonderful, the drive in the mountains spectacular, strolling past the various art displays, ranging from limited-edition animated watercolors, to tribal textiles, to fine ceramics, humbling, but none compared to where she was now: sitting at the Grayson family booth.

Faith wrapped her hands around her diet cola and tried not to fidget. When Brandon dropped her off at her hotel, he'd invited her over for a late dinner. She'd accepted before the words were barely out of his mouth. On arriving a little after nine, she'd expected to be seated at a table.

Instead, the smiling hostess had shown Faith to the family table. The surprise must have shown on her face. They'd sat there the night Brandon fixed dinner for them, but she thought that was because it was closer to the kitchen. The young woman had taken her drink order and said she'd let Brandon know she had arrived.

In seconds, Marlive was there with a diet cola. "Hi, Ms. McBride. Brandon is finishing up an order and will be out shortly. Do you want to order or wait?"

Faith wrapped her hands around the drink. "I'll wait."

Marlive nodded. "I'll bring chips and salsa. If you change your mind, just catch the attention of any of us."

"Thank you." Faith flipped through the menu, trying to reconcile her mind to where she was. Brandon dated a lot of women; so had his brothers . . . except

Luke. The family table was usually reserved for the family. Rumors and speculation had started flying when Luke and Catherine, then Morgan and Phoenix, were seen sitting there. Both women had married the two elusive bachelors.

"Here you go." Marlive set the food on the table along with a glass of water. "Still want to wait?"

"Yes, thank you."

"No problem. If you need anything, holler." Marlive moved away.

Faith followed the direction the other woman took and saw Brandon coming toward her. Her heart swelled with love. Who wouldn't love a caring man who was also drop-dead gorgeous, sexy, and built like a warrior?

He slid into the booth beside her, their bodies touching from their shoulders to their thighs. He leaned over and whispered, "Keep looking at me like that and I'll have to close the place down early."

"Promises, promises," she teased back, earning her a bark of laughter from Brandon. It felt good being able to tease him, to know she could make him laugh.

He put his hand on the table, brushing lightly against hers. "What would you like?"

"You can't be serious," she said, her brow arched.

He chuckled, then said softly, "That comes later."

Her body tingled with anticipation. "In that case, I'll put myself in your hands."

"I'm counting on it." His voice stroked her.

She gulped her drink.

"Will you be all right by yourself? A lot of people don't like dining alone." He frowned. "I'll come back as much as I can, but things happen. I guess I didn't think past having you here."

No one had ever said anything as wonderful. "That's as far as I got to, being here with you."

His gaze dropped to her lips, then slowly lifted. "I'll be back as soon as I can. We close at ten on Sunday, so the place should be cleared out by ten thirty."

"Which means eleven," she offered. "We have until two, and I'm sure we won't waste a second of the time."

"Count on it." Brandon slid out of the booth and went back to the kitchen.

Brandon's crew must have sensed his urgency, because they worked like Trojans to have the place cleared out and cleaned up in record time. By 10:33 he let Michelle out and locked and bolted the door. He grabbed Faith's hand, and they ran up the stairs and into his room. She was in his arms, his mouth devouring her, by the time the door closed.

Her hand went to his belt. He unfastened her skirt. He toed off his loafers. She stepped out of her heels as they moved toward the bedroom. He slipped her blouse over her shoulders. She let his shirt fall to the floor. With her in black lace bra and bikini panties and him naked, he picked her up and stepped into his bedroom.

"Look."

Faith glanced over her shoulder and gasped. The bed was covered with white rose, gardenia, and orchid petals. Tears crested in her eyes. "Brandon, it's beautiful."

"So are you." He placed her among the fragrant ivory petals, then took a creamy orchid petal in his hand and brushed it across her lips. "Ever since I saw you do that, I've wanted to do that and much more to make you scream in ecstasy."

"Show me."

"With pleasure." He stared at her a few minutes longer simply because he couldn't help himself. She moved him in so many ways. It was both powerful and humbling to have her submit her body to his with such complete trust.

He gave in to the urge and trailed the petal once again across her lips; his own lips followed. He inhaled her warm breath, which trembled over her slightly parted lips, caught her sigh of pleasure on his tongue. Without looking, he knew she'd closed her eyes, her senses savoring each touch.

He unfastened her bra and ran the petal down the slope of her breast to the turgid point of her nipple. He moistened the point with his tongue, then blew. Faith arched, her hands lightly cupping his head. Heeding her need, he lavished kisses on the glistening peak before going to the other one. She twisted beneath him, her legs moving restlessly, her moist center brushing maddeningly against his full erection.

Gulping air to maintain control, he began to move the petal downward, his mouth following, pausing at the indentation of her navel, going lower still to the waistband of her panties. Impatient, he slipped them off. He came back to the inside of her thighs, the beckoning nest of dark curls.

He replaced the petal with his mouth. Faith's sharp intake of air cut through the room. Her hips arched off the bed. She clutched at Brandon's head, then the sheets.

"Brandon." His name was a wild, restless cry of rapture on her lips.

Her cry excited him, drove him on. He was relentless. He loved her, worshipped her.

Soon he felt her body tighten. Lifting his head, he fastened his mouth to hers, joining them with one powerful thrust. Sensations rocketed through him. Her scream of release, the clench of her muscles around him, pleasured him as nothing else ever had.

Cupping her hips, he surged into her tight sheath again and again, bringing her to a second, a third orgasm before he let himself find his own release. For a long time, the only sound was their labored breathing.

Faith felt boneless yet powerful. She had been thoroughly loved. Each time was better than the one before. Ripples of pleasure still washed over her. Brandon lay sprawled on her, his head tucked between the curve of her shoulder and chin. Weakly, she stroked his damp back, wishing they could always be like this.

"Brandon."

He lifted his head. He looked at her with passion and possession. "Yes?"

Her heart swelled with love. For this time he was hers and hers alone. "You certainly know how to fulfill a promise."

"I haven't finished." Good at his word, he proceeded to take her on another long, hot ride of ecstasy.

Each day afterward for Faith was sweeter than the one before. She wanted to pinch herself to make sure she wasn't dreaming. She and Brandon had breakfast every morning and were together every night at her place or his. They'd even managed to take in a movie and go to the theater. She'd cooked dinner for them again with help from Henrí, but she hadn't breathed easy until Brandon had taken a bite of his roast pork tenderloin. She'd never forget what he said. "Forget Henrí, how about I hire you?"

She'd kissed him and the meal was an hour late while they feasted on each other. She'd never grow tired of being with Brandon, seeing him smile, loving him. She knew she walked around with a goofy smile on her face and she didn't care.

The only thing that would make things perfect

was if Brandon loved her. He cared, but she wanted to be more than another lover. She tried not to be greedy when she'd already been given much more than she had ever thought possible, but she was finding that it was impossible not to want a lifetime instead of weeks.

Checking her lipstick and hair in the bathroom, the next morning Faith dropped her compact in her bag and headed for her office door. She was meeting Brandon for lunch. She'd be busy well into the night with several events at the hotel. Since he didn't like her coming to his apartment after eleven, she'd given him the key to her place. The knock on her door came just as she was about to leave. Hoping she could get rid of whoever it was quickly, she opened the door.

"Phoenix."

Phoenix glanced at the handbag in Faith's hand. "I knew I should have called, but I thought I'd just drop by since I'm having lunch with Morgan."

"That's quite all right." Faith stepped back. "Please have a seat."

Phoenix entered the office but continued to stand. "I won't hold you. I just wanted to tell you I'm in on the art project."

Faith squealed. "This is wonderful. Which pieces?"

"*Defender* and two new pieces," Phoenix told her.

"This is more than I had hoped for. Critics around the world have wanted to see *Defender*, the bust of Morgan, since its only public showing was the night of your first opening," Faith said. "I can't thank you enough. I have the press release ready in hopes you'd come on board. I'll send it out as soon as I return from lunch."

"I won't keep you," Phoenix said. "I'm meeting Morgan at Brandon's restaurant."

Butterflies took flight in Faith's stomach. "I'm meeting Brandon there for lunch."

"Wonderful. Would you like to ride over with me?"

The butterflies settled. Phoenix's warm smile didn't falter. She might suspect something, but there was no way for her to be sure that Faith and Brandon were having an affair. Faith wasn't sure if she wanted Brandon's family to know. She couldn't be 100 percent sure they'd approve. She was nothing like the shapely, artistic women Mrs. Grayson had chosen for her two older sons.

"Is there a problem?" Phoenix asked, her brows puckered.

"No. Everything is fine." Faith indicated Phoenix should precede her out the door. As she walked beside the svelte, beautiful woman Faith's earlier happiness plummeted. She'd been fooling herself. She might have Brandon for a season, but not a lifetime.

The Red Cactus was jumping and so was the staff. Brandon hadn't had time to take a breath since the restaurant opened. Two busloads of women shoppers heading for the Santa Fe Premium Outlets had stopped to eat lunch before they hit the stores. They were a friendly, fun group, but trying to feed that many and get them out together was challenging, especially when many of them wanted separate checks . . . after the tab had been rung up.

"They're starting to get antsy, boss," Luis said.

Brandon blew out a breath. What a time for Michelle to have a dental appointment. "Tell them it will be just a few moments longer."

"Will do." Luis turned away only to turn back. "Faith and Phoenix just came in."

Brandon's hand racing over the computer screen stopped. "Please tell Faith to come here."

Brandon had finished the ticket and picked up another by the time Faith arrived. "Hi. You want to save my sanity?"

"What can I do?"

No questions. No "maybe." Faith was the most generous, caring woman Brandon had ever met. He quickly explained the problem. "The separate food items are circled. Just punch it into the computer and give to the waiter. Use the computer next to mine."

Faith picked up a receipt and moved to the computer next to Brandon's. He watched her for a few seconds.

"Instead of watching me you should be working."

Luis smothered a laugh.

"Yes, ma'am." Brandon went back to work. Together they had the new receipts printed out in minutes. Faith didn't even surprise him when she went to the various tables to give the women their receipts and collect payment. She did surprise him when she enlisted Sierra, who had arrived several minutes earlier, to tell the women the best places in the outlet mall to shop.

Sierra went one better by recommending Casa de Serenidad as the place to stay to relax and enjoy the city. Somehow they pulled Phoenix into the act as a renowned artist. After one woman asked for her autograph, others wanted it as well. The bus left thirty-five minutes later than planned, the women vowing if they didn't close the outlet stores they'd come back through to eat.

"You three make a good team," Brandon said.

"Feed us and prove it," Sierra said.

Brandon threw one arm around Phoenix and the other around Faith. "Do you think she will ever grow out of being bossy?"

"It's called assertiveness," Faith said, surprising herself.

Sierra applauded. "That will show him."

They all went to the family table. Pierce and Morgan showed up moments later and sat in the booth with Phoenix. Brandon slid in next to Sierra and Faith, then picked up her hand. "Thanks."

"You're welcome." Faith tucked her head, pulled her hand free and placed both hands in her lap.

Brandon frowned until he noticed his brothers and sister staring at him. *Caught.* "So what will everyone have?"

Brandon took the orders and went to put them in

instead of giving them to Marlive, since the restaurant had calmed down. He needed a minute to himself. Reaching for Faith had been instinctive. If she hadn't pulled her hand back, he would have kissed her palm. They were two consenting adults enjoying each other. He didn't want Sierra and Pierce making more of it than it was. He certainly didn't want Faith to feel embarrassed or uneasy around them.

"Boss, cancel Faith's order. She needed to get back to the hotel," Marlive said on passing.

Brandon rushed back outside, but she was already gone. "What happened?"

"She said she had forgotten an appointment and left," Morgan said, watching Brandon closely. "Faith never impressed me as the forgetful type."

Brandon's gaze cut to Sierra, then Pierce. Both innocently held up their hands.

"I like Faith," Phoenix offered. "I'm going to enjoy working with her on the art project. She seems fun and intelligent."

"That and more. I'll be back in a minute." He went to his office and called her cell and got her voice mail. "Remember to eat, and I'll see you tonight. Miss you." He hung up, realizing how much he did. The precious time they were together couldn't come fast enough. First, he had to have it out with Pierce and Sierra.

"How could you have done this?" Pierce asked as soon as Morgan and Phoenix left the table.

Sierra picked up the attack. "You beat Luke and Morgan's record for falling."

"Whoa." Brandon slid into the booth facing his baby sister and brother. "Faith is a great woman and I enjoy being with her, but it's not for a lifetime."

Sierra looked at Pierce, then leaned across the table and rapped Brandon's head.

He batted her hand away. "Stop that."

"I was just seeing if you had air instead of gray matter." She folded her arms. "Men."

"Brandon, how could you? I wonder if Mama knows she can start celebrating her latest victory." Morose, Pierce drained his glass of raspberry tea.

"You two have been in the sun too long, and let's leave Mama out of this." Brandon braced his arms on the table. "I tell you, we're just enjoying each other."

Sierra tsked. "That's why you were all over her, playing with her hand, looking proud and cocky."

"I was not."

"Afraid so," Pierce said. "Luke and Morgan looked the same way when they fell."

"And denied it just as vehemently." Sierra shook her head in disgust. "Only a man wouldn't know when he fell in love."

"Will you stop saying that?" Brandon hissed. "I am not in love."

"You're so far gone you can't even see it." Sierra frowned at Pierce. "As analytical as you are, you won't figure it out until you're halfway down the aisle of the chapel."

"That's precisely why I *won't* fall," declared Pierce.

"I have not fallen," Brandon told them, tired of repeating himself. His mouth was compressed in a thin line.

Sierra threw her hands up in the air. "You're in deep denial, and to think I helped in your downfall."

Brandon stared at her. "What are you talking about?"

"Faith came to me about the time she started dating and asked for my help in updating her looks. I knew she was after a man, but I didn't know it was you."

Brandon felt on firmer ground. "Now I know you're wrong. Faith asked me to teach her how to get a man. She wasn't after me."

Sierra rolled her eyes. "I'd rap you again if your head wasn't so hard. She used the oldest trick in the book, jealousy, to get to you."

Brandon was already shaking his head. "You're wrong, Sierra. She changed her mind. She didn't want my help."

"It pains me that a brother of mine is so gullible. Her refusal brought out your protective instincts and made you look at her not just as the little sister of your best friend but as a desirable woman." Sierra sat back with a smug smile. "Catherine might be a psychologist, but any woman worth her mettle knows the best way to attract the attention of a man is to dangle in his face what another man wants."

Pierce whistled. "You scare me sometimes."

"Remember that and put up a better fight than Brandon." She picked up her purse and stood. "If I didn't love you and like Faith, I'd disown you."

Pierce came to his feet as well. "You didn't have to ask, but I'll be your best man. On second thought, I'll pass. I'd probably cry all through the ceremony knowing I'm next. It's a good thing I'm not a drinking man."

Brandon continued to sit at the table alone, the chatter and noise of the restaurant fading to a distant drone. They were wrong. They had to be. Faith was too honest. She wouldn't have tricked him.

# 18

Faith was nervous. She wiped her sweaty palm on her skirt and hurried home along the walkway. After Brandon had taken her hand in his and then left to turn in the food orders, she'd been too aware of the speculative looks from his family to stay. They'd known something was going on. She wanted their approval so much and had been too much of a coward to stay and find out if she had it.

She was barely out the door when she'd received a call from Brandon. At the time she was still too unsure to pick up. What worried her was that he hadn't called again. It was half past eleven. He should be waiting.

Passing through the gate, she opened her front door. Brandon sat on the sofa, facing her. His head lifted. If she'd seen an angrier man, she didn't remember when.

Her first thought was that she'd left out her book with the *Operation Get Brandon* written in bold letters until she recalled putting it up the night before. "What's the matter?"

"You know the answer to that better than I do."

Uneasiness crept through her. She tossed her notebook on the side chair and knelt in front of him. "I don't understand."

"Let me enlighten you. I'm through being used." His cold eyes drilled into her.

Her uneasiness turned into panic. Needing to touch him, to somehow take the anguish from his face and his voice, to make things as they had been between them, she placed her trembling hand on his thigh. "Used? Brandon, what are you talking about?"

"You schemed to let me think you were interested in another man when all along I was your target."

Her breath caught. Icy fear clutched at her heart as she stared at his closed, angry face. The way he said it made it sound wrong. "You weren't a target. I wanted you to look at me as a desirable woman and not as Cameron's little sister."

His accusing gaze bore into her. "You tricked me, used me. I trusted you."

Frantic, more frightened than she had ever been in her life, she placed her other hand on his thigh and searched for the words that would make him understand. "Brandon, please. I might have gone about it the wrong way, but I was desperate and so afraid you'd fall in love before I had a chance."

"There is no excuse for what you did."

"I love you. I've always loved you. Please believe me," she pleaded.

"Like a fool, I believed your lies once. Never

again." He brushed her hands from his legs and rose to his feet. "Good-bye, Faith."

Her chest felt as if it were in a vise. Unsteadily she came upright, her eyes and voice pleading. "Brandon, please try to understand. I did it because I love you."

"If you call that love, I don't want it." He walked out without a backward glance.

Desolate, tears streaming down her cheeks, Faith crumpled to the floor. Brandon was gone. This time he wasn't coming back.

Faith woke up groggy, in the fetal position on the sofa. Brandon walking out on her came rushing back. Whimpering, she curled tighter. She'd considered going after him, begging him to please try to understand. In the end, all she'd been able to do was drag herself to the sofa and cry. She'd cried herself to sleep only to wake up with tears on her cheeks to cry some more and repeat the ritual.

She'd lost the only man she'd ever love. She'd never ached as deeply or felt as hopeless, yet the world went on. Sun shone through the sheers in her room, her staff was getting ready for the day, and Brandon . . . She bit her lip. Was he up? Was he still angry? Sitting up, she put her feet on the floor.

If she didn't get moving soon, she never would. The only way to fight the crippling pain was to fill her mind with things other than the anger on Brandon's face when he walked out. Pushing to her feet, she picked up the notebook from the side chair and flipped to her agenda for the day.

Tears formed and dropped on the page. *Breakfast with Brandon.* Her fingertips brushed over the words; then she went down farther and stopped on *Media alert/Santa Fe Arts Council.* Her head fell.

Once Phoenix learned Faith and Brandon were at odds, she might withdraw her support. Faith had already spoken with the president of the arts council. He had been ecstatic about the idea of bringing art to the hotel guests, bridging the gap to people who might not have time to visit art galleries to sample the creativity of Santa Feans' work.

Now that might never happen. Ruth Grayson and Morgan were on the arts council and had powerful family connections in Felicia Falcon and her son, Daniel. Besides destroying any chance for happiness for herself, Faith might have jeopardized her plans for the art partnership. The day was going to be a rough one.


Brandon had been determined to sleep in his bed, to ignore the emptiness of his arms, the need for Faith pulsing through him. He'd succeeded from sheer force of will until shortly after six that morning. Deciding that was as good as it was going to get, he headed to the bathroom.

Showering had tested his control further, as he'd

lathered and recalled Faith's hands running over his body, his hands over hers, lifting her breasts, kissing them, sucking them.

Desperately he sought something else to think about. What came to him was much worse: Faith with tears sparkling in her eyes, saying she loved him and begging him to stay. His stomach churned. He slapped his hand against the wall.

"Faith." Her name was a hoarse whisper of sound, a groan of denial that he still cared, that her tears could bring him to his knees. Wrenching the faucet to off, he stepped out of the shower, telling himself that she was the cause of her own tears. But as he dressed and went downstairs to his office, the cause didn't seem to matter as much as the irrefutable knowledge that, regardless of why, she was hurting.

Precisely at 9:00 that morning, Faith called Phoenix. Yesterday on the way to Brandon's restaurant, Phoenix told Faith that she and Morgan always had breakfast together before he left for work. At the time, Faith had thought of how she and Brandon did the same.

"Hello."

For a moment Faith couldn't speak. She swallowed convulsively.

"Faith, is that you?"

Glad at least that Morgan apparently had Caller ID and Phoenix hadn't hung up, Faith finally managed to speak. "Yes. Good morning, Phoenix."

"Are you all right?" The other woman's concern came clearly through the line.

*I'm not sure I'll ever be all right again.* "This . . . this is about your partnership with Casa de Serenidad. Brandon and I . . . had . . . We're not friends anymore." Her voice broke, but at least she'd gotten it out.

There was a long pause, then, "I'm sorry; is there anything I can do?"

"I wish there was." She took a sip of water for her dry throat. "If you want to withdraw your sculptures from the project, I understand."

"The art stays. Have you finalized a date?"

Faith wished Phoenix's support helped her feel less like putting her head on her desk and bawling. "The third Sunday in June, as you requested. I'm meeting with the president of the arts council and members of the media this afternoon at four in the Matador Room."

"I'll be there with *Defender.* If Morgan is free, I'll bring him."

It was more than she expected. "Morgan might—"

"If possible, he'll be there. I'd better get to work. Bye!"

"Good-bye, and thanks." She hadn't thought of Phoenix as the assertive type. Faith almost smiled; then she thought of Brandon and felt tears roll down her cheeks.

◆ ◆ ◆

"Tell me you didn't do what your face says you did."

Brandon didn't look up from his desk. Sierra had come inside with one of the early staff members before the restaurant opened. "Don't you have an appointment or something?"

"I have never understood why men are so long on pride and short on common sense," she huffed.

"If you'll go to the kitchen, I'm sure Antonio would be happy to fix you fresh tamales."

Her hand came down in the middle of the schedule for his staff. It remained there until he lifted his head. Her face softened. "I never would have said anything if I had known you would break up with her. I don't want to see either of you hurt."

"I know." He moved her hand aside and went back to staring at the schedule that he hadn't made any headway on in the hour he'd been working on it.

"Faith will probably never forgive me."

His hand clenched on the desk. "Your name wasn't mentioned. Besides, she's the reason we're not together."

Sierra rounded the desk and swiveled his leather executive chair around until she faced her. "If she hadn't decided to shake things up, you'd still be dragging your feet and dreaming about some mysterious woman."

"She was the woman," he confessed. Since he and

Faith had made love, his dream woman's identity had become clear.

"See, even your subconscious knew." Sierra picked up the phone. "Call and invite her to lunch."

He took the phone and replaced it. "I don't like being manipulated. I was so busy trying to avoid a trap Mama set for me, I didn't see the one Faith set."

"That's not going to be any comfort on a long lonely night."

Brandon threw her a look. She snorted in disgust. "I know about desires even though I'm not indulging."

He came to his feet. "You'd better not."

Shaking her head, she went to the door. "Do as I say and not as I do, huh? Big brothers should be banned. One final word: did you forget that Faith is Duncan and Cameron's little sister?"

The door closed and Brandon took his seat. He hadn't forgotten, but somehow his need of her overshadowed every other consideration. He'd deal with her brothers when the time came.

Now he was more concerned with how to stop thinking about Faith every waking moment, and wondering if she still had tears in her eyes.

It was the longest day of Faith's life, and it was barely four in the afternoon. At least the Matador Room looked beautiful, with a fresh floral arrangement on the table surrounded by delectable goodies prepared by Henrí and his staff. No thanks to her.

That morning when she was going over the final details of the menu with Henrí she couldn't seem to stop crying. He'd finally said he'd take care of it and left muttering something about "if I had a gun."

She sniffed and nodded to the editor of *Santa Fean* magazine. It wasn't Brandon's fault. Perhaps she should have been bold enough to just tell him how she felt. She'd been too afraid of being rejected. He'd rejected her anyway. Her eyes teared at exactly the worst possible moment.

Into the room stepped Phoenix, Morgan, and his mother, Ruth. Faith sniffed, used the soggy tissue in her hand, and made herself move toward them. "Hello, everyone. Morgan, please put *Defender* on the pedestal in front by the podium so it will be easily seen during the news briefing."

None of them moved. Faith kept her gaze locked on Phoenix.

"Hello, Faith. I see you have summer allergies as well," Ruth said.

Faith's gaze whipped to Brandon's mother, serene and regal as usual. She wore her hair in a chignon, and a pale green suit with matching bag and shoes that would rival Sierra. Ruth had dressed to impress. Her eyes were clear, black, and so reminiscent of Brandon's that the tears Faith had been trying to control pooled again.

"Please take my handkerchief." Morgan handed her the white linen square. "I'll put this up."

"The president of the arts council couldn't make

it, so I volunteered," Ruth went on to say. "I so admire what you're trying to do. Since you're battling allergies, with your permission I'll take over this afternoon."

Tears crested and rolled down Faith's cheeks. She was afraid to open her mouth.

Phoenix took the handkerchief from Faith's hand and dried the tears from her cheeks. "You have our full support."

"Of course she does." Ruth patted Faith's hand in reassurance. "Please don't be concerned that you aren't at your best today. We share a vision, and together we'll achieve our goal."

"Yes, ma'am," Faith finally said. With their support, the success of the art project was almost assured. Faith's other vision, the one of her and Brandon together for a lifetime, was another matter entirely.

"Why don't you have a seat and I'll let everyone know we're ready to get started?" Ruth said. "Everything will be just fine. You'll see."

"Yes, ma'am." Faith took a seat, wishing with all her heart Ruth's prediction would come true, not just for the collaboration but for her and Brandon as well.

"Brandon, Mr. Montgomery tells me you had more than the bathroom renovations done. I can't wait to see the changes."

Late that afternoon Brandon trudged up the stairs ahead of his mother. She'd dropped by during the lull between the lunch and the dinner crowd and wanted to see the apartment. He unlocked the door and stepped back, trying to think if Faith had left any of her things there. Memories of her certainly hung around.

His mother stepped past him. In the kitchen, she ran her hand over the new details on the cherry cabinets, the extension of the island, pulled out the baskets on the hidden shelves beneath.

In the sitting area, she picked up a pillow he'd tossed aside and replaced it on the end of the sofa, lightly touched the saxophone case, tested the dryness of the dirt surrounding the plant. In his bedroom she studied the new leather headboard, the cherry bookcases already filled with books and keepsakes.

He tensed on seeing on the bottom shelf the crystal bowl of fading flower petals he'd saved and hadn't been able to throw away. He hoped his mother didn't notice them. When her gaze moved on, Brandon stuffed his hands in his pockets and tried not to look at the bed he and Faith had spent so many wonderful times together in.

Still silent, Ruth went to the bathroom. She stared into the shapely etched mirror, touched the sconces with the leafy design and glossy black finish on either side. She turned to see the matching black and brown striped fluffy towels on the nickel-plated rack Faith had insisted he take as a gift to replace his mismatched ones. That morning he'd been so intent on getting in and out of the bathroom, he hadn't remembered.

Leaving the bathroom, his mother went to his walk-in closet. Instead of the usual hodgepodge and jumble, his clothes, thanks to Faith, were now color coordinated and grouped. He didn't like to fuss with clothes. The organization now meant he didn't have to.

"Faith put her stamp on this place," his mother finally said.

Brandon's hands whipped out of his pockets. "What do you mean?"

"It's warm yet functional, with a touch of elegance," his mother explained. "You feel the same way at Casa de Serenidad."

Brandon relaxed. "I guess."

Her brow bunched. "Mr. Montgomery was under the impression that your stay at the hotel helped influence your decision to remodel and was the reason you asked Faith to help. Was he wrong?"

"No," Brandon quickly said. His mother was too sharp to let his mind wander.

She went back to the living area. "Are you playing the saxophone again? I hope so. Music should be shared."

Brandon's gaze snapped to the instrument against the sofa. "Faith put it there."

"I'm glad. I'd like to hear you play again." Ruth glanced around the room. "I can't imagine one thing different. I hope you thanked her. At the very least, sent her flowers," his mother continued.

A vision of Faith on a bed of flower petals, her arms outstretched, flashed before him. He'd kept the flower petals as a memento of that night. He wheeled and went to the kitchen. Pouring himself a glass of lemonade, he positioned himself behind the counter. Those were not the kinds of visions you had when your mother was present. "She got flowers. You want anything?"

"No, thank you." Ruth placed her purse on the granite counter. "You were always a gentleman and so thoughtful of others. You'll make a wonderful husband."

Brandon's glass hit the counter. "Please, Mama."

Her brow drawn, she rounded the counter. "Are you all right?"

"I'm fine." He managed a smile for her. "I'd better get back."

She studied him a long moment, then picked up her purse. "I can tell you're troubled by something, but I won't push. Just remember the answer to most of our problems is right before our eyes, if we'd just look. At least you have your place back, and it's better than ever. Good-bye."

Yeah, he had his place back, but his life was a mess.

Two days later the door to Brandon's office opened abruptly, then banged against the wall. He looked up, saw Duncan and Cameron, their expressions angry. He didn't need two guesses to know why they were there.

Brandon rose to his feet. He was just keyed up

enough to give them the fight they were probably spoiling for.

"Duncan. Cameron."

Duncan shoved the door closed, the sound reverberating around the room. "What the hell did you do to Faith?"

Brandon reached Faith's oldest brother in two long strides. "What's the matter with her? Is she all right? Dammit, answer me!"

"You tell us," Duncan said, punctuating each word with a finger in Brandon's chest. "Esmeralda called us because she was worried about Faith. She said she was crying at the drop of a hat, not eating, moping. We arrived last night, and Esmeralda was right."

Eyes narrowed, Duncan inched closer. "Esmeralda said Faith was happier than she's ever seen her when you two were dating. After you broke up, she's miserable."

"Henrí says you should be shot," Cameron added.

"Henrí should mind his own business, and that goes for you two as well," Brandon said.

"Protecting Faith *is* our business." Duncan jutted his chin. "How many times did you take her out?"

Brandon knew where her brother was heading, the sexual question behind it, and hesitated too long.

"You bastard!" Duncan's fist plowed into Brandon's chin, sending him sprawling to the floor. "Get up so I can hit you again. I trusted you. *We* trusted you. You shouldn't have touched her. You know the

McBrides are unlucky in love. You just used her for a good time and she was gullible enough to believe you."

Brandon saw red. He came off the floor like a bullet. His right hook knocked Duncan flat. Fists balled, Brandon stood over him. "Don't you dare say anything about Faith. She's the best there is. Any man would count his blessings if he caught her attention."

"Then you care about her?" Cameron asked mildly.

Brandon turned on him. "Of course I care about her. She's the air I breathe, the first thought I have in the morning, the last thought I have at night. She's . . ." Brandon's voice trailed off. He staggered back, turned, and plopped into his chair. "I can't be," he mumbled.

Cameron reached out and pulled Duncan to his feet. "From the shocked look on Brandon's face, I think the McBride luck has finally turned. Maybe there's hope for us to find love."

Brandon shuddered. "I'm not in love."

"Then you won't care that she's going out with another man tonight?" Cameron asked.

Brandon's eyes flashed dangerously. His mouth flattened into a thin, compressed line.

"Seems you're right, Cameron." Duncan reached for the doorknob. "Looks like Mrs. Grayson is three for three, but Brandon, if I were you, I wouldn't wait too long to tell Faith."

Brandon barely registered the closing of the door. He wasn't in love. He just cared about her. If she wanted to date someone else, that was her business. He started to reach for his pen and found his fist clamped around a cactus-shaped paperweight on his desk.

"Damn!"

Faith didn't want to attend the party, but it was a business mixer for people in the hotel industry. Esmeralda was scheduled to attend as well, but she said she didn't feel well and asked Faith to please take her place with her date. Faith wished she hadn't agreed. Carl Bright thought he was God's gift to women and was way too full of himself.

"Did I tell you that my family is one of the oldest in the city and among the wealthiest? I have relatives in key positions from the state to the nation's capital."

*Several times.* "Yes."

"I'm only in the city for a short time; then I'm heading back to New York, where the real action is, to run my import/export business." He leaned over and whispered, "It's making millions."

Esmeralda owed her for this. "I'm pleased for you."

Carl stared at her as if wondering why she wasn't suitably impressed. "Would you like a glass of wine?"

She was about to say no when Brandon came into the room with a tray of drinks, gorgeous and devastatingly handsome in a white dinner jacket. Her first instinct was to run to him and beg his forgiveness. She stiffened her spine instead. Her only crime had been in loving him. "Please."

Carl lifted his hand and snapped his fingers. "Over here."

Faith cringed. People around them frowned. Carl had the manners and subtlety of a rhinoceros. Where had Esmeralda gotten this guy?

"Here."

Brandon finally looked their way. His gaze dismissed Carl and seared Faith. She felt the punch all the way to her toes. He started toward them. Faith's grip on the wrap loosened, letting the shimmering red silk slide sinuously over her bare shoulders. The knee-length fitted gown molded her body. She wanted Brandon to see and remember every detail and know what he was missing.

From the slight pause, he was doing just that. Faith wished she could be happy about it. She couldn't because she was remembering what she was missing as well.

Stubborn man.

Taking two glasses of wine from the silver tray Brandon held, Carl gave one to Faith. "To us and a night we'll both remember."

Out of the corner of her eye she saw the dangerous expression on Brandon's face and was happy Carl could not. He might have fainted dead away. She tilted the glass to her lips but didn't drink.

Carl emptied his glass and took hers. He placed

both glasses back on the tray with a clink. "Shall we dance?"

Faith let him lead her to the dance floor. He pulled her into his arms, then put his sweaty hand in the small of her bare back. It was all she could do not to squirm or look at Brandon.

*I could be in his arms if he wasn't so stubborn.*


Brandon pictured the annoying man with Faith without his teeth, but as pleasing as that was, the man's arm was around Faith, his hand on her soft, fragrant skin. The only thing that kept Brandon from flattening the man was the irrefutable knowledge that it wasn't any of his concern any longer. Faith shouldn't have tried to trick him.

The man's hand slid lower, toward her hips. Brandon moved before he was aware of it.

"Where are you going with the drinks?"

Brandon jerked his head around to see Cameron. "That guy is making a move on Faith."

Cameron lifted a flute of champagne from the tray, then looked at his sister on the dance floor. "I don't see a problem."

"He has his hands all over her," Brandon bit out, only partially relieved that the song had ended and they were leaving the dance floor.

Cameron twirled the glass by the stem. "Why should you care where he had his hands?"

Brandon opened his mouth, then snapped it shut.

"It's about time Faith had a social life outside the hotel. She deserves a great guy, since you didn't want to stick around."

"Your chin is begging for my fist," Brandon snarled.

"Truth hurts." Cameron strolled off.

Brandon felt like following Cameron and dumping the tray of drinks over his head. He, of all people, should know how susceptible people on the rebound were. Faith was vulnerable. Brandon looked around for Duncan. Their older brother, like Luke, had always guided Cameron and Faith.

Less than a minute later, Brandon located Duncan. Brandon blinked, blinked again. Duncan had his arm around the shoulder of the jerk who earlier had his hands on Faith where they had no business being.

Disgusted, Brandon headed toward the kitchen to reassign serving duties. Unlike Faith's poor examples of brothers, he didn't shirk his duties as the caterer or as a friend. Seems it would be up to him to set the man straight.

But when he returned from the kitchen, Faith and the man were gone.

# 19

Unable to sleep, Faith wandered through her house. Memories of Brandon permeated every room, yet despite the pain his leaving caused, she'd never regret a moment spent with him. She'd been loved and cherished by the man she loved. She had been given a precious gift that she'd once thought she'd never have.

What had finally pulled her out of despair and given her hope was the conversation he'd had with her brothers earlier that day at his restaurant. They thought he cared, but he was just in shock. That she could understand.

Her revelation of always loving him had probably thrown him, perhaps more so since he was running from being next on his mother's list to marry off. That list had given Faith herself some bad times because she was sure her name wasn't on it.

But Mrs. Grayson loved her children more than anything. If Faith could show his mother that she was the best woman for Brandon, maybe she would give them her blessings.

The problem was, Brandon wasn't even speaking to Faith now, let alone ready to propose. Her only hope was that eventually he'd calm down and come to understand that she'd acted out of desperation and love, not deceit.

Her fingertips trailed over the memory book that held the first corsage he'd given her and the last flowers. He cared. The fact that he'd tried to protect her from Carl tonight proved as much. A small smile tilted her mouth upward.

Duncan had done that nicely. Carl's eyes bugged as Duncan, pretending to give him a manly hug, squeezed instead and whispered what he'd do to Carl if his hands wandered again. Her date had decided he had an early appointment in the morning and needed to leave immediately.

Duncan and Cameron had followed them all the way back to the hotel. As soon as Carl stopped and the valet opened her door, he'd pulled off with a squeal of brakes.

She'd commented that she'd lost another man and almost started crying again. Duncan and Cameron had put her in their rental and taken her to a sports bar to play pool. She might have lost the game, but a man had tried to pick her up and had given her his phone number. She sighed. She only wanted one man.

The sudden pounding on her door startled her.

Her head came up. Frightened, she reached for the phone. Then she heard Brandon's voice.

"Faith. Open this door."

A broad smile on her face, she ran to the door. In her haste her nervous fingers took longer than usual to operate the locks. Finally they clicked into place. She swung the door open, her arms reaching for Brandon, but he stalked past her.

"Where is he?" He didn't wait for her answer. He kept going, searching each room, opening the doors to her closets, her bathroom, dampening her enthusiasm.

*How dare he imply I had another man here.* She refused to dignify Brandon's question by following him. Leaving the front door open to show her displeasure, she waited for him to reappear.

"I called you several times."

Since his hands were on his narrow hips and his eyes narrowed, his comment meant he thought the worst of her. "There were no messages on my phone from you."

"I didn't leave any."

"How intelligent." A muscle leaped in his jaw. *Good.* "If you don't mind, I'd like to go to bed."

As if he had just realized she was dressed in a hot pink long satin robe and gown that caressed her body, his gaze slowly swept over her, pausing at the swell of her breasts, the junction of her thighs. Her body hungered, heated.

"Good night, Brandon."

His gaze snapped up. "I don't want you making a mistake on the rebound."

Any lingering goodwill or passion vanished. "So you think I'd jump into bed with the first guy to come along? I seem to remember you had a fit when I thought you were seeing another woman the night after we made love."

His hands clenched. She hoped he was visualizing them naked and driving each other wild with desire. "It's been over a week."

"So naturally I'd hook up with the first man to come along. Don't insult me further." She folded her arms. "Good night."

He hesitated, then headed for the door. When he was even with her, he stared down at her. She saw remorse when she wanted to see love. "I don't want you hurt."

Her throat constricted. He cared; he just didn't love her. She swallowed before she could speak. "It's a little late for that."

He flinched. "It can't be the way you want."

"Because you won't let it. Forget about being next on your mother's list to marry off, and just think of what we mean to each other," she said fiercely, her arms coming to her sides.

"How can I? You tricked me," he accused.

"Ugh. I made a mistake because I was desperate for you to look at me as a woman, to love me. I'm beginning to wonder why I thought I loved a man with such a narrow, one-track mind." With both hands, she shoved him out the door, and slammed it in his face, but not before she saw his shocked expression.

She marched to the bedroom to kneel in front of the blue porcelain wastebasket to search inside for the business card she'd thrown out earlier. Finding the card of the man she'd met at the sports bar, she sat back on her heels. *Randal Hemming, Hemming Restorations, President.* She'd call him tomorr— Her hand fisted, her head fell.

She'd been down that disastrous road before. The only man she was interested in was the pigheaded one she'd just tossed out her front door. She wasn't going to pretend interest in another man. It wouldn't be fair.

In the meantime, she was going to stop feeling sorry for herself, stop imitating a leaky faucet. She'd just have to hope and pray that Brandon got over his anger before his mother threw a potential bride in his path and *he* became the one on the rebound.


Brandon slammed doors all the way to his bedroom. Not one made him feel one iota better. He was too steamed. Instead of Faith being grateful that despite the way she'd betrayed his trust, he had tried to protect her, she had insulted him, then shoved him out the door.

No women had ever treated him so abominably. Just the opposite, they went out of their way to be friendly and accommodating. Not Faith. She hissed and spit like a cornered cat.

He jerked his shirt off and tossed it in the direction of the suit valet. Women. If he lived a million years he'd never understand how their illogical brains worked. Sitting on the bed, he yanked off his boots, then shucked his pants and Jockeys. Naked, he grabbed his pants and began emptying the pockets onto the brass tray connected to the valet, muttering to himself about ungrateful, unpredictable women.

"She should be thankful. I did so much for her. I . . ." He paused, stumbled, his brain trying to think of things he'd done for her.

There had to be plenty of things. He was just so angry he couldn't think straight. But the more he thought, the more he came up with things she'd done for him, each one more generous than the one before. The most precious thing was giving him her innocence.

His head hung. Even the bed of flower petals had been for his enjoyment as much as hers. The clothes valet had been her idea, after she'd seen how helter-skelter he tossed his clothes when he undressed. It shamed him that he couldn't think of one tangible thing he'd done to let her know how much she meant to him, that he valued her, her friendship, her smile . . . her love.

His head came up. He looked around as if afraid someone was there to hear the words his heart had spoken. "No. No." He shook his head in denial. That wasn't right. He cared about her. He didn't love her, because if he did that would mean the end of his freedom.


Midmorning, Faith was sitting in her office going over the budget the business manager had submitted to her when her phone rang. She glanced up to see that the call came from the front desk. She hit the speakerphone. "Yes?"

"Ms. McBride, you have a special delivery at the front desk."

"Please sign for it and send it back to my office," Faith said, running down the column of figures.

"The delivery requires your signature."

Faith's head came up; a small frown knit her brow. There had been laughter and something else in Grace's voice. Faith looked at the figures, then sighed. She'd been at this all morning. Perhaps she needed a break. "I'll be right out."

"Thank you."

Disconnecting the call, Faith left her office. It wasn't unusual that her personal signature was required on certain high-ticketed deliveries. However, she couldn't recall authorizing any such items recently. Rounding the corner leading to the front desk, she came to an abrupt halt, her mouth gaping.

Standing shoulder to shoulder were at least a dozen men and women. Each held a bouquet of flowers. The woman who had delivered Blade's earlier arrangement stepped from the end and held out an electronic pad. "Ms. McBride."

Somehow Faith got her feet to move. Her gaze went from one arrangement to the next, each one more beautiful than the one before. The flowers ranged from roses to orchids.

The deliverywoman grinned like a Cheshire cat as Faith signed her name. "Which one has the card?"

"No card this time," the deliverywoman said cheerfully. "He said you'd know eventually who sent them. I'm to give the message." She straightened her shoulders. " 'As I carry you in my heart, please pick which one you'll carry on our special day.' "

Faith gasped, then closed her eyes for a moment. How could Blade have done this to her? But even as the thought came to her, she knew it wasn't Blade. It had to be the unpredictable Shane.

"Where shall we put them?" asked the deliverywoman.

Faith looked at the beautiful arrangements and wished she had enough willpower to refuse the delivery. She didn't. "Half of you, please come with me to my office. The rest of you, please wait here." She started to her office. She'd call Shane to thank him, then tear a strip off his hide.

Two hours later, Faith hung up the phone. Blade was out of the country and his secretary wasn't sure how to reach Shane. Only Blade had his contact information. On impulse, she asked for Holt. It hadn't

taken long to discover Holt was almost as elusive as
Blade and Shane. She just hoped this was the last of
Shane's attempts to make Brandon jealous. His be-
ing protective couldn't compare with loving her.

The only thing the flowers had accomplished was
to make her the hot topic of gossip for the guests
and, unfortunately, the staff this time around. The lat-
ter was done with affection. Everywhere she'd gone
afterward, she received thumbs-ups or big grins. They
were happy for her.

After a brief knock, her office door opened.
Cameron and Duncan entered. She'd obtained them
rooms at a nearby hotel. Both whistled. "Brandon really knows how to grovel," Cameron said with a
chuckle.

Faith's heart winced. "Brandon didn't send them."

"Then who sent them?" Duncan asked, his smile
gone.

"A man who liked doing the unexpected." She
came around the desk. "How about a late lunch before you take off?"

Cameron and Duncan exchanged looks. Duncan
said, "Last time you were begging us to stay; now
you're rushing us to leave."

"Because I know Cameron has a race coming up
this week and it's time for you to harvest feed," she
said. "I love you both for coming here, but I'm going
to be all right." She held up her right hand. "Scout's
honor."

Cameron threw an arm around her shoulder. "If you aren't I'm going to pay a visit to a certain person who won't be happy when I leave."

"Cam—," she began.

"Nothing you can say will change our minds," Duncan said, cutting her off. "He only has a pass for now."

She looked at the stubborn expressions on their faces and knew they'd spoken the truth. But since they hadn't drilled her on who sent the flowers, she considered herself getting off lucky. "Let's go eat lunch."

Brandon's gaze narrowed on seeing Duncan and Cameron enter the Red Cactus. He moved toward them. It was safe to assume they hadn't come to pick a fight. "I'll take them." He picked up two menus. "Good evening. You want a table?"

"Nope. We'd like a moment of your time. The bar will do," Duncan said.

Replacing the menus, Brandon went to a quiet corner and pulled out a chair at a bar table. "What?"

Neither man sat. "Just thought we'd give some friendly advice," Cameron said.

"Seems you have some stiff competition," Duncan said, his face gleeful.

"I can tell you're really broken up by it." Brandon took a seat and placed his folded arms on the table.

"We're happy she's not moping over you any

longer." Cameron rocked back on his heels. "He filled Faith's office and her house with flowers."

"Why are you telling me?" Brandon asked, his face and voice giving away none of what he was feeling.

"Better the devil you know." Cameron slapped Brandon none too gently on the back. "But if you make her cry again, we'll come down on you like a hard rain. Bye now."

Duncan tipped his Stetson. "Bye."

Brandon eased back in his chair and watched the brothers walk away. They could have saved their breaths. He'd already made up his mind about Faith, and nothing on earth could make him change it again.

The next day Faith received another call. "Ms. Mc-Bride, you have another special delivery."

Faith's lips pursed. "Thank you," she said into the receiver of her headset, then disconnected her cell phone and turned to the head gardener for the hotel. "Please excuse me. I'll be back as soon as I can."

"Take your time, Ms. McBride. You think it's from him again?"

There was no sense being evasive or coy. "I don't know," she answered, and headed for the lobby, hoping it wasn't. Three steps inside the lobby, she knew it wasn't to be.

This time there were ten men and women. Each held a twenty-by-thirty poster of places around the world . . . a ski chalet in Switzerland, the Ritz in

Paris, a hidden cove on St. Thomas, and on and on. The last breathtaking photo was of the balcony of a Navarone Resort and Spa on Maui overlooking the Pacific Ocean. Her lips tightened. Oh, if she could just get her hands on Shane.

A smartly dressed middle-aged woman stepped forward and extended her hand. "I'm Cassandra Eldridge, owner of Unique Travels. I have a message for you."

"I bet," Faith said under her breath.

"The journey is important, but so is the destination. Choose one, choose them all, as I have chosen you to continue the journey of a lifetime," Cassandra finished, her voice unsteady.

Faith snorted. She wouldn't have thought Shane had a poetic bone in his hard body. Intelligent—extremely. Sensitive—no way. Perhaps he'd hired someone to write the words. He'd unwittingly picked spots she'd always wanted to travel to but never had time to do so. How had he been able to be so accurate?

A prickling sensation ran up her spine. Stepping around the travel agent, Faith went to each enlarged picture. She'd wanted to travel, planned to until her parents divorced and she took over running the hotel. The only person she'd admitted her longing to was Brandon, but that was years ago, while she was trying to deal with her parents' separation and pending divorce.

She hadn't wanted to add to Duncan's and Cameron's own pain or have them worry about her, so she'd said nothing to them. She'd confided in Brandon. He couldn't have remembered.

"Here is the packet of brochures. My card is attached."

Her hands trembling, Faith took the folder. "Thank you."

"My pleasure," the travel agent said with a little sigh. "He was so romantic."

"He came to your office?" Faith pounced on that bit of information. Any woman who saw Brandon would never forget him.

Cassandra sadly shook her head of short dark curls. "It was all conducted by telephone. Where do you want me to leave the prints?"

"My office, please." Faith headed in that direction, daring to hope that Brandon, not Shane, was behind the deliveries. She was too big of a coward to ask him.


Faith didn't care that she was obviously waiting behind the check-in desk the next day for the delivery. She wasn't the only one. Several guests milled in the lobby. Mae, one of the housekeepers, had been polishing the brass door handles for the past ten minutes. A short distance away, the three-by-three spot James kept running the vacuum over had to be the cleanest in the hotel. Even Henrí had passed through a couple of times.

If Brandon embarrassed her by not coming through, she was going to the Red Cactus and give him a piece of her mind. In fact, she might do that anyway. She came around the desk.

She'd spent a restless night vacillating between happiness and despair because she couldn't be 100 percent sure that he was behind the flowers. Brandon could make a simple walk beautiful just by holding her hand. She cherished the ordinary because she'd never quite let herself believe any of it would happen. Dinner with just the two of them at his restaurant, a drive in the mountains, a bed of flower petals were all precious gifts she'd always cherish.

Suddenly James cut the vacuum and beat the doorman to grab the door and step back, a wide toothless grin on his brown face. Faith swallowed. There were four men, two in front and two slightly behind a fifth man who carried a black attaché case. When the man in the middle neared, she saw the chain hanging from his wrist. He stopped in front of her. The four men encircled her and the fifth man.

"Ms. McBride?"

"Yes," she said, her throat dry, her heart thudding like she'd run for miles.

"Is there someplace we can talk in private?" he asked.

"Yes." She went to the office behind the front desk. She didn't want to wait a moment longer than necessary.

Two guards came inside the room while the other two remained outside. They looked around, then went back out, quietly closing the door. "Please have a seat," the fifth man said, placing the case on the desk.

Faith sat. From the inside of his suit jacket the man removed a key. Then he unlocked the case. Faith gasped. Diamonds, emeralds, rubies in round, square, princess, and emerald cut sparkled. She wasn't an expert, but she didn't think any were less than three carats.

"All A-1 clarity, certified—flawless. He said they were just like you."

Faith felt tears prick her eyes. She took the crisp linen handkerchief the man offered. Brandon's restaurant was doing well, but he couldn't afford this. Even if he could, he didn't go in for extravagance.

"He thought you might have difficulty, so he asked me to inform you that at the right moment he will choose, just as he's chosen you and you him." The case closed. The click of the lock sounded overly loud in the room.

At the door, the man paused and looked back. "He asked that I tell you one more thing."

"Yes?"

"Hold on to your faith." With a slight tilt of his dark head, he was gone.

Faith's hand clutched the handkerchief as thoughts bombarded her. She wanted so much to believe it was Brandon but was afraid to.

*Hold on to your faith.* "All right, Brandon, but I think it's time I took my courage in hand and paid you a visit."

❖ ❖ ❖

Despite the demands on his time with two of his wait-staff and Michelle out with unexpected illnesses, and him trying to divide his time between managing the floor and helping in the kitchen, he noticed Faith the moment she crossed the room behind the hostess. When they passed an open table, Faith stopped and said something to Carol. The hostess who had been heading for the family table turned and looked at him. Faith's gaze followed. The kick was as sharp as he remembered.

With a small nod of approval, he turned to finish trying to soothe the ruffled feathers of a patron who thought his rare prime rib was dry and overcooked. The man had eaten the entire meal, then wanted the meal credited. The woman with him had her head tucked as if she wanted to disappear. Brandon didn't like being taken advantage of, but he didn't have the time to argue with the wide-shouldered man who appeared to be in his midthirties. "I'll comp half the meal."

"I want—"

"Half, and the next time it will be a fourth."

The woman's head came up, her eyes wide as her gaze went from the speechless man up to Brandon.

"Decide now."

"I've eaten in some of the finest restaurants in the world, and I've never been treated so rudely," he claimed, his voice rising.

"If it's been your practice to eat a meal, then demand it be comped because it was inedible, then I'd say you're long overdue," Brandon said just as loudly. "I'll tell your waiter half. Have a nice day." He turned and should have headed to the kitchen, but he detoured to Faith's table. Although she was familiar with every item they served, she had her head hidden behind the oversize menu.

"Hello, Faith."

The menu slowly slid down over her beautiful face to reveal chocolate eyes that would always get to him, mauve-colored lips that haunted his dreams. "Hello, Brandon."

Bracing one hand on the back of her chair to get closer to her, he said, "I see you're over your pique at me."

"I don't like to see us at odds," she admitted, tucking her lower lip between her teeth in a gesture he'd come to recognize as nervousness, or she was concentrating as she'd been the first time she'd put on his— he blocked that thought and shifted away in time to see the diner he'd just spoken to shake off the hand of the woman he was with and come toward them.

"You got a nerve brushing me off in front of my girlfriend, then coming over here to talk to some wo—"

Brandon snatched the beefy man, who outweighed him by thirty pounds, off his feet by his shirt collar. Suddenly there was absolute quiet in the restaurant. "That's a line you don't want to cross."

The man squirmed, prying ineffectually at Brandon's clenched fists. His eyes bugged.

"When I release you, I want you to apologize and do us both a favor and don't come in here again. Understood?"

The man nodded. Brandon unclenched his hands. The man staggered, clutched at his throat, and backed up.

"I believe you forgot your apology," Brandon said mildly, his eyes as cold as ice.

The man stopped, moistened his dry lips. "I-I'm sorry, miss."

Brandon's gaze went to the silent woman behind him. "You're welcome anytime. Your first meal is on the house. You didn't ask, but you can do better."

She stared at Brandon, and when the man with her tried to take her arm she stepped away. "Thank you. I apologize. I think I'll take you up on the offer and the advice." She left, the man trying to catch up with her.

Applause erupted. Brandon ignored it. "Sorry about that."

"He was bigger than you," Faith said, her voice trembling.

"I was madder."

"Why?"

Unable to resist a moment longer, he tenderly brushed the back of his hand against the smooth curve of her cheek. "I think we both know the answer to that."

"We do?" she asked, her eyes huge and hopeful.

"We do." He straightened. "Enjoy your lunch. I have to get back to work."

She picked up her purse and came to her feet, shoving the strap over her shoulder. "I need to get back as well."

"You haven't eaten."

"Doesn't matter. I have what I came for." She kissed him on the cheek.

"You know that's going to spread like wildfire," he said.

"I know, and you had better not let me down." She walked away. Brandon's hot gaze followed her every step of the way.

*Would he come tonight?* Faith asked herself that question over and over as the day progressed. She bounced between thinking he would and being deathly afraid he wouldn't. She was sure . . . well, almost sure that he was the one who'd been romancing her. She smiled and stared into space. Laughter outside her office door snapped her back into the present. Hunching her shoulders over the budget that she should have approved days ago, she had started over the figures one more time when the door opened abruptly.

"Faith, there's a problem with the lights in the Matador Room," Esmeralda said.

Frowning, Faith threw a quick look at the clock

on her desk as she came to her feet. "The Peterson party only had the room until six. It's almost nine."

Esmeralda threw up her hands. "You know how these things go sometimes."

Indeed she did. "Have you called maintenance?" Faith asked, heading out the door.

"They'll meet us there."

Faith hoped the problem was easily fixed. She opened the door . . . to find that her most cherished dream had come true.

The immense crystal chandelier overhead threw soft light over the flower-filled room interspersed with exact replicas of the travel posters in her office. Standing in the middle of the room was an incredibly handsome, well-built man in a black dinner jacket playing a tenor sax. She closed the door behind her without taking her eyes off him.

The song ended on a long, mournful wail that made her heart weep. "You finally played for me, but I don't think I've ever heard anything so sad."

"That's how I felt these last days without you in my life."

"Brandon," she whispered, going into his open arms. Her mouth fastened to his. She groaned with pleasure as their tongues mated.

"I missed you so much," he said, holding her tight.

"Me, too. I'm sorry about—"

Holding her away, he put his fingers to her lips. "I'm the one who's sorry. I'm glad you had the courage to shake things up. I should have known when I started having dreams about you that what I felt had gone beyond friendship."

Her fingers curled around the lapels of his jacket. "Do you think you might tell me what your exact feelings are?"

His hand tenderly cupped her cheek. "I love you."

Tears pooled in her eyes. "Oh, Brandon."

Panicked, he hugged her again. "Honey, please don't cry. I promised that I'd never make you cry again."

She smiled through her tears. "Since I cry when I'm happy, that might not be a promise you can keep."

"There's one I can, though." Taking her hand, he went down on one knee. "I love you, Faith. You're irresistible to me and so beautiful. Will you marry me?"

A deluge of tears flowed down her cheeks, but she croaked out, "Yes."

He came to his feet and pulled a ring from his pocket. He slid it on her finger and kissed her hand. "Do you like it?"

Faith couldn't see through the sheen of tears. She tried to blink the moisture away.

Brandon removed his pocket square and dried her tears. "I guess these monkey suits have their uses."

"You wore the jacket and did all this for me?" she asked, already knowing the answer.

Taking the hand with the ring on it, he kissed her

palm. "I wanted this moment to be perfect for you, just like you made my life perfect before I almost messed things up. I've been practicing on the sax every chance I got."

"You played beautifully. I've never forgotten the first time you played for me. It's one of my most cherished memories," she told him, her voice trembling with emotion.

He shook his dark head. "I was trying to show off. Something I never did. Guess I should have known then that you were the one for me."

Her free hand tenderly palmed his cheek. "Just so you know it now."

"With every breath I take," he assured her. "But you haven't even looked at the ring."

Faith was surprised to hear the anxiety in his voice. Brandon was one of the most self-assured men she knew. Leaning against him, she looked down, gasped, and straightened.

"You can get another one if you want," he quickly said. "I picked it out by myself. I just thought the pink diamond would be unique, just like you. I haven't given you anything else."

Her head jerked up. "What are you talking about?"

He glanced away. "You gave and I took. I finally realized that the night you tossed me out of your place. My so-called freedom wasn't worth anything if you weren't in my life. Your love and generosity humbled and shamed me. You gave me your most precious gift: your innocence."

"Brandon," she said, taking his face between her hands. "If you ever again say anything so idiotic I will hide your precious knives and cookware. Every time you touched me, every time you smiled, every moment with you was a gift that for so long I feared I'd never have. You gave me you, your love. Nothing material can ever compare to that."

He hugged her to him. "You're the best thing that ever happened to me."

"I feel the same way about you, and by the way—" Her gaze swept the room. "The ring is absolutely perfect and so is this."

"Whew. Esmeralda was great in helping me set this up tonight." His mouth twitched. "I think Henrí is warming up to me. He cooked the dinner we're having later since I happen to know you didn't eat. But first we have to visit my mother, then call your parents. We'll tell the rest of the family tomorrow."

She bit her lower lip. "What if your mother picked out someone else and is upset?"

"You're the one I picked," Brandon said adamantly. "Mama likes you and will soon love you. You'll see."

Faith wasn't convinced. "Maybe we should wait until tomorrow morning. Maybe she's asleep."

"She doesn't go to bed until after the last news program at eleven. Tomorrow morning, you're going to wake up with a very satisfied smile on your face. Mama would take one look at you and know," he told her frankly.

She blushed. "But you never let us stay together past two."

He grinned devilishly. "I figured out a way for me to stay longer at your place."

Her grin matched his. "Then we'd better hurry."


His arm around Faith's waist, Brandon walked up the steps of his mother's house and rang the doorbell. Five-foot topiaries graced each side of the double wrought-iron doors. Viewed through the opening was the recessed front door and a huge pendulum wrought-iron chandelier.

Waiting for his mother, Brandon kissed his fiancé on the top of her head and reassured her, "Mama will love you."

"I hope so. I really like and admire your mother."

"She's going to be so surprised," he said with a broad grin. "For the first time, one of us got the best of her. I picked my own wife."

The inner door opened. Ruth Grayson saw them in the light and hurried to unlock the grilled doors. "Brandon. Faith. Is everything all right?"

"Everything is perfect." Brandon ushered them both inside the house, then lifted Faith's left hand and had the pleasure of seeing his mother's eyes go wide with surprise. "Mama, I'd—"

His mother squealed like a teenager meeting her idol, then enveloped Faith in a hug. Keeping one hand on Faith, Ruth hugged Brandon with the other. "This is wonderful. Have you set a date yet?"

Faith glanced up at Brandon with love shining in her eyes. "He just asked me less than half an hour ago."

"I'm the first to know?" At their nods, Ruth hugged them again. "The others will be as pleased as I am."

"You really are happy?" Faith asked.

"Of course." Ruth smiled down at her. "I will have another beautiful daughter who is talented and gifted and loves my son. What more could a mother ask?"

At the words "talented and gifted" Brandon's antenna went up. "You think Faith is talented and gifted?"

"Of course. Don't you think so?" Ruth asked, her expression unreadable.

"Yes," he hastened to say.

His mother chuckled. "I should hope so. Now, let's sit down and, Faith, tell me every detail of how he asked you to marry him."

Brandon sat beside Faith on the sofa while his mother sat in the nearby side chair. Watching his mother, he let Faith tell her about tonight. His mother looked at him with pride when Faith, her voice a bit shaky, recalled receiving the flowers, the travel posters, the engagement rings. Both women's eyes misted when Faith told how Brandon proposed on one knee.

"I could keep you all night talking, but your

parents deserve to have the good news as well. I expect both of you here tomorrow night at seven for dinner to celebrate with the family." Ruth went with them to the door, and after one last hug she bade them good-bye and closed the door.

"Something isn't right here. She was too happy."

"Why do you say that?" Faith asked.

Lines radiated across Brandon's brow. "It's something Sierra said about a woman doing one thing when her object was another. Mother was trying to push the Albuquerque designer down my throat. She even went to you for help. Then we show up engaged, and she's doing handsprings." He shook his head. "We already figured out she wants talented and gifted daughters-in-law."

Faith, her eyes huge, looked at the house, then back at him. "She said I was gifted the time she came to see me at my office."

"She did?"

"She told me talent lay in many areas and my gift was as a nurturer, like you," she told him quietly.

"Why didn't you tell me?" Brandon almost yelled.

"I didn't think it mattered." Faith shook her head. "Besides, when you came into the office afterward I was miserable thinking your mother had picked out the Albuquerque designer for you. I was almost in tears," she explained, then bit her lip. "If you're right, then . . . then—"

"You were the one she picked for me."

Faith's squeal of delight imitated that of Brandon's mother earlier as she hugged him. "Oh, Brandon! This is so wonderful! I was so afraid I wouldn't measure up to the other wives."

Brandon had been about to go off on a tangent about being manipulated, but hearing the happiness in Faith's voice he asked instead, "My mother's scheming makes you happy?"

"Immensely. Despite the McBrides' curse and the fact that I'm not as slender as her other daughters-in-law, she thinks I'm good enough for you and can make you happy."

He snorted. "I love every delectable inch of you, there is no curse, and you're too good. Besides, I'm the only one you have to worry about pleasing."

She gave him a quick kiss. "Then we'd better get back to my place so I can get started."

Laughing, they ran down the steps to the car.

# Epilogue

Inside the house, Ruth let the curtain fall as soon as Brandon's Porsche pulled out of the driveway. She rushed to the phone and dialed.

"Mr. Montgomery. I'm sorry to call so late, but I thought you'd like to hear that everything worked out as we planned. I must admit I felt better as well knowing the pipes *really did* have a leak behind the wall. By simulating a false leak we actually prevented what could have been a major catastrophe."

She smiled. "Yes, it's wonderful how things work out for the best sometimes. Good night."

Almost unable to contain herself, Ruth dialed another number. "Felicia, they're engaged. They just left. They were both glowing." She looked at the wedding pictures of her two older sons and their wives on the mantel. Soon Brandon and Faith's would be there as well.

"I think Brandon actually thought he had pulled a fast one on me when he arrived, but then he became too quiet." Smiling, she took a seat on the sofa. "He'll figure it out, but he's so happy he won't mind. But I'm almost positive that he'll never guess that we faked the leak or made the hotel reservations for Mr. Nolly, then let nature take its course."

She laughed, then sobered. "Pierce and Sierra won't be so forgiving, I'm afraid."

She sighed. "Yes. I agree. I don't usually second-guess myself, but I have reservations regarding my next two choices. Both are as unpredictable as Pierce and Sierra. The friction between them will be immediate and intense. Making this work will test even our combined ingenuity."

Ruth stared at the family photo with all the children smiling and crowded around their parents. The photo had been taken the week before her husband flew on his fatal flight to Brazil. At times, her heart still ached for him.

"No, I have every intention of going through with things as planned." Marriage had heartaches, but it also held great joy. "Let me tell you about the woman I've chosen. Trouble is coming to Santa Fe and as a famous actress once said, 'Fasten your seat belt.' Pierce is next."

Read on for a sneak peek at Francis Ray's
unforgettably provocative mainstream novel

# In Another Man's Bed

Coming in trade paperback from St. Martin's Griffin
Winter 2007

Justine Crandall had seduction on her mind and in less than ten minutes she would be in bed with the man she adored.

The racy thought made Justine grin, then she laughed out loud at her uncharacteristic naughtiness. Both she and Andrew, her husband of five years, were as conservative as they came, but since they'd been apart for two weeks, she didn't think he'd put up much resistance.

In the cocooned luxury of the Porsche Carrera, she sighed in pleasure and anticipation as the sports car easily took the sharp turns up the Appalachian Mountains. She'd been on the road since five that morning and couldn't have picked a better day for the drive.

Spring was in full force. The air was crisp and clean, the sky a startling blue, and the roadside bursting with wildflowers. She smiled and slowed as a deer bounded gracefully across the road and disappeared over the steep incline. She'd seen several this morning. It was a good thing DEER CROSSING signs were posted. As owner and operator of It's A Mystery Bookstore in Charleston, she seldom had a chance to enjoy nature.

Last night, after Andrew had finished his last workshop at the men's retreat in Gatlinburg, he'd called to say he was too tired to make the four-hour drive back to Charleston on Sunday afternoon. Justine suggested he stay at their nearby cabin for a few days before returning. He could work on the book he wanted to write.

As soon as she hung up, she'd begun planning to surprise him. They were going to have two whole days by themselves, something they hadn't had in a very long time. They'd built the cabin as their retreat two years ago, but it had been almost a year since they'd been there together.

Justine patted the Gucci overnight bag in the seat beside her. Inside was a new blue negligee. Andrew loved blue and he loved her.

She'd be the happiest woman in the world if they could begin planning a baby. Andrew wanted to wait until he wasn't away from home so much, but she was hoping she could change his mind.

However, for the past nine months Andrew had been on a grueling schedule conducting a number of men's retreats across the country. There hadn't been very many occasions for "trying." Justine didn't begrudge the time Andrew spent away from her because she felt his work was important. Perhaps if someone had counseled her father he might not have left her mother for another woman.

Justine knew she'd never have to go through divorce. She and Andrew were committed to each other for a lifetime. Not just because they loved each other, but also because neither wanted to repeat the mistakes of their parents.

Shortly after nine she pulled up to their cabin, a two-story structure with a gabled roof and a balcony that ran along the back of the house. Disappointment hit her on seeing another car parked beside her husband's Escalade. She'd wanted them to have this time alone. Annoyance crept in. He should be resting instead of counseling someone.

People sometimes took advantage of Andrew's goodness. He didn't know how to say no. Usually she stayed out of his business affairs, but lately he'd been preoccupied and easily distracted. It was time he was a bit selfish and put himself first, she thought.

Getting out of the Porsche, a birthday gift from Andrew, she shoved the keys into the pocket of her white slacks and started toward the hand-carved front door. She and Andrew could unload the car later. Now, she couldn't wait to see her husband after being apart for two weeks.

Going up the stone steps, she inhaled the sweet fragrance of the peace roses in full bloom on either side of the house. She made a mental note to put a bouquet of the lush pink flowers in their bedroom.

Entering the spacious interior she had lovingly decorated in warm earth tones and comfortable easy-to-care-for leather, she turned, expecting to find Andrew and his guest in the kitchen. The big plate-glass window in the breakfast nook gave a spectacular view of the heavily wooded mountains and always beckoned them to begin their day there as they ate a leisurely breakfast together.

She started in that direction, then heard a sound from upstairs. She glanced at her watch. Nine-ten. Andrew was an early riser. Worried, she started up the stairs. He didn't take care of himself when he was away from her. She wished he were home more. He was a wonderful, loving—

Her thoughts abruptly halted as an unmistakable moan of sexual pleasure drifted out to her from their bedroom. Stunned, she stood at the top of the stairs, a tightness in her chest, her throat. She wasn't aware of how long she remained immobile before she moved down the hallway in a daze. Her tennis shoes were soundless on the wool runner on the polished oak floor as she stopped at the open door of the master bedroom.

Justine's heart clenched, her breath snagged as she caught a glimpse of a woman's naked butt and shoulder going into the master bath. Her gaze stayed glued to the closed door as if putting off looking at the bed as long as possible. Her hands clenched, she finally made herself look. Hot rage rolled through her.

Her husband lay naked on the wide bed. His eyes were closed, one long leg was drawn up, and a satisfied smile curved his soft mouth upward. Justine tried to remember if she'd ever seen that look of complete satisfaction after they made love. She couldn't.

She must have made a sound because Andrew's eyelids flew up. Stunned, he stared at her with those light brown mesmerizing eyes that had swayed and motivated thousands, then he sprang out of bed to cut her off from the bathroom.

"You lying, cheating bastard!" Justine snarled.

Andrew looked as taken aback by the harsh words spewing from his wife as by her appearance. "Justine, please let me—"

The open-palm slap across his face echoed through the silent room. He stared at her as if she'd gone mad.

There were so many hot emotions running through her that she thought she might just have. She'd always been quiet, had never raised a hand to another person, had never given her mother or her teachers one moment of trouble, but right then she wanted to scratch Andrew's handsome face to shreds.

She'd given him everything, and he'd left her with nothing. The only reason she didn't slap him again was the fear of not being able to stop. He would defend himself and that meant he'd have to touch her. She never wanted his hands on her again.

"I trusted you. I loved you," she said, her voice trembling with rage and pain.

"It only happened once," Andrew told her, his hand on his cheek, his eyes wide and uncertain.

She fought the urge to hit him again. "Do you think that makes the betrayal any less?"

"Hon—"

"Don't." Justine stepped away from the hands reaching for her. "Who is she?"

"It doesn't matter. She means nothing to me."

Justine raised her hand to hit him again, then clenched it into a fist instead. "That takes you even lower." She swallowed the painful lump in her throat. "Don't come home. I'm filing for divorce as soon as I get back."

Fear leaped into his eyes. "You can't throw away all that we mean to each other, all that we've shared."

"I didn't. You did. Now, get out of my way."

"No!" Andrew said, spreading his arms wide so she couldn't go around him. "Let's go downstairs and talk."

Hysterical laughter burst forth. "You're naked and your lover just left the bed I picked out for us. Nothing you can say will change anything. Good-bye."

"Jus—" His hands lifted purposefully toward her.

"Try to touch me and you'll regret it," Justine promised. She looked over his shoulder at the closed door. There was no sound coming from the bathroom. Whoever was behind that door could hear them.

Justine had a few words for her. "There's a word for women like you, but I don't want to foul my mouth saying it!" With that parting shoot, she turned and walked from the room. What she really wanted to do was scream and kick and howl.

Her world had just been torn apart, her heart yanked out of her chest. One arm wrapped around her heaving stomach, she stopped on the stairs for just a second, then continued downward. She had to get away.

Her pace increased. She didn't want to give Andrew or his lover the pleasure of seeing how much their betrayal had hurt her. She ran faster, stumbling on the way out the door, picking herself up to stumble forward again.

By the time she reached her car, her hands were shaking so badly it took several tries to get the key into the ignition. As she pulled off, Andrew, always well-groomed and fashionable, ran out of the house with his shirt open, his slacks unfastened. He was carrying his shoes. She gunned the Carrera and spun out of the driveway, fighting the upheaval in her stomach, the gut-wrenching loss of her dreams as Andrew leaped into his own vehicle and began to chase her.

Justine was an excellent driver, and she used that skill to pull farther and farther away from Andrew. She tried to keep the image of her husband's deceit at bay, but it kept returning.

Her hands gripping the steering wheel of her sports car, Justine threw a quick glance in her rearview mirror. Andrew was at least a quarter mile behind her. On the winding mountain road, his Escalade was no match for her Porsche on the sharp turns of the narrow descent. With each rotation of her wheels, he lagged farther and farther behind. It would be laughable if it weren't so tragic that he had given her the means to evade him.

*"This car will be carrying the most important and precious person in my life."*

Justine's hands flexed on the steering wheel as she fought to keep the tears from falling. Lies. A man didn't love one woman and have sex with another.

Her mind shied away from the scene she had just witnessed. She wouldn't let herself think about it, or she'd never be able to get down the mountain and make good her escape. She had surprised her husband all right, but not in a way either of them had expected.

Her eyes shut tightly in an attempt to keep the sickening picture of Andrew's betrayal at bay. It was useless. She heard the moans, saw the backside of the woman, her husband's naked body and satisfied expression.

The blast of a car horn jerked her eyes open in time to see an oncoming truck directly in front of her. She yanked the Porsche back into her own lane and out of the truck's path with only seconds to spare. Her heart pumping with fear and anger, she glanced in the rear-view mirror again. There were so many questions running through her head she couldn't sort them all out. She'd worry about that later. Now, she needed to get away.

*"Let me explain."*

There was no way in hell he could explain away what she'd just witnessed. If it hadn't taken her those several moments on the stairs to stop shaking and compose herself enough to drive, he wouldn't have gotten this close to catching her.

Out of the corner of her eye she caught a flicker of movement in the thick brush on the side of the road. Three adult deer and one fawn emerged as she passed by. Instinctively she glanced in the rear-view mirror.

She eased off the gas and onto the brakes. Her heart pounded even more as she glimpsed the deer crossing the road. She hit the horn just as Andrew's car rounded the curve.

The fawn froze. The others scampered away. Andrew didn't brake; he swerved around the animal, putting his vehicle perilously close to the edge of the ravine.

Justine didn't realize she'd stopped and gotten out of her car until she felt the imprint of the door handle biting into her clenched hand.

She could see Andrew desperately wrestling with the steering wheel, his eyes wide with terror. Then the back wheels began to lose traction. For a moment their eyes locked, then the Escalade slid down the cliff.

Justine screamed, then she was running. She stared in horror as the vehicle flipped over and over before coming to a halt. Through the dense trees and shrubbery, she barely distinguished the gleam of the gray exterior of Andrew's SUV. A plume of thick, black smoke spiraled upward.

Justine hesitated for a moment, then began to scramble down the hundred-foot embankment toward her lying, adulterous husband.